CW00447311

THE FOX

Published by arrangement with Salka, Iceland.
www.salka.is

Cover art courtesy of Aðalsteinn Svanur Sigfússon

Corylus Books Ltd

corylusbooks.com

ISBN: 978-1-9163797-3-2

Sólveig Pálsdóttir

THE FOX

Translated by Quentin Bates

Published by Corylus Books Ltd

CORYLUS
BOOKS

She could see only the white flakes spinning towards her out of the darkness and for a moment it occurred to her that it was time to give up, walk out into the teeth of the storm and leave the snow to pile up and cover her. She could let herself drift into unconsciousness before they could catch up with her. She could fall asleep in the cold and dream her way to the warmth of home. She glanced into the mirror and moaned at the sight of her face, swollen, the cuts turning septic and the clumsy stitches.

'I will,' she whispered to herself, feeling the old determination return. 'I will go home,' she told herself, out loud this time as a gust of wind made the car bounce. She gripped the wheel so tightly that her knuckles turned white as she cautiously put her foot on the accelerator.

February

1

The man sitting next to her had a friendly face. He was fair-haired, his beard bushy but neat, and he held a paper coffee cup in one hand. His eyes went from the aircraft's window to the back of the seat in front, and back again. It looked as if he was trying to stare the flight out, just as she was. The turbulence started ten minutes after takeoff. The aircraft juddered at first, and then lurched as it lost height. Sajee snatched at the man's hand and hot coffee spilled over him.

'I'm so sorry,' she said, letting go of his hand and transferring her grip to the seat's steel arm rest. He took a serviette from the pocket of the seat and wiped off most of the spilled coffee.

'Did it burn you?' she asked, mortified. 'I'll wash your shirt for you.'

'It's all right,' he said with a mild, beautiful smile. He was a handsome man, but there wasn't much expression to be seen. His hair was cropped close at the sides, but thick on top and a fringe flopped over his forehead. He looked at her with curiosity. 'You speak Icelandic?'

'Just a little,' she mumbled. That wasn't true, as she had a good command of the language, but often people failed to understand her because of her mouth. Right now she hardly trusted herself to speak, not until she had solid ground under her feet again.

'You're travelling alone?' he asked, leaning towards her.

She nodded cautiously, not sure that she was ready to shift even slightly in her seat.

'What takes you to the east at this time of year?' he asked politely, without seeming to pry.

'Work,' she gulped.

'Where?' he asked.

'At a beauty salon.'

'Really?' he said with a note of surprise in his voice. 'In Höfn?'

'Yes.'

He gave her a warm smile.

'It'll be over soon. Just try to take deep breaths and relax,' he said, patting her hand. 'Don't try to fight it. Go with the plane's movement instead of tensing against it,' he said sympathetically.

She tried to follow his advice, until the aircraft began to shudder again.

Each shovelful dispatched more snow as it formed a white wall alongside the steps leading up to the olive-green, two-storey house on Höfn's main street. Guðgeir Fransson, former Reykjavík police chief inspector, had rented the ground floor, an apartment that was big enough for a single person, although the low ceiling could sometimes make a tall man feel as if the walls were closing in. The place was halfway to

THE FOX

being a cellar, but Guðgeir counted himself fortunate to have got the place, as the growing flow of tourists had resulted in a shortage of housing in Höfn.

The previous summer had seen records broken as more tourists than ever before had turned up and even more were predicted for the next summer. So everyone who had an opportunity to rent out a room to tourists was busily doing just that. All the same, not many had turned up so far. The winter had been a hard one and spring was still a long way off.

That February morning it had turned unusually warm, so the snow was wet and heavy, and clearing it had become heavier work than usual. He worked as hard as he could, as if he were determined to set a speed record for clearing snow. His mental state always felt better for physical exertion. Since making the move to this quiet coastal town a day's drive from Reykjavík, he had made an effort to get daily exercise. He swam, walked a lot and ran when the weather allowed it. His aim was to fall into an exhausted sleep every night. If he wasn't able to fall asleep quickly, thoughts of his old life and the pain of missing it would keep him awake far into the night and he would imagine the person he loved asleep at his side, while he craved the warmth of her body beside him.

Sajee had little experience of travelling by air – or travelling at all. This was only the second time she had been anywhere. Before that had been the long journey, all the way from Sri Lanka to Iceland. Now the aircraft's metal frame shivered and the lights

9

above the seats flickered, people took deep breaths and small children wailed. Over the crying she heard the pilot make an announcement over the loudspeaker. She wasn't able to make out his words, but sensed the tension around her. The aircraft dropped sharply, banked hard and climbed so quickly that the airframe shook.

She kept a tight grip on the armrest with one hand and reached with the other for the sick bag in the pocket in front of her. She vomited a slimy liquid containing the remains of the sandwich she had eaten at Reykjavík airport. She felt her companion lifting her hair with both hands away from her face while she retched into the bag. She remembered little more of the flight until the bumpy landing at Höfn's airport. Not a sound could be heard inside the aircraft apart from the whine of the engines and the squeal of wheels on tarmac. The children had stopped crying and the adults sat stiff in their seats. The aircraft taxied slowly up to the airport building, and a round of applause broke out as it came to a halt.

She stood exhausted among the pale-faced passengers waiting for her suitcase. The man who had been next to her on the flight came over, wearing a coat zipped half-way up. The dark brown stain on his shirt front gave her a pang of guilt.

'Can I offer you a lift? he asked.

Sajee was so taken by surprise that she declined, speaking in her own language before realising what she had done.

'No, thank you. I'm being picked up,' she said in Icelandic. 'I'm so sorry about the coffee.'

The man laughed and was about to say something else when a dark-haired older woman came to stand by them.

'That was appalling,' she fumed. 'The plane should never have left Reykjavík!'

Others around joined in to agree with her, arguing loudly that passengers deserved counselling after a flight like that. The man took a card from his pocket and put it in Sajee's hand.

'Thank you,' she said, looking at the drawing of a house overlooking a blue sea. The door was framed within a handsome portico and flanked by deep tubs filled with flowers. He looked at her questioningly.

'Is it difficult to read?'

Sajee nodded.

'I run a guest house here in Höfn, called the Hostel by the Sea. If you're stuck, come to me,' he said in a low voice. 'My name's Thormóður.'

'Thank you,' Sajee said and backed away. She was sure there had to be a bad smell about her. There was vomit on her sweater and on the many-coloured scarf around her neck. When her large, black suitcase finally appeared, still wet with snow, she took herself to the toilets, relieved that nobody from her new workplace was there to see her. She unwound the colourful scarf, pulled off her sweater and leaned over the sink to wash as well as she was able. She brushed her raven hair and put on a clean sweater from her suitcase. By the time she felt she was presentable, the arrivals area was practically deserted. Through the window she could see where her companion on the flight was standing by a Land Rover, and the angry woman with the dark hair was still talking while the man had a look of resignation on his face. He finally got into the car and drove away, and before long there was only one car left outside the airport building.

Höfn was a place where heavy snow was nothing unusual, but this winter had been exceptional. It had begun to fall early in the autumn, just a few weeks after Guðgeir had been taken on by a small security company after many miserable months of searching for work. There were only two staff who took alternate shifts, and their paths almost never crossed. Guðgeir wasn't sure that the fledgling company would even stay afloat to the end of the year, but so far wages had been paid on time. The family had been left behind in Reykjavík, in the terraced house in Fossvogur.

He would have preferred to have sold the place after the horror that had taken place there when his colleague and old friend Andrés had become the victim of the killer they had been tracking, but Guðgeir's wife Inga hadn't been prepared to let the place go – at least, not while things between them were so uncertain.

She told him that it was just a house and there were no memories stored in the concrete walls around them, while people had feelings and they were the ones who needed to make sense of their own emotions in the aftermath of what had happened.

For weeks he had kept to the shadows, hiding away in a room he rented out of town, and returned home when the worst of the storm had abated. They had tried to pick up where they had left off, to act as if nothing had happened, as if there had been no betrayal – the first and only time he had been unfaithful to Inga. A second's lapse of judgement had triggered a series of horrific events, with the end of all this still not in sight.

The pain was too sharp for them to be able to talk to each other and their home life turned into a poor imitation of what it had once been. The harsh note of accusation was never far away, in both Inga's voice and that of the two youngsters as Guðgeir was constantly wracked with guilt. An atmosphere of brooding silence had replaced the positive closeness of the family home. When there had been an offer of a job in Höfn, Inga had made it plain that he should take it. They could examine their feelings again at the end of the one-year contract. Guðgeir felt that a year was too long a time and tried to convince her, but she wouldn't be swayed.

Now he could see that Inga had been right to hang on to the house. It made sense to wait with the big decisions until they had reached some sort of balance once more. Their existence had been in turmoil; over a short time everything had changed and lives had been lost. Sometimes he wondered if the Höfn weather was some kind of a symbol of the turbulence in his own life, as it could rarely be predicted and often turned wild. There had hardy been a full week without a blind blizzard descending, and several times avalanches had blocked the Hvalnesskriður road to the east. In between the falls of heavy snow there had been days when the temperature lifted and things began to thaw. Then there was every chance of a downpour of rain before it froze again. The streets were so slippery with ice that getting from one house to the next could be a challenge.

2

It was too cold to wait outside in the February darkness so she sat on a sofa upholstered in fake black leather. Surely the man would be here soon to collect her? A burly man with brush-cut hair was finishing some paperwork behind the reception desk.

'That was quite a landing,' he called out and disappeared through a door with a box in his arms. Sajee nodded her head in agreement, but the man was already gone. She was alone in the arrivals lounge and closed her eyes. A few minutes passed and she was almost asleep when she realised the man was speaking again from where he sat tapping at a computer behind the desk.

'It was pretty bad and the passengers don't like it, but there was never any real danger,' he said. 'It's rarely like this in Höfn, so it's understandable that some people get more upset than others.'

He laughed again and went back to his work. For a while only the whine of the wind could be heard. Sajee checked her phone. Nobody had called or sent a message, so she walked over to the window and stared out.

'Can I help you?' the man asked, looking up from his computer screen.

Sajee hesitated and looked down. Her long black hair fell over her face.

'You understand Icelandic?' the man asked, as if he had only just registered her appearance, switching to English. 'Can I help you?'

'Yes, I speak Icelandic,' Sajee replied, pleased that he could understand her. Often she had to repeat each sentence, which could be exhausting. Sometimes it was easiest to say as little as possible. 'I've lived here for a few years.'

She stood up and went over to the window again. There was nothing to be seen in the parking lot, so she took out her phone, but could reach neither Kristinn nor Liu. After a couple of unsuccessful attempts she went back to the sofa.

'Could you help me get a taxi?' she asked, tucking her hair back behind her ears. 'There's so much snow that I won't be able to carry my case if nobody comes to collect me. I don't understand what's wrong. I've tried to call again and again.'

'There's no taxi around here. There was a couple in Höfn who ran a taxi, but they gave up in the autumn. Hopefully someone else will start up in the spring,' the man said. 'Where are you going?'

'It's a local beauty salon,' Sajee said, repeating the words in English as the man raised an eyebrow.

'Understood,' he said with a laugh. 'I'm Sveinn, by the way.'

He laughed again, but not at her. It seemed to be a habit, finishing each sentence with a short snort of laughter.

'My name is Sajee,' she said, trying to smile. 'It's sometimes difficult to speak clearly, because of this,' she said touching her upper lip with her index finger and covering her mouth. It was an old habit she struggled to break. As a youngster she had not only covered her mouth to speak to strangers, but had let her thick hair fall over her face like a curtain.

'Couldn't you get that seen to?' Sveinn asked. 'It doesn't look that bad. Probably wouldn't even have known it was there if you'd had treatment right away...' He hesitated, and barked with laughter. 'Well... these plastic surgeons are so smart, they can do pretty much anything,' he said, looked ready to laugh again, and stopped himself, as if realising that it was time to let the subject lie.

'My father didn't have much money,' Sajee said. 'Things in Sri Lanka are very different.'

She said no more, knowing that people frequently didn't give themselves time to listen to anything more than the most straightforward explanation, either interrupting her or else letting their attention wander. She ran a finger under the hair tucked behind her ear and let it fall over her face. His attention went back to the desk in front of him.

'Is that right that you're going to a beauty salon?' he asked after a pause, looking up at her.

'Yes, I'm starting work there,' Sajee assured him. 'I'll be doing pedicures, massages and that kind of thing. I'm good at this kind of work, and learned it all at a really good salon. Lakmal would only have the best people working at his place.'

She hesitated when she saw that Sveinn had a curious look on his face and assumed that he hadn't understood.

'And what's this salon called, the one you're going to work at?' Sveinn asked with the usual laugh, this time a little forced.

'It's called Höfn Beauty,' she said. 'It's on the main street.'

'I don't know the place. This isn't a big town and I know pretty much everyone here.'

'Wait a moment,' Sajee said, fumbling for the phone. She quickly scrolled through the messages and showed him the old phone's cracked screen.

'I'm going to buy myself a new one. When I have been paid,' she said apologetically, searching for the right message. 'I think it's this one.'

Sveinn took the phone and read the message. His brow furrowed and he squinted to read it a second time. 'Höfn Beauty,' he said out loud. I've never heard of it,' he said and this time his laugh sounded forced. 'Is that all?'

'No,' she said and shook her head. 'There are two more messages. They're next, look.'

A heavy finger tapped at the phone.

'I had forgotten how difficult it was to read anything on these tiny screens,' he muttered, elbows on the desk. He moved the phone closer to see it better. 'Then there's more from the same number.'

'That's right,' Sajee said. 'It says that Kristinn who owns the salon will meet me at the airport.'

'I see that, then there's the same text as in the other messages,' he said and passed the phone back to her, a serious look on his face. 'I know a few people of that name, but not anyone in this kind of business. You didn't get any paperwork? A business card, or a leaflet like the ones over there?'

'No, just text messages,' she said, shaking her head. 'But Liu, the woman who rented at the same place as me in Reykjavík, said it's a good place to work,' she said, lowering her voice without finishing what she had meant to say.

'Liu?' Sveinn asked, clearly intrigued.

'She's Chinese and helps me read the messages because I don't read Icelandic. Liu helped me book the ticket for the flight here.'

'And what's her link to this salon?'

'Her friend worked there but had to leave. I'm supposed to take over her work and the apartment where she lived.'

'So that's the way it is,' Sveinn said, looking at her and scratching the back of his neck. 'So you can't read what's here in your phone?' he asked, hesitating as if he were anxious not to offend her.

'No,' Sajee replied. 'Well, of course I read Sinhala and write to my family.'

'Do you have a return flight booked?' he asked, tapping at the computer, to check.

'Look, it says here,' he read out in a clear voice. '"To Sajee. Can you come and work for us right away,

27th February. Good wages and apartment. Best regards, Höfn Beauty." I have to say the wording is very strange. Who sent you this message?'

'Kristinn. The man who owns the salon,' Sajee replied, twisting the ring on her index finger, a narrow gold rope. 'Liu told her friend about me because she had a problem. Her relative in China is very ill and she had to leave. Liu asked me if I could take the job and I was so pleased. Then this message came. There are four women working there so it will be good for me because I work alone and don't know many people. And I don't have to write anything because the man looks after all that kind of thing.'

'Which man?'

'Kristinn,' she said with a sigh.

'Höfn isn't a big town. You're sure about all this?'

'Yes. Read it yourself,' she said shortly, irritated by his questions.

Sveinn looked through the messages again.

'There's a third message from the same number,' he said, concentrating on the screen.

'Yes,' Sajee said eagerly. 'The one that says Kristinn who owns the salon will pick me up at the airport.'

'That's right, and with the date and time,' Sveinn said. He put the phone down, crossed his arms and looked at her with concern. 'Then there's the same text again, exactly the same as in the other messages. I don't want to be unpleasant, but like I said, I know most people here and don't know anyone who runs a beauty salon. Could you have misunderstood?'

She quickly looked down at the tiled floor. The remnants of slush ice were melting there into a brown puddle. She was tired and out of sorts after the flight. On top of that, a nervous feeling was gathering inside her.

'But what do I know?' he said quickly, hoping to lift her spirits. He was the type who liked people around him to be happy, always ready to help and to make every effort to solve to any problem. 'Have you tried to call the number?'

'Yes, of course. Many times, and I've tried to call Liu, but her phone is out of range.'

'Let's give Adda Lísa a call,' Sveinn said, turning back to the computer. 'She's the only beautician I know of around here.'

He punched numbers into the phone and offered it to her. She took it and after a moment's thought passed it back to him.

'Would you speak for me? Sometimes people don't understand me easily.'

'Of course,' he said and turned away. Sajee watched in agitation as he walked back and forth as he talked.

'Adda Lísa has never heard of this place,' he said eventually. 'She works by herself and shuts the doors when she takes time off,' he said and stood for a moment in thought. 'To tell you the truth, I don't know what the best thing to do is. You're welcome to have a ride into town with me later. It's a bit of a distance,' he said, glancing at his watch. 'Between us we ought to be able to get to the bottom of this.'

He gave her a look that was supposed to be encouraging, but this time there was no laughter.

3

Worried and frightened, she sat on the couch to wait, staring out at the snow, the empty car park and the distant mountain peaks. She tried to push aside the uncomfortable feeling that she had been duped. Sveinn strode over to her and picked up the black suitcase.

'Shall we be on our way?' he asked cheerfully.

She looked at him in confusion for a moment as she gathered her wits. She stood up, zipped her coat up to her neck and went out into the cold.

Darkness was already falling as they drove away from the airport and flakes of snow spun past in the wind. Posts with reflectors attached to them showed the way, until the street lights of Höfn appeared. Sveinn stopped at a few places, either making phone calls or knocking on doors, while Sajee waited in the car.

There was nobody to be found who remembered offering her work.

'It doesn't look promising,' he said after the last call, turning up the heater as he noticed her shivering.

'Could you drive me to this place?' she asked, holding out the card that Thormóður had handed her.

'Sure,' Sveinn said, with relief, and his habitual bark of laughter. 'I need to be on my way home as well, and I hope it all gets sorted out for you.'

She nodded and stared out through the windscreen. The road passed through the town, almost down to the harbour and the boats at the quays. Sveinn turned and drove along a row of low terraced houses. The hostel was at the end of the row, and it didn't look as smart as the picture on the card Sajee had been given.

'I'll look after myself from here,' she said, opening the car door. 'Thank you for your help.'

She was about to say more, but Sveinn had already got out of the car to open the boot.

'You don't want me to come inside with you?' he called to her, lugging her suitcase to the door where the flowerpots were almost buried by snow.

'No. That's fine, she said firmly. 'It'll be fine. Thank you.'

'Sure?'

'Yes, of course,' she said in a clear tone, waving him goodbye.

'All right, then. I'm sure it'll sort itself out,' he replied. 'Good luck.'

Her companion from the flight stood behind an old-fashioned reception desk with the phone to his ear. Still wearing his coat, he looked busy.

'Hello again. Are you on the way out?' Sajee asked, stamping the snow from her shoes. 'I'm so sorry, I'm making a mess.'

'Don't worry about it. Good to see you,' he said, coming around to the front of the desk. 'Welcome to the Hostel by the Sea.' He bowed his head courteously and put his hands together as if he wanted to offer her some kind of Asian welcome. 'You need a room?'

'Yes. At least for tonight,' she said. 'How much does it cost?'

She was unable to hide the concern in her voice.

'We always have the best prices,' he said, slipping out of his coat. 'There are no tourists at the moment, so we have plenty of empty rooms. If you clean up after yourself then I won't charge you.'

'I can pay,' she said quickly. 'I just hadn't expected to have to find a place to stay.'

'Really? Is there a problem?' he asked, stroking his neatly trimmed beard.

'I think so. It looks like there was some misunderstanding about the job,' she said.

'You're in trouble, then?'

'Yes...' she said slowly. 'Maybe there isn't a job.'

'Really? That's a shame,' he said with concern as he took a set of keys from a hook. 'Who offered you this job?'

'A man called Kristinn, but his phone's dead. So is the woman's, the one I was supposed to be working for. He was supposed to come and collect me. And there's no salon here. I don't understand this...'

Sajee fell silent and covered her mouth. She knew how ridiculous this sounded, but Thormóður didn't appear to be surprised, but looked at her curiously.

'So who is this woman?'

'Her name's Liu,' Sajee said.

'She's a friend of yours?'

'No.'

'How did you make your way here?' he asked, running fingers through the thick, fair hair at the top of his head.

'A man who works at the airport drove me. I showed him the card you gave me.'

'I see.'

He held out his hands like a priest bidding parishioners stand.

'Maybe chance has thrown us together? I had a good feeling when I looked into your beautiful eyes on the flight today,' he said and gave her a warm smile. 'I hope you've managed to recover after that experience.' He patted her shoulder, picked up her case and set off along the corridor. 'Don't worry, we'll sort something out for you.'

She tried to think back as she lay in bed a few hours later, still wide awake. The bed was soft, the duvet was snug and the door was locked, but painful thoughts kept her from sleeping. The more she thought about it, the clearer it became that this job offer had been a trick to get her out of the apartment on Snorrabraut. Things had been tense between her and Liu who rented the other room. They shared a kitchen and a little living room, but the bathroom was out in the corridor and was shared with even more people. The place was small, and even so, Liu's friend Jinfei had spent most evening with them and frequently slept in the living room. There was every chance they had plotted to get rid of her so that Jinfei could have her room. Their sudden interest in Sajee's wellbeing must have been an act. As she thought things over, it seemed almost clear-cut, but she was still unwilling to believe that Liu could be so manipulative. But what was she supposed to think after having tried all evening to call both numbers?

She sighed and burrowed deep into the duvet. How was she going to get herself out of this situation? It would be expensive to fly back to Reykjavík, and what was she supposed to do there now that she was homeless and unemployed? It wasn't easy to find a place to stay in Reykjavík, and it would be expensive.

The longer she lay in the darkness the more obvious it all became. How could she have been so gullible? Little things came to mind that began to fit together. Sometimes the two of them would fall silent if Sajee appeared in the shared kitchen, and would sit and wait until she had left the room – even though she didn't understand a word of Chinese. Last week she discovered that the food she had put in the freezer compartment of the fridge had been thrown in the bin, and Liu pretended not to understand when she questioned her about it. Most of the time they struggled to understand one another and often resorted to gestures as there were so many words neither of them knew in Icelandic.

Maybe Liu didn't even know where Höfn was, just that it was a place a long way from Reykjavík. Sajee squeezed her eyes shut and pulled the duvet over her head. It was painful to be duped, but the shame in every fibre of her body was even worse.

4

After a bad night's sleep and a couple more attempts to contact Liu and Kristinn, Sajee went along the gloomy corridor to the hostel's kitchen. The man had told her the night before that since there were no guests, she could help herself. In the fridge was a yellow tub of skyr, decorated with a tempting picture of pineapple and mango. She spooned some into a bowl with sugar and some milk, and sat down to eat as she looked out of the corner window at the harbour. Men in padded overalls hurried back and forth as tubs of fish were swung ashore from the boats. Sajee sat and ate without much of an appetite, watching the activity.

The synthetic fruit flavours made her shudder and she felt a wave of homesickness.

She conjured up images of people at home in Sri Lanka with an occasional familiar face appearing from the crowd. She imagined her sister Chamundi, with tired eyes and surrounded by her brood. Sajee always felt a stab of conscience when she thought of her, and sent her money whenever she could. Then there was Janitha, who had bought himself a motorbike when he turned fourteen and a year later roared away and out of their lives. She missed them all, as well as the crowds, the smells, the noise and the heat. She wanted to call Hirumi or her sister, but couldn't bear the thought of telling them how she had been tricked. They'd say it was her own fault and wouldn't hide their disappointment in her. Hirumi had often told Sajee that she could just be grateful for the work she had cleaning houses, and that she should forget dreams of any other life. All the same, she couldn't help herself. Sometimes she'd add a man and a little girl with a dot of red dye between her eyes into her dreams. There might even be a boy as well, but as the number of imaginary children grew, her sister's tired eyes always came to mind.

5

'Good morning.'

Thormóður's voice was deep and cheerful. This was the man with the gentle smile who had held her hair from her face while she had retched and thrown up during yesterday's dreadful flight, and he was genuinely pleasant. The previous evening she had been about to go out to find something to eat when he had called to her.

'I've made soup and baked some bread,' he had said, pushing the blond fringe back from his forehead. 'Would you like to join me?'

Over their meal she had told him the whole story and left nothing out. She showed him the text messages and told him her suspicions of what Liu and her friend had plotted. It was a relief to share all this with someone. Thormóður had listened attentively to every word, without interrupting.

'I'm so ashamed,' she said, staring out of the window. A few points of light sparkled in the darkness, but the harbour was deserted. 'Now I have no work, because I told all the people I have been cleaning for that I was going away. Some of them weren't happy that I left without much notice and I've definitely lost my room in Reykjavík.'

'Do you have anyone in Iceland who can help you?' he asked thoughtfully. 'Anyone at all?'

Sajee shook her head. Liu wasn't picking up, and Hirumi was away in Sri Lanka. There was nobody else she was close to and this was a difficult situation that she wanted to solve for herself.

'If you want something desperately, it's easy to become blind to what's around you,' Thormóður said gently. 'Those lovely dark eyes of yours shouldn't be sad. I'll see what I can do to help you.'

'Thank you,' she said, repeating her words after a moment as Thormóður didn't appear to have heard her. He was engrossed in his phone as she went back to her soup.

'Could I work for you?' she asked, and he looked up. 'I can do all sorts of things.'

'I'm sure you can, but that wouldn't work out and I have an idea,' he said. 'Something that could help us both out of a problem,' he added cheerfully as he got to his feet. She was confused, unsure of what he meant, so she just smiled and started clearing the dishes from the table, until he stopped her.

'Don't worry about that.'

Guðgeir tightened his grip on the shovel and doubled his effort. He had cleared the steps and cleared around the cars on the drive, and he needed to finish the job properly. He didn't need to be at work until midday and this would kill time until then. The door of the olive-green house swung open and his landlord, Sveinn, appeared and made his way down to the little wooden decking platform that had been built beside the house with screens sheltering it on two sides. He was a man of quick movements, bundled up in a heavy brown coat and the chequered scarf he wrapped around his short neck made him look even bulkier.

'That's a fantastic job you're doing there, Guðgeir,' Sveinn called out, with the short burst of laughter that ended most of his sentences. Guðgeir still hadn't figured out of this was the product of some deep-seated inferiority complex, or just a habit. 'You're making life easy for us all. I told the old lady that if you move back to Reykjavík it would do me in completely. You're the best tenant we've ever had. We'll never even think of renting to tourists as long as you're downstairs.'

'Good morning, Svenni. Thanks,' Guðgeir said, without pausing from the task he had set himself. Sveinn pulled the door shut with a bang behind him and took cautious steps along the cleared steps between snow a metre deep on each side.

'I didn't mean that literally,' he said awkwardly, reaching out to place a hand on Guðgeir's shoulder, but instead landing in in the middle of his back. 'I mean about you going back to Reykjavík being the end of me. I didn't mean … You know. Just a manner of speaking.'

His laughter died on his lips.

'No problem. I don't take it personally,' Guðgeir said, slowing his pace. He gave Sveinn a cheerful smile to make it plain that he hadn't given the remark a moment's thought. But that wasn't quite true, and he was well aware that things that were prominent in people's minds were often the ones that clumsily broke the surface. He was also often made aware that people were uncomfortable that a man who had been a senior Reykjavík police officer was now working as a security guard in a coastal town. The higher you climb, the further you fall, people said. There was gossip everywhere and he knew all about it. Höfn had welcomed him, but there was a curiosity there as well, and he sensed the unasked questions. Guðgeir was the man who had screwed up so much; a solid reputation, a good job and a family. He had made a serious mistake and had then made an error of judgement in keeping quiet about sensitive information that concerned him at a personal level. There had been weeks when his name had been in the media practically every day, as often as not accompanied by his picture. Little was held back in the comments that had become part of any media coverage, even though it was obvious that most of them had minimal understanding of the actual events. Gradually the story faded away and disappeared from public consciousness, but the hurt done to the family remained. The children were devastated and sleeping pills helped Inga cope as she struggled with insomnia. It had been a terrible time and nothing would ever make up for the loss of his colleague's life. Before leaving for Höfn, Guðgeir had paid regular visits to Andrés's parents and his relationship with them had helped more than anything else to think his way through this debilitating experience and to get on with life. While Guðgeir recognised that nothing would ever again be as it had been, he was determined to regain as much as possible of his old life. He needed to rebuild trust and his family were at the top of the list. After some tough months he was becoming optimistic and every new day strengthened his belief that fortune would again come his way.

'Good morning, Thor… I'm sorry, I'm not sure how to say your name,' Sajee said and laughed apologetically.

'Don't worry about it. There's no need to strain the brain too early in the morning, and it looks like I've found you a place to work and live,' Thormóður said with satisfaction, pushing his fringe aside. The red wine stain stretched from his hairline down to the middle of his forehead. It was broadest at the top, narrowing like the leaf of a water lily.

'You're serious? Where? At a salon?'

She jumped to her feet. The table lifted, the bowl was overturned and sugar spilled everywhere. Sajee was mortified. Yesterday she had spilled coffee over him, and now there was splashes of skyr all over the table. Thormóður laughed, pulled some sheets from the roll of kitchen paper and crushed them into a bunch. It was clear that he didn't need to count the pennies. She looked away, as she still felt a twinge of discomfort at the sight of unnecessary waste.

'Actually, no. But at a lovely place. It's a household that needs your help. So it's work and a place to stay all in one,' he said, delighted at what he had found for her. 'It's a good household, with decent food and well paid. That's as good as it gets, isn't it?'

He unwound another handful of paper and finished wiping up the spilled skyr.

She struggled to say anything, swallowed and stared at him.

'How many children are there?' she asked, taking a deep breath.

'No children. Why did you think that?' he asked. 'Don't you like children?'

'Yes, of course,' she replied quickly. 'But they can be difficult, and they can get sick sometimes. I've been an au-pair before and it's really badly paid,' she said with a stiff, forced smile. 'But of course I need somewhere to live, and work.'

There was something charming about the way he laughed and he put an arm around her shoulders.

'There are no children at the farm, just a lonely old lady and her son. They live in an out-of-the-way place, Bröttuskriður, about an hour's drive from here. The old lady, Selma, needs some company, and the place could do with cleaning up. She can't cope with it any more now that her hips are bad and I'm sure she'd be grateful if you could massage her feet once in a while, so you'd get to use your skills. And the son... Well, let's say that while he's younger than I am, Ísak is no modern man. I can promise you that he can just about fry an egg and load the washing machine. His mother has always looked after him.'

'I've met men like that before,' Sajee said, looking down so that her black hair fell across her face.

'That's what I thought after what you told me yesterday, so I thought I'd get in touch and see if they could use your help.'

'Are they your friends?' Sajee asked. She was doubtful about whether or not to accept this offer.

'Yes, we can say so. I help them out with all kinds of stuff.' He clapped his hands together. 'What do you say to trying it out for a while? Free food and board, and a decent wage. That's a good deal, isn't it?'

Sajee gave him a thin smile, looked out into the cold outside and rubbed the ring on her finger. The boats had finished landing their catches and the last of the trucks had driven away. She was torn in both directions and her heart hammered. She glanced at him, saw the dark coffee stain on his otherwise pristine shirt, and looked away. This man had treated her well, she decided. He had been polite and agreeable. She would have to take care not to distrust people, even though Liu had cheated her.

'Well?' he said. 'Do you have a better offer?'

'No. No better offers,' she said and straightened her back.

'You're a proper grafter!' Sveinn called, a little too loudly considering how close they were to each other. 'The old lady's enjoying watching you work.'

That meant his wife, who was barely forty, and who worked at the local authority's office. It was as if a softness crept into Sveinn's voice as he spoke those words.

'I've nothing better to do and it's good exercise,' Guðgeir said, pushing the shovel deep into a heap of snow so that its handle stood up.

'All that shovelling kills two birds with one stone and guys like you need to keep fit, so I wouldn't dream of interrupting you,' Sveinn said, taking a step closer. 'But what do you reckon happened to me yesterday?'

'What was that?' Guðgeir asked. He leaned on the shovel to give himself a break. He could sense there was a tale coming, and Sveinn's stories were usually worth listening to.

'You'd never believe it,' he said, drawing out the moment.

'Let's hear it,' Guðgeir said, and took hold of the shovel again, ready to get back to work. That had the effect he had intended.

'You see, there was this young woman who was sitting in the arrivals lounge just as I was closing down after the flight. Some foreigner who had no idea where she was supposed to be. She was a bit shocked after the flight, because it was an unusually rough ride. By rights, they should have cancelled it. Didn't you hear about that?'

'No, I didn't know,' Guðgeir said, zipping up his coat. After all that exertion it wasn't good to let yourself get cold.

'Well, this poor girl was just sitting there,' Sveinn said, the excitement palpable in his voice.

'Really?' Guðgeir said, trying to show more interest than he felt. 'What was she doing in Höfn at this time of year?'

'She'd been offered a job at some beauty salon here and all she had was a couple of text messages, pretty badly written to say the least. But it turns out she can't read or write Icelandic even though she could speak it pretty well.'

'So how had she been able to read the texts?'

'A Chinese woman she rented a place with read them for her. She said she was from Sri Lanka,' Sveinn said. 'She showed me the messages and they looked dubious to me, a sort of Google Translate feel about them. She reckoned she'd come all this way to work at a salon, replacing someone nobody knew anything about, someone from China,' Sveinn laughed. 'Have you ever heard anything like it?'

'Does this salon have a name?' Guðgeir asked.

'It just said Höfn Beauty Salon, that's all, and nobody answered either of those phone numbers. I imagine it was a mistake and she went to the wrong place,' he said with another burst of laughter. 'You know what I mean.'

'So what was the upshot of all this?' Guðgeir asked. He was curious, and tried to echo Sveinn's laughter.

'The poor girl was distraught, so I tried…'

'Was this a teenager?' Guðgeir broke in.

'No, what makes you think that?' Sveinn asked in surprise. 'She must be around thirty or so, I'd say. Said her name began with an S, Saj or Suj, or something, if my memory's not playing tricks. A pretty enough girl, but a tiny little thing, like these Asians usually are, y'know. Terribly small and bony.'

'Sure,' Guðgeir said, scraping some snow aside with the shovel. 'So what did you do with her?'

'Well, I was more or less stuck with her out at the airport, and tried to help her as best I could. She was adamant she was going to work at some big salon, so I thought I'd check a couple of places that might have possibly offered her work, so I took her up to the old people's home.'

'The old folks' home?' Guðgeir said. 'Why there?'

'Well, the oldies need all sorts of care, but nobody there had any idea, so I tried everything I could think of. Took her up to the hotel, and even called Adda Lísa, but the whole thing's a mess and nobody knows anything about it. Adda has her own business, and she just shuts up shop when she takes a holiday,' Sveinn said and clapped his gloved hands together. 'Finally I took her to the hostel down by the harbour, the new place that opened last year.'

He looked at Guðgeir, who shrugged.

'You mean those houses out on the end? The one with the romantic name? The Hostel by the Sea?' he asked, exaggerating the syllables as he spoke the name as he swung the shovel again.

'That's the place,' Sveinn said, laughing again. 'The owner's name is Thormóður, moved here a year or so ago and fixed up the inside of the old factory, even though the outside isn't done yet. He'll have to get it done this summer when it warms up so they can paint it…'

'And she got to stay there?' Guðgeir asked, trying to keep Sveinn to the subject.

'Yes,' Sveinn said. 'I wonder if she's a bit backward?'

'Why's that?' Guðgeir asked.

'You have to wonder, considering everything that happened. Her looks make her stand out, though.'

'Hopefully nothing's happened to her,' Guðgeir said, wielding the shovel again to keep himself warm. Sveinn didn't appear to be feeling the cold.

'No, of course not,' he muttered. 'At any rate, she stayed there last night and with luck she'll stay there a little longer, as there's a lousy forecast,' he added.

'She must have been upset when she realised how wrong things had gone,' Guðgeir said, feeling a deep sympathy for the woman.

'Too right! And the messages on her phone were weird,' Sveinn said. 'Downright weird,' he added with a burst of laughter. 'It's like the tourist who thought he was heading to Laugavegur in Reykjavík, chose the wrong option on the satnav and ended in in Siglufjörður instead. Don't you remember that? There was even a skit about it on TV.'

'I saw it on the news, but don't remember the jokes. Some English or American tourist who should have taken the trouble to read the instructions, but if this woman is illiterate then it's no surprise that she found herself in difficulties. They use a completely different script in Sri Lanka,' Guðgeir said. 'A sort of flowing script, quite beautiful and complicated, for us, at least. I can't recall what it's called...' he said and paused, searching his memory for the name.

At one time he had remembered everything. But after months of mental tension, he had found that the answers were no longer always at his fingertips.

He knew that a slight loss of memory was one of the effects of the pressure he had been under, and that it would be temporary, but it still irritated him.

'A very beautiful script,' he said again as he went back to clearing snow.

'I wouldn't know about Asian letters,' Sveinn said, looking ready to be on his way now that he had exhausted the subject. 'See you,' he said and marched towards his jeep. 'And thanks for clearing the snow. The weather's going to break again later.'

The car door slammed behind him and the wheels spun as he drove off. Guðgeir stuck the shovel into the snow and gazed into the distance to check the weather. A bank of heavy cloud had formed around Vesturhorn. A storm was brewing.

'Shouldn't we turn round and try again tomorrow?' Sajee asked, worried as she peered out into the blizzard. Moments ago the car had spun right around on the icy road.

'Not at all. It's not that bad. This is a good jeep and I'm used to this. There's nothing to be gained by hanging around in Höfn,' Thormóður said in his mild voice. 'We have to go through the tunnel and then drive through the countryside to get to Bröttuskriður.'

He seemed confident and it didn't appear to bother him that the wind buffeted the car and they could hardly see the road ahead for falling snow. It was as if he relished getting to grips with the challenges nature put in their way, as there was a smile on his lips.

It was a relief to enter the tunnel, escaping the blizzard. Here there was shelter and they could see ahead. On the far side of the mountain the weather turned out to be less wild and before long the snow had stopped falling. Sajee found herself relaxing and enjoying the view over the rolling countryside. They drove over a long bridge that spanned a glacier river churning with brown water. On one side black sands glittered between long tongues of snow that stretched towards a long lagoon, and on the other side the crags of mountains loomed over them. The peaks were jagged, as if they had been sketched in a hurry. The magnificence of nature all around them was mesmerising and she was spellbound as she gazed out of the car's window. This place felt as if it had been plucked out of some fairy tale. To begin with there were a few farms, but these became increasingly fewer. Then they crossed another river and there were no more farms to be seen.

The farmhouse stood on rising ground beneath the scree of an imposing, steep-sided mountain. They turned off the main road and drove along a rutted track that looped past a deep lagoon. The powerful jeep vibrated and fishtailed in the snow, but Thormóður laughed. He seemed relieved that they had reached their destination without any mishap. Sajee looked around curiously. On the slope lay a large boulder that had fallen from far above, and as far as she could make out, not too long ago. Birds wheeled around the jagged peaks.

The house itself was an imposing one, with two storeys built on a concrete basement sunk into the ground. The place looked as if it had never seen a paintbrush as it rose from the white of the snow and its walls blended in with the grey basalt of the scree behind it. As she approached, she saw that the steel sheets on the roof looked to be brand new and the black window frames appeared to be freshly painted. There were curtains in a coarse, dark material in the windows. The same material had been used everywhere, except the narrow basement windows which had been covered with black plastic.

'Don't the people who live here feel the need of a little colour? It's all so grey,' she muttered.

'What was that?' Thormóður asked without looking up. His attention was on adjusting a small lever which appeared stiff. As it moved, the note of the engine changed. She shook her head and smiled politely.

'Nothing,' she said.

To the western side of the farmhouse was a long barn and a small animal with a tail as long as its body ran back and forth. Clearly tethered, it ran the same distance again and again.

'What animal is that?' she asked.

'A fox,' he replied shortly, without looking. His attention was clearly elsewhere.

She asked no more questions, but watched the animal's quick movements with interest. Further to the west was a copse where gnarled trees stood packed together inside iron railings, standing out against the bleak landscape.

'What kind of garden is that over there?' she asked curiously. This time he didn't reply, but instead focused on a green car that had been parked beside the house. It seemed to irritate him, and he stopped, taking out his phone to make a call.

'Who the hell's that and why didn't you let me know?' he snarled into the phone, glancing around as he listened to the reply. It clearly wasn't something that agreed with him, as he scowled.

'No, it's too late now,' he said angrily, ended the call and drove around to the eastern side of the house. 'Nothing but trouble, these people,' he mumbled to himself.

'Something wrong?' Sajee asked, wondering what was going on.

'Nothing you need to worry about,' he replied and got out of the car to open the rear door. He picked up a couple of boxes and carried them down the steps leading to the basement and then picked up two carrier bags from the back seat. A little bottle of nail varnish remover dropped from one of them, and as he opened the bag to put it back, more could be seen in there.

'You're sure you don't have a salon after all?' she suggested, hoping to lighten the atmosphere a little, but he either didn't hear her or didn't understand, and disappeared without a word, the two bags in his hands. A moment later he returned and asked for her phone, saying he wanted to add his number to the directory.

'That's my name,' he said, showing her the screen. 'You see? If you need me, call.'

He seemed to be in a hurry, effortlessly swinging her heavy case from the car and dropping it at her side.

'You can tell Ísak and Selma that I've done their shopping,' he said and patted Sajee's shoulder. 'I'm going to be on my way. You can never tell when the weather's going to close in again.'

'Aren't you coming inside with me?' she asked forlornly.

'No, you'll be fine. I don't want to meet...' he nodded towards the green car. 'Must rush. Don't worry. I'll drop by,' he said, and was gone, his hurry to be away taking her by surprise. She hardly managed to say goodbye or thank him for everything he had done.

6

She stood alone by the house under the scree. The mountains surrounded her. She looked up at the needle-sharp peaks, mesmerised by the rags of cloud that swirled around the points that jutted upwards like the teeth of a saw.

'Hello, you must be Sajee. Has Thormóður already gone?'

Sajee was so taken by surprise at the sound of the voice that she started.

An upright older woman stood at her side. She was dressed in black trousers made of some fine material, and a grey polo-neck under a grey woollen cardigan with silver buttons. Her skin was clear, although tiny bags had formed under her cheekbones and the skin hung under her neck like a wattle. Her hair was as grey as ash, her forehead low, with dark eyebrows and with an alertness in her deep-set, blue-grey eyes.

'Were you born with a cleft palate, or did you have an accident? She asked, looking Sajee critically over.

'I was born like this.'

'Good,' the woman said, a hint of friendliness in her voice, holding her cardigan around her in the cold. 'That's just better.'

Sajee nodded politely, as if she knew what the woman was talking about.

'Come indoors. You're so poorly dressed that you'll freeze if we stand out here much longer,' she said, heading for the door.

They went through a little entrance hall and up wooden stairs to the second floor. Sajee went cautiously as the steps had become so worn that they sloped downwards. Upstairs the ceiling was low and the room the woman showed her into was sparsely furnished with items that showed their age. A picture of a little boy with fair hair hung in a gold frame on the wall under the gable. Next to it hung a second picture, painted in dark shades and difficult to make out.

'My name is Selma, but I suppose Thormóður already told you that,' she said. 'I live here with my son, Ísak. You can push that under the bed when you've unpacked,' she added, looking curiously at Sajee's case. She seemed intrigued to know what it might contain, as if it might tell her tales of travels in distant lands.

'This is fine,' Sajee said.

The room had a comfortable feel to it, but had clearly been unused for a long time. A crocheted purple spread covered the bed and a lamp made from a wine bottle stood on a dark wood bureau. Next to the lamp was a photograph of a handsome young woman. The picture was old and the frame looked as if it had not been polished for many years.

'I need a little time to sort things out.'

'That's no problem,' Selma said quickly as she turned to go. 'Make yourself at home and you can rest. There are visitors downstairs who will be leaving shortly, so there's no hurry to come down.'

It was astonishing how life could take a new direction so quickly. A rocky shore and the grey sea could be seen out of the little gable window. Only the day before yesterday she had left her basement room in Reykjavík. From there she had seen feet pass by, young and old, some young, some old. Occasionally a cat had come up to the window, rubbed itself up against the glass and tried vainly to get in. Life on Snorrabraut was so completely unlike what she had grown up with in Sri Lanka where most houses were open and there was little to separate what was indoors from the world outside. Icelandic houses were shut up tight and she had the feeling that this house with its grey concrete walls was shut tighter than most.

She leaned against the old woodwork of the window frame and looked out. The expanse of the ocean in the distance sparked mixed feelings inside of both freedom and confinement. This was a step in the wrong direction, but hopefully something positive would emerge from this unexpected turn her life had taken. It was far from being her dream job, but at least she would have free board and lodging. After everything that had happened, things could have turned out worse.

There was a corner shelf in the room, and this was where she placed the Buddha. He was the most important one. Next came the statue of Ganesh, whom she asked to bless the change in her life's fortunes. After a moment's thought, she added the figurine of the Virgin Mary to the shelf. A woman she had once worked for had given her the little statue as a parting gift, and Sajee was fond of it. She stood back and smiled as she looked at the group. She would bring them an offering when she had found out what kind of food there was at Bröttuskriður. Food for the gods shouldn't pass through ordinary people's kitchens, so she would ask Selma to let her bring a little fruit or vegetable upstairs.

Once she had put the room in order, she rubbed avocado oil into her hands and feet. The oil always reminded her of the happy time when she had worked at Lakmal's salon. They had laughed good-naturedly at the owner's foibles and swapped stories. After work they cooked together in the back garden and Sajee felt her mouth watering at the thought of the food they ate there.

She massaged her cold feet with soft, quick hands, and pulled on her socks before she stepped onto the cool floor. Then she padded carefully down the stairs and along the gloomy passage towards the loud voices.

7

The house was old and it was obvious that it hadn't been looked after. Shabby walls could have done with a coat of paint and the grubby sockets and switches needed a good scrub. Sajee stopped for a moment outside the closed kitchen door before opening it. The chatter ended abruptly as she appeared in the doorway. As well as Selma, there were a man and a woman, both past middle age and noticeably skinny. The woman sat on a chair at the end of the table and the man on a white wooden bench by the wall. They looked in surprise at the unexpected visitor, while Selma's eyes narrowed in displeasure.

'This young lady is going to give me a hand for a few days,' she explained shortly, hands on her hips.

'Well, is that so? Pleased to meet you,' the man said as he ran a hand over his bald head. 'My name's Karl and that's Marta,' he added, nodding to his wife. They both continued to look her up and down without trying to hide their curiosity.

'My name is Sajee…'

'These are our neighbours, but out here it's a long way between farms,' Selma interrupted before she could say any more. 'Take a seat, now that you're here.'

Sajee looked around curiously. Like the rest of the house, the kitchen was shabby, but most of the kitchen implements were new and some of the better brands. On a side table stood a red kitchen mixer and a blender of the same make. Sajee had seen the same machines in one of the mansions she had cleaned in Reykjavík. The coffee machine on the worktop was a big one, offering endless combinations and it wouldn't have been out of place in a restaurant. The air was heavy with the smell of cooking and she glanced at the window. It was shut. A blizzard again raged outside, hurling snow at the glass. There were two candles in holders on the windowsill. Selma noticed where she was looking, but instead of opening a window, she struck a match and lit the candles, releasing a strong aroma of fruit that quickly filled the room. For a moment Sajee felt that she was back home and closed her eyes. In her thoughts she could see the bustling crowds and hear the blare of horns.

'Are you tired? Marta asked.

She wore a silver bracelet, and fiddled with the clasp, opening and closing it. Sajee opened her eyes.

'No, not at all,' she said, and sat up straight in the chair. The stuffy atmosphere was making her drowsy and she tried to shake it off. Everything about this house seemed to oppress her, but maybe that was just the outcome of yesterday's disappointment. By now she had already had more than enough of cleaning other people's houses.

'How do you like being out here in the country?' Selma said, fiddling with the coffee machine. 'Don't you feel it's a little isolated?'

She pressed buttons here and there, finally gave up and filled an old-fashioned kettle from the tap.

'I couldn't see much because of the weather.'

'Tell me about it,' Karl grumbled. 'Our electricity went off, so we came out here.'

'As we drove up here I saw a little garden by the mountain, with trees around it,' Sajee said.

'Did you see the cliffs above the road as well?' Karl asked and Sajee looked at him in confusion, wondering what he was talking about.

'No,' she hesitated. 'I just saw the garden. Is it for growing vegetables in the summer?'

They looked perplexed and she repeated words several times to make herself understood, until Selma anger burst out.

'Vegetables in the family plot!' she snapped, her face flushed as she waved the dishcloth. 'Vegetables! What the hell are you talking about, girl?' She threw the cloth into the sink, and stretched for scissors and a bag of coffee from the shelf. 'Planting cabbages in the family plot,' she said through teeth clenched. 'The thought of it!'

She tapped the scissors several times on the worktop as if to add emphasis to her words before she snipped open the packet.

'Ridiculous,' Marta muttered, snapping her bracelet closed, while Karl seemed to relish the furore and grinned to himself.

'You mean it's like a churchyard? Where people are buried?' Sajee asked nervously, looking from face to face. Selma's anger had abated and the couple acted as if nothing had happened.

'Yes. But just our people,' Selma said in a dry tone. 'All my people are there. Mother and father, my grandparents, and others.'

She pushed the ash-grey hair back from her low forehead and her blue-grey eyes looked searchingly at the foreign guest.

'Oh, I understand,' Sajee said, a hand to her mouth. 'I didn't mean to … I'm so sorry.'

'The dead are in the family plot, but the cliff to the east is where the hidden people are. Believe me, they're more than just folk tales,' Karl said in a hushed tone of voice, lounging in his seat.

'Of course,' said Sajee, who had no idea what was being discussed.

'You know what kind of people they are?' he asked.

'No,' Sajee said cautiously, with a polite smile and wary of upsetting anyone a second time. 'Would you explain for me?'

'The hidden people are people like you and me.' Karl patted his chest with the palm of his hand, leaned towards her and his voice dropped as a secretive expression appeared on his face. 'But we don't see them. At least, most of the time we don't, because we humans have our limits in so many ways. Our senses are very poor unless they're carefully trained.'

'What on Earth makes you think she understands all that?' Selma said. She seemed to have regained her equilibrium after her unexpected outburst and now she looked at Sajee with concern. 'Please, help yourselves,' she said, placing a bowl of pastries on the table.

'The hidden people are called that because they're hidden from us, they aren't visible and can't be seen be seen by normal eyes,' Karl said, his explanation accompanied by hand gestures. 'They're not elves, because that's just rubbish. But the hidden people exist and they live among us.'

'Do you mean spirits?' Sajee asked with interest. She pushed her hair back behind her ears and paid attention. There was no mistaking her curiosity. 'Good spirits or evil ones?'

'Not exactly. The hidden people are like us, except that they're taller, more dignified and in every way more handsome that we humans are. They dress in shades of blue and they live in the rocks. That's not in every rock, but just in some places.'

'Have you seen hidden people?' Sajee asked in excitement.

'Of course he hasn't seen any hidden people,' Marta sniffed. 'Don't listen to his fairy tales. These are just old folk tales that people told in the dark before we had electricity. Back then people had to have ways of explaining things they didn't understand.'

'The hidden people are usually good, unless they're mistreated. If you harm them in any way, they're merciless in getting their own back,' Karl continued, not inclined to let his wife spoil his tale.

'How do they do that?' Sajee asked 'Like evil spirits do? I know a lot of stories of that happening.'

'They do, and they can be both very cruel and without a shred of mercy,' Karl replied quickly. He spat the words out and a vein in his neck pulsed as he spoke.

'He's trying to frighten you,' Selma said. She stood in the middle of the room with the coffee pot in her hand. 'That's a fine sort of reception you're getting here.'

'I understand well. At home in Sri Lanka we also have spirits,' Sajee said. 'Some are good and others are terribly evil. My grandmother believes in many spirits. She's old and...'

'The hidden people aren't spirits,' Selma said, her voice again harsh. 'They are people like us. But they have a higher consciousness and they watch us humans. Sometimes they come to our aid when it's needed, but if they're wronged then their revenge can be bitter.'

She banged the coffee pot down on the table so hard that boiling droplets erupted from the spout. Sajee watched in astonishment. It was difficult to get the measure of these people, what they meant and what they didn't. Just a moment ago Selma had talked as if the hidden people didn't exist, and now she seemed to be saying the opposite.

'Well, no more of that superstitious claptrap, Karl. What's got into you?' Marta said to her husband as she jabbed him with one elbow. 'Let's just have coffee and talk about something pleasant instead.'

She lifted the ancient coffee pot and poured into four cups. Droplets continued to fall from the spout, collecting in little puddles on the flower-patterned plastic tablecloth. Sajee looked around for a cloth and her gaze ended at the magnificent coffee machine that stood unused in the corner.

Karl didn't seem to notice Selma's and Marta's words and he continued speaking. Nothing seemed able to interrupt his flow. He planted his elbows on the table and his chin on one hand. The index finger of his left hand was missing the tip.

'There are many tales of the hidden people helping people in trouble, and that's something the people here at Bröttuskriður know very well,' Karl said slowly, crossing his bony arms and catching Sajee's eye meaningfully. 'On this farm they know about hidden people who not only provide help in need but who spirit problems away ... yes, and there are other kinds of hidden people as well. Those are the up-to-date ones who bring all kinds of presents.'

'Shh! Stop that stupid talk!' Selma snapped, pacing the floor. 'It's not good manners to frighten folk, especially disabled people who don't have the wit to know what you're on about!'

Karl bubbled with laughter, as if he had been playing a complex game and had won.

'There, there. Calm down, Selma. Your new little friend needs to get to know us better,' he said, purring with suppressed anticipation. 'You know the hidden people can also make unpleasant people disappear from our world.'

'Where do they take them?' Sajee asked, her heart in her mouth.

'Into the rocks,' he replied quickly.

'Karl! Stop it, will you? Are you losing the little sense you had?' Marta said sharply. 'What's got into you, man?'

'Nothing at all!' he said, glancing from Marta to Selma. 'Nothing,' he repeated, placing a finger on his lips as he turned to Sajee. 'Nothing at all, but whenever the hidden people have to do an uncomfortable task, then they leave behind them some mark that's difficult to erase.'

'Of course,' Selma said, as if she had experienced a revelation. 'That's the way of it.'

She stopped her pacing and stopped in front of Sajee, grey eyes inspecting her.

'Stop this rubbish right away, Karl,' Marta snapped. 'You're frightening the girl.'

'I'm not frightened,' Sajee said. 'How do the hidden people make bad people disappear?'

'Isn't that just it?' he whispered to her, his eyes on Selma. 'Sometimes they just go up in a puff of smoke, but there are others the hidden people drive completely mad.'

The outside door banged and the floorboards creaked. A fair-haired man with startlingly thick, dark eyebrows and who looked to be somewhere between forty and fifty made a sudden appearance in the kitchen. He was heavily built, with broad shoulders that slumped. He and his mother were strikingly alike.

'Is this her?' he asked, slouching forward as he picked up a crocheted red cloth from the table and used it to wipe oil from his grimy fingers. In a moment the cloth was black with oil.

'Who else would she be? Won't you wash your hands at the sink, Ísak?' Selma said tenderly, putting out a hand to stroke his cheek. 'Did you lock the cellar?'

Ísak nodded, but the look on his face indicated that any further questions would be unwelcome. Selma smiled affectionately and poured more coffee into everyone's cup without asking if they wanted more.

'Do you have tea?' Sajee asked, but nobody replied.

'What are you doing here?' Ísak demanded. His eyes flashed across all the faces in the room, but the question was clearly meant for the couple from Gröf.

'They came because the power went off,' his mother replied. 'But she,' Selma said, nodding towards Sajee, 'is going to help us for a while, and as I said earlier, she can do massage and do my old feet some good.'

'Yeah. All right. You do massage too? I thought you were just here to clean,' Ísak said. He glared at Sajee, and helped himself to a pastry.

'What have you been tinkering with?' Karl asked.

'Oiling the transmission,' Ísak replied and his expression lightened.

'How's it going?'

'It just needs attention and a bit of a massage,' he said with a grin.

'I learned massage,' Sajee broke in, eager to tell them what she could do.

'You all do massage, don't you?' Karl muttered with a gurgle of laughter.

'Massage and a bit of oil does the trick,' Ísak said, laughing at his own joke as he caught Karl's eye.

'Stop it, will you?' Selma said. 'You're talking as if every woman from Asia is some kind of whore.'

The silence that fell was deafening. There was something behind their antics that couldn't be said out loud. Sajee sipped her coffee and her hand shook. She had experienced all this before, in another place. She reached into her trouser pocket for her phone. If she were to feel genuinely uncomfortable here, then she could call Thormóður and ask him to fetch her.

'Of course not,' Marta said after a long silence. 'Who on Earth would suggest that?'

'Don't take it personally, my dear. They're just making fun,' Selma said as she poured more coffee into Sajee's cup, even though she shook her head and raised her hand to stop her, but was too late. The coffee was almost spilling onto the table.

'Making what?' she asked, looking in dismay at the coffee.

'A joke,' Ísak explained. 'You can take a joke, I hope?' he asked with a bark of nervous laughter.

Sajee forced a smile.

'There was a bit of a wild one turned up in Djúpivogur a year or two back,' Karl said.

'Wasn't that one from the Philippines?' Marta asked. 'She liked a good time and had a child with some lad from around there. Or was she Thai? I reckon all that went on somewhere near Breiðdalur...'

'The one you're talking about wasn't in Djúpivogur,' Selma said, wiping up spilled coffee with the crocheted cloth her son had used. 'She was somewhere further east, wasn't she?'

Sajee stared at the greasy cloth as it swept across the table.

'Asians are there for anyone,' Karl said, licking his lips. 'They just laugh and take it, these girls.'

'That's enough,' Ísak said with unexpected determination. 'The power must be back on at your place by now. The wind's dropped so you'd best be on your way.'

There was silence again as they stared out of the window. Selma put down the cloth and offered the dish of pastries to Sajee, who declined.

'Don't take their talk seriously, my dear. Boys will always be boys. They won't be told and the whole lot of them are as stubborn as any donkey.'

She poured even more coffee into Sajee's cup, which had hardly been touched, and pushed the pastries again towards her. She shook her head again, but Selma appeared not to notice, so she took one of the twisted doughnuts and took a small bite. Greasy and with a cardamom flavour, it stuck to her palate.

'Where are you from?' Marta asked.

'I come from Sri Lanka. It's an island, like Iceland, in south-east Asia,' she said gabbled. She spoke too fast, but made herself intelligible all the same.

'That's it. Used to be called Ceylon,' Karl said, clearly proud of his general knowledge.

'Like the tea,' his wife added.

'Are you a Tamil?' Ísak asked, and Sajee shook her head.

'Mr Knowledgeable,' Karl said, the sarcasm clear in his voice. 'That's a man with years of learning behind him.'

'I've just heard them talk about the Tamils on the news. There's always trouble brewing over there. I expect you're relieved to be here,' Ísak said.

'Are you from the country?' Selma asked, breaking her own silence.

'No,' Sajee said. 'I come from a district near a huge city called Colombo. There are millions of people living there.'

They stared at her and silence fell again.

'Thormóður said you're alone here,' Selma said. 'He told me you don't read or write.'

'My aunt will come back soon from Sri Lanka and she has been away for a long time,' Sajee said, keeping to the truth and not correcting the misconception.

'Don't you people have anything better to do than talk?' Ísak broke in.

There was a long pause, that ended as Marta and Karl got to their feet at the same time, and Sajee started at the sound of their chairs on the floor.

'Well, my dear. It's been interesting to meet you, and I can tell you that I'm not the type to be prejudiced but I'm all for keeping the stock pure. The Icelandic stock, I mean,' Marta said with a smile of farewell for Sajee that seemed also aimed at Ísak. 'In my opinion, it ought to be kept as pure as possible, preferably completely pure. It's the same with sheep. There's no good that comes of mixing dark wool with light. That's my experience from years of keeping livestock.'

'Quite right, Marta,' Karl said. 'There's no value in mixed wool, no value at all.'

Ísak fidgeted in the doorway. His agitation had grown with every passing minute, but the visitors appeared to be paying him no attention.

'Will you be staying long here at Bröttuskriður?' Marta asked, this time speaking directly to Sajee, but didn't wait for an answer before turning to Selma. 'I thought we'd agreed that we'd ask for a home help from Höfn? There's more chance of that if there's two of us need some support. Didn't we agree on that?'

'No, she's not stopping long,' Ísak interrupted before Selma could reply. 'She's not stopping long at all.'

April

8

A storm had been forecast for the whole of the south coast, all the way to Vík. Gale force gusts could be expected and there wouldn't be weather for travelling over Easter. Guðgeir had meant to drive to Reykjavík after work, returning on Good Friday, as he was on the rota to work both Saturday and Easter Sunday. But now it was Thursday morning and it was clear he wouldn't be going anywhere, so he called Inga to let her know. His mood was gloomy, a mixture of disappointment and claustrophobia.

'How about you? Could you make it?'

He opened his eyes wide and took deep breaths, as if mental energy could be enough to make his own unspoken wish come true. 'Could you get a flight and come here for a couple of days?'

He heard her hesitate, knowing he had been too eager, but decided to stick with what he had said. What the hell? They were still married, and if it were up to him, they'd stay together.

'Actually, no,' she replied in a slow tone. He sensed her stepping away from the phone.

'I can't hear you very well? Is it on speaker?' he asked.

'No.'

'I can hardly hear you,' Guðgeir said, trying to hide his disappointment. 'Hello? It's a bad connection. Hello?' he called, louder this time. Had she put the phone down, or had the connection been dropped?

'It's fine this end, and I can hear you clearly,' Inga said. 'But I'm exhausted. There's a lot of pressure at work and I was going to make the most of Easter to get some rest. Plus I need to clean the house and make a start on the garden.'

'Can't the garden wait?' he asked, too eager, again.

'It's not going to clear itself up, is it?'

He felt he could hear the hint of accusation in her voice. He smarted, but managed to hold back a sharp retort. She was the one who was making this long-distance relationship happen, not him. A year, she had said. After a year, we can take stock. They had spent Christmas together, and after that he had allowed himself to hope that they would come together again. All the same, he had slept on the TV room sofa the whole time except for New Year's Eve when friends and family had vanished out into the smoky darkness. The two of them had been left alone in the house, and it was the way it had been before. In fact, better, more passionate, more urgent. But in the morning Inga acted as if nothing had changed. She had helped him pack his stuff and took it with him out to the car. There had been no drama, no accusations, not the slightest hint that he would be missed. That had hurt the most.

'I'll call, you, darling. See you at Easter,' she had said cheerfully, giving him a fleeting kiss on the lips, but he held her tight.

'You know I'll do whatever's needed to make amends, and maybe we won't need a whole year,' he whispered in her year, feeling her relax in his arms, just for a moment before she slipped out of his embrace and walked along the drive to their house; their home.

They hadn't seen each other for three months. The children had spent a few days with him in the middle of February, but Inga wouldn't let herself be persuaded to come, and now it was Easter. The thought that she could have embarked on another relationship troubled Guðgeir more and more. It preyed on his mind, and it was painful – more painful than he was prepared to admit.

As a child Sajee had frequently retreated into daydreams as an escape from difficult and often painful reality. The family lived in one of the many chaotic districts on the outskirts of Colombo. The house had never been properly rainproof, but provided shelter from the heat of the sun. Few of the streets lay in a straight line, but snaked through the district like veins pulsing vigorously with blood, alive with noise, smells and life. Sajee was the youngest of three siblings and only six years old when her mother, who had suffered from epilepsy, died. Her brother Janitha was thirteen at the time and her sister Chamudi was twelve. A little while later their mother's sister Hirumi came into the household to care for them, but it wasn't long before she was gone. Sajee wept until her eyes were sore, but her father said it was for the best and that the evil eye followed their mother's family. Hirumi would visit occasionally when their father was away, but never stayed for long, and eventually she stopped coming altogether.

One day a postcard arrived from Iceland, a country they had never heard of. Hirumi had met and married a man from Iceland, and now she worked cleaning houses in the capital, Reykjavík. Over the coming years more postcards with pictures of mountains and waterfalls arrived, and Sajee hung them over her bed.

Janitha left home as soon as he was able, and when Sajee was ten years old, her sister Chamundi was married off to a middle-aged man in another district. That left Sajee alone with her father as he grew increasingly bitter at his lot and frequently vented his anger on her. She learned young that it was best to do as he wanted, and otherwise stay out of sight. She often spent as long as she could on the way home from school, playing with other children until she started spending time at Lakmal's shop, the local massage and beauty salon.

The women who worked for Lakmal were cheerful and talked endlessly. They treated Sajee kindly while she watched as if in a trance as their gentle hands massaged the tired feet of those who came into the shop. Before long she was running errands for Lakmal, who was pleasantly surprised at how quick she was to learn.

She quickly picked up techniques from the women and before long Lakmal asked her to join them. Her father was relieved, got rid of the shack they had lived in and moved in with his elder daughter while Sajee slept with the other women in a room above the salon. The next few years were the happiest of her life. She was respected and no longer needed to sweep the pavement outside or stand with a smile on her face to encourage customers to stop. Her foot massages were popular, as she had the softest hands and knew how to use them, and she made a point of not chatting endlessly with her customers as some of the other women did.

One day there was no sign of Lakmal at opening time and the women wondered what to do. They waited outside for hours as customers came and went, without being able to do anything for them. Late in the day a stranger came, and gave them the news that Lakmal had suffered a heart attack. For the next few days they waited in hope and fear, and the salon stayed closed as he was the key holder.

They made offerings and they prayed, but without success. On the seventh day Lakmal died and they all lost their jobs, and most of them became homeless. Sajee was devastated. She sent a desperate letter to her aunt Hirumi asking for help. For the next few weeks she was able to lodge with a charitable family, but nobody seemed to have any use for her skills. At dawn she would rise and go out, but there was no work to be found. The patience of the family with its own numerous mouths to feed began to wear thin.

Before long she would have no choice but to join the beggars in the street, as she was reluctant to impose on her sister who already had her hands full with a brood of children and a father who became more difficult by the day.

Guðgeir brewed coffee and switched on the television. He channel hopped until green fields and steep slopes caught his attention. Next there were brightly dressed women with giant baskets on their backs, which as far as he could see were made of plastic. The women picked tea leaves, throwing them behind them into the baskets. They sang as they worked and the narrator explained that tea was Sri Lanka's most important export. Then a bare-chested farmer riding an elephant appeared on the screen as Guðgeir drank the last of his coffee and switched the television off. He remembered that the woman Sveinn had talked about came from there. He went to the hallway, and pulled on his coat and boots. The gloom that waited for him outside was the complete opposite of the colourful scenes he had just seen on the screen.

He strode rapidly down to the sea where there was a walkway that followed the shoreline. It was known as the Nature Trail and it provided spectacular views over Hornafjörður and to the distant ice caps. This was where Guðgeir had often spent time when he wasn't feeling his best, and it had helped him through some dark days. As usual, he stopped at the large model of the solar system. Every time he stopped and examined it, he was gripped by the sense of his own smallness compared to the universe, and by a feeling that was strange, yet familiar. This was what he had called his 'alien feeling', when he was a child, failing to connect with the kids in the new district in Reykjavík after having been uprooted from the countryside in the west.

His thoughts went back to the woman from Sri Lanka who must have experienced similar emotions while she had been weatherbound in Höfn. It must have been frustrating to be shut away in such an isolated spot because of circumstances beyond her control. He he had become painfully familiar with loneliness and homesickness, and felt an instinctive sympathy for her

After the seismic events that had culminated in Andrés's death, he had been plagued with such guilt that the physical pain he had endured was almost mild by comparison. If only he could turn back the clock and change the course of events, like an author tinkering with a plot.

Guðgeir set off, gradually lengthening his stride until he broke into a run. The ice was starting to release its grip and as his pace increased, he could feel his mood improve as he ran. It was unfortunate that he was overdressed and knew that he should have stuck to his usual running gear. The weather was fine and there was nothing to complain about here, even if the wind was blowing hard further down the coast. He picked up the pace a little more, not slowing down until he had reached the end of the walkway.

He turned, running with sweat, and on the way back he stopped at the swimming pool. He cursed silently when he saw that it was closed, and peered at the note on the door that displayed the Easter opening hours. He had left his glasses at home, but as far as he could make out, the pool would be open again tomorrow. That was a small consolation for the walk home.

After a shower and a shave, he dressed and went out, this time to the coffee shop on the corner. It was opposite the flat, so he often went there and was on good terms with the staff, especially Linda, who seemed to take every extra shift offered.

He was surprised to see that the place was full. Over the last few days there had been a steady increase in the number of tourists arriving in the town, but he hadn't realised quite how many there were. Fortunately, Linda was at work and quickly found him a seat, with a warning that with business booming it could take a while to get something to eat.

'The tourists are coming thick and fast. It's never been like it at this time of year,' she said, handing him a menu.

'I'm in no hurry to eat, but a beer would help,' Guðgeir said with a smile. 'A large one.'

The smile she sent back his way filled her whole face and lively eyes. Like Inga, she was slim and petite, but with a fairer complexion. He followed her with his eyes. She had tied her apron at the front so that the two tapes crossed above her bottom, which flexed gently with each step until she vanished through the swing doors. Guðgeir looked out of the window and at the people around him, before putting on the glasses he had this time remembered to bring with him to look through the menu. It hadn't changed for a couple of days.

A babble of languages could be heard around him as he picked out familiar words from English, Swedish, German and French, as well as languages he couldn't identify. An Indian family sat at one table, clearly recovering from some adventure in the wild weather on the hills below the Vatnajökull ice cap, as they had plenty to talk about and their exhausted children were half asleep where they sat.

He took a long draught of ice-cold beer and called Inga, who answered breathlessly, telling him that she had trimmed the hedge and pressure-washed the patio. These were the kind of garden chores he had always disliked, but now found himself missing.

'You could have waited for me. I've a long weekend coming up so I'll come down and get on with it,' he said, watching Linda placing plates on the neighbouring table. He could smell the lamb cutlets.

'Well, I'd had enough of seeing the garden looking like that,' Inga said, without a trace of irritation in her voice. 'A bit of exercise doesn't do any harm,' she added. 'It's as good as a workout.'

'And there was me thinking you were so tired. Didn't you say something about taking it easy over Easter?'

'I'm fine,' she replied, quickly.

'You can leave the clippings and the rubbish. I'll borrow a trailer at the weekend and clear it all up,' Guðgeir said.

'Don't worry about it. Finnur stopped by with his jeep and a trailer and offered to give me a hand,' Inga said, words tumbling out.

An image of the newly qualified Finnur, Inga's colleague at the legal practice, flashed into Guðgeir's mind. He felt a tightness in his chest. If he remembered correctly, this was the smooth guy who wore expensive suits when he wasn't pedalling at speed around Reykjavík on his top-of-the-range bike, open-water swimming in the freezing cold or sweating at CrossFit. The caricature of the man stuck in his thoughts and was like a needle punched into his heart.

'Finnur? Is that the new guy who spent ten years getting his law degree?' Guðgeir asked, unable to hide the scorn in his voice.

'Don't be like that. Finnur had to work alongside his studies, plus he was always doing competitive sports as well. You ought to know we don't take on just anyone. It's not as if lawyers are in short supply,' she retorted.

He didn't reply, and rubbed his forehead hard. Why had she become so defensive? Because she had taken the man on, or was there something else?

'Are you there? Hello!' Inga called out. 'Now the bad connection's my end. Guðgeir?'

'Yes,' he said, staring at the pine-panelled wall. A gold-painted fan swirled about his head as if it wanted to break free and drift away.

'There's no need to sulk.'

'I just feel it could have waited until I could get home. You shouldn't need to get your colleagues to help you round the house. Of course I'll deal with it,' he said and watched the Indian family as he spoke. One of the children had fallen asleep in the father's arms.

'It's not as if I'm sleeping with Finnur. He just gave me a hand in the garden,' Inga said and her voice had suddenly become clearer and harsher. Sometimes it's as well for those who live in glass houses not to throw stones for fear of smashing something, Guðgeir thought to himself and shut his mouth tight. How had he managed to let the conversation go on this direction? He rubbed his jaw, angry with himself, and looked around in discomfort. Linda was serving the Indian family's meals.

'Inga, I didn't mean to…'

'Sorry, Guðgeir. But when you don't mean this or that, it gets on my nerves,' she snapped.

'I'm sorry, my love,' he said quickly. 'I'm in a café and the place is full so it's not a great place to talk. It's good to know you had some help around the garden and I wasn't trying to imply anything. Please say thanks to Finnur and give him my regards. I'll call tomorrow and talk to the children.'

He held the phone in his hand and pressed the red button before she could say anything in response. He stared out of the window to calm himself down. It had started to rain.

The beer deadened some of the pain in his chest, and when his cod arrived, he asked for a glass of white wine to go with it.

'The place is packed,' Guðgeir said, looking around. He was the only one with a table to himself.

'It's starting to quieten down now and I should get a break soon,' Linda said. 'I'll come and keep you company if you don't mind.'

'Linda!' a voice called from the kitchen and she turned in response.

'Please do,' he said quickly, taking off his glasses.

After a while she re-appeared, with a glass of wine and a portion of fish on a plate for herself.

'It's all right renting from Svenni and...?' She sat down and started on her food without finishing her question. 'Wow ... I hadn't realised how hungry I was.'

'Matthildur, you mean? Yes, I was lucky to find that place,' Guðgeir replied. 'You know them?'

He knew perfectly well that she could hardly not know them, and that she naturally knew where he lived, but this was as easy a way to kick off a conversation as any. He had no desire to spend another evening alone with his phone.

'You must be joking. I'm a hundredth generation local and I'm pretty sure their roots here go back to the Saga age. Everyone like that knows everyone else,' she laughed. 'This place is like a living museum, a cross-section of East Skaftafell's population.'

Guðgeir smiled and Linda continued, clearly keen to cheer him up.

'You've noticed how Svenni talks, with that little laugh after every sentence? It makes no difference what he's talking about. He could be telling you about some disaster, but there's always that giggle that ends every sentence.'

'That's right,' Guðgeir said as he ate his fish. 'I had noticed.'

'Svenni's mother was just the same, and so was his grandfather and his great-grandmother, although all of them are long gone. They were Höfn people going back generations and we're all more or less related to each other. We're a prime example of inbreeding,' she said. 'Svenni and I ought to be stuffed and put in a museum for the tourists to look at,' she said with a laugh of her own.

'And talking about you and Sveinn … did he mention to you the woman from Sri Lanka who arrived here thinking she had a job to go to?' Guðgeir asked, determined to keep the conversation going. 'That was back in February when the weather was pretty wild.'

'February, you said?'

'Yes. Around the end of the month, as far as I recall,' Guðgeir said. 'In fact I had forgotten all about this, and then the woman came to mind when I had a touch of claustrophobia when I heard the forecast. It's uncomfortable not being able to go anywhere, let alone when you're in a strange place.'

'There weren't many tourists about in February. The weather was so lousy last winter that they only started to show up around the end of March,' she said, shivering at the recollection.

'This woman wasn't a tourist. It seems she came here because she was sure she had been promised work in a salon, or something like that,' Guðgeir repeated.

'That's it,' Linda said. 'Reminds me of the American who wanted to go to Laugavegur and ended up in...'

'Siglufjörður,' Guðgeir said, doing his best to be patient. 'Except he was in a hire car and punched in the wrong street name into the satnav. But this woman was under the impression that there was a job and a place to live waiting for her. The problem is that she can't read or write Icelandic, but I hope she managed to get back safe and sound.' He rubbed his cheek with one hand and gazed out of the window. 'Have you heard of a Chinese woman who either works or worked as a beautician around here?'

'No,' Linda said, raising an eyebrow as the question took her by surprise. 'What's that about?'

'This girl from Sri Lanka was under the impression she was taking over from some Chinese woman.'

'That's weird.'

'This woman appears to be non-existent,' Guðgeir said.

'Do you think the one from Sri Lanka could have gone somewhere with the guy who owns the Hostel by the Sea?' she asked after a pause. 'I think his name's Thormóður. My brother Jói is a plumber and he did some work for him. Would that fit?'

'What was that?' Guðgeir's attention had wandered and he had lost the thread of the conversation. The

Crossfit lawyer with the trailer had sneaked back into his thoughts. 'That's more than likely. That's where Sveinn said he took her.'

'I think I saw them at the Ólís filling station some time back in the winter,' Linda said. 'The woman went inside to use the toilet and Thormóður sat in his car. I was on the way out to the lagoon with Jói because the family has a summer house out there. We had been told there was a leak in one of the pipes, so we went to check. I remember we stopped off at the filling station for something and I had to wait for the toilet to be free. Jói wasn't impressed because the forecast was bad and he wanted to be quick. Thormóður and the woman were ahead of us all the way through the tunnel and past Jökulsá. Then we turned off and they carried on. I remember because we were wondering where they could be heading and who the woman was. It was pretty bad that day, and the roads were practically blocked.'

'The girl we're talking about has a cleft palate, which is distinctive,' Guðgeir said.

'Exactly. Then we're talking about the same person. I couldn't help noticing her hair, thick and beautiful,' Linda recalled, her voice lower.

'Maybe he took her sightseeing?'

'Surely not in that lousy weather,' Linda said. 'It improved later in the day, so I hope they didn't get stuck anywhere.' She glanced quickly at the clock. 'We wondered at the time where they could be going, and my brother reckons the guy goes out to Bröttuskriður now and again.'

'Bröttuskriður? Where's that?'

'It's a farm right under the mountain slopes. On the far side of the lagoon,' Linda said. 'It's a grim sort of place and very isolated. I gather the farmhouse itself is something of a wreck. They're flat broke out there.'

'So why would he be taking her all the way out there in such terrible weather?' Guðgeir said, as he went into police mode. 'What would take Thormóður and this woman to such an out-of-the-way place in the dead of winter?'

He was starting to feel a deep foreboding.

'Who knows? They must have been on the way somewhere. There are only two places that far inland. There's Gröf, which is closer, and then Bröttuskriður,' Linda said. 'He can hardly have been hoping to drive for a few hours to catch a flight from Egilsstaðir. In any case, he wouldn't have had a hope of getting through.'

Lost in thought, Guðgeir didn't reply straight away. It was all a while ago, but it wouldn't do any harm to check it out. Casting around to find what had become of the girl would be something to keep him occupied.

'Are you done?' Linda asked suddenly, looking at him enquiringly. It took him a moment to realise she was asking if she could take his plate.

'What? Yes, of course,' he said, forking up the last piece of fish. 'My compliments to the chef. The fish was really good.'

'I'll tell him. Thanks for the chat,' she said, getting to her feet. 'I have to get back to work. See you.'

'Certainly,' Guðgeir said. 'But tell me. Does anyone live there?'

'At Bröttuskriður? Selma and Ísak. An elderly woman and her son.'

'Ah. That's good. I was imagining an abandoned farm and all sorts of horrors.'

'Like what?' Linda asked, a curious expression on her face.

He shrugged and smiled. He had no intention of explaining. Sometimes he felt he had seen and experienced too much to be able to live a normal life.

'I reckon they don't have an easy time of it out there.'

'Why's that?' Guðgeir asked, making an effort to show interest. 'They keep livestock, don't they?'

'I'm not sure. They must have some animals. But everyone's either up to their ears in debt or they've sold their milk quota. The only ones who make a decent living are those who cater for tourists. And there are more and more farms bought up for summer places. Foreigners, a lot of them,' she added.

'And do they do that? Cater for tourists, I mean?'

'No. The old lady's a bit odd. Half crazy, I suppose. She went through some terrible shock when she was young, but the son was more normal … as far as I know, but I don't know what opportunities there are now for him,' Linda said, and hesitated. 'He used to keep to himself, which is understandable, considering, and he managed to hang on up there. His name's Ísak, and he was a couple of years ahead of me at school. Then he went down south to university in Reykjavík and everyone thought that would be where he'd stay, but he dropped out. I guess he's stuck out there.'

'Maybe studying was too difficult for him?' Guðgeir said, just to say something.

'No, I think he struggled with leaving home. He was always very reliant on his mother, and maybe he found it difficult to get on with other people. He was always on his own, never had fun with the rest of the kids or anything like that. Every summer most of us worked in the fish plant, and there was always work in the prawn season. But he never did any of that.'

'Was his father from out there by the lagoon as well?'

'No, it was always just Selma and him, and she lived at Bröttuskriður with her father. As far as I know, her mother died a long time ago. I once heard my grandmother say that Ísak's father had been a Yank from the base at Stokksnes. Did you know that they were once here in Höfn? It wasn't exactly a military base, nothing like Keflavík, but there was a radar station. Have you been out there?'

'I've heard about it,' Guðgeir said, reflecting that he had to be at least fifteen years older than Linda and there was a clear difference in their awareness of the past.

'Ísak's father was supposed to have been stationed there. If I remember the gossip correctly, he came off the road on the pass. He was coming back from Bröttuskriður when the roads were icy and the car ended up going straight down the mountainside. The man was killed instantly. Selma was adamant she wanted the car, which was a complete wreck after rolling down the mountain. For years it was outside the farmhouse at Bröttuskriður and she used to stand there and stare at it with the baby in her arms. It's no surprise she turned out to be on the odd side. But I don't know the details, and for all I know I could be making stuff up. Anyway, I have to get back to work.'

He saw Linda nod to her colleague, indicating that she knew she had talked for long enough and started collecting crockery.

'Interesting,' Guðgeir said as more questions began to come to mind. He wanted to know more about Bröttuskriður and the tale had sparked his curiosity. 'Remarkable that the boy should have gone off to university and then ended up in that remote spot with his mother.'

'It's not that remarkable, even these days. You and I fail to understand how he can live there, but some people are just much more in touch with nature. They can't live in a town like Höfn.'

Guðgeir hid a smile. He recalled that Höfn's population was around fifteen hundred people and he saw the place as a long way from being a town where the crowds could overwhelm anyone – the lack of people was more likely to be uncomfortable.

'I've obviously lived too long in Reykjavík to be able to understand how anyone can live somewhere so isolated in winter,' he said.

'True. But Bröttuskriður is a wonderfully beautiful place in summer,' Linda said. 'Awfully beautiful. You ought to go for a drive out there.'

'Awful beauty in an awful place?' Guðgeir said. 'Who lives at the other farm you mentioned?'

'You mean Gröf? An elderly couple with no children who are a bit cracked, as my grandmother always said. The woman was always involved in local politics and knew everyone, but I can't remember their names,' Linda said, her brow furrowed. 'Haven't you been up to the lagoon?'

'No, but now I'll make sure I do. Didn't she get any help? The mother, I mean.'

'No, definitely not. There was no counselling or anything like that back then,' Linda said. 'The best she could have hoped for would have been a sedative from the local doctor.'

'Poor woman,' Guðgeir muttered. An image of a young woman with a baby in her arms gazing at a wrecked car had taken root in his mind. He felt a stab of sympathy for her.

'It was seen as a terrible thing to be sleeping with a Yank, so she had to put up with the shame of that as well,' Linda said.

'So she didn't have much of the man while he was alive and couldn't mourn him when he was dead?'

'Exactly,' Linda said. 'Back in the old days people weren't supposed to talk about anything like that. There was no way to work these things out. People just had to bottle up all their emotions and act as if nothing was wrong. I remember the terrible stories my Dad used to tell me about the shipwrecks out here in the Hornafjörður estuary when husbands and fathers drowned before the eyes of the families waiting for them. Nobody said anything much. They'd just sit there and stare silently into a mug of coffee, as the old man said. So people suffered from depression, or turned into alcoholics, or they hardened against everyone and everything, or else they went completely off the rails.'

9

Over the last couple of weeks she had scrubbed practically every corner of the house at Bröttuskriður, wiped away stains and done her best to restore the place to its former smart self with pure elbow grease. The farmhouse was spotless, with the exception of the cellar, and Sajee was thoroughly relieved not to have to go down there. Now she was on the way over to Karl and Marta at Gröf, as the previous evening Marta had showed up at Bröttuskriður and demanded that Sajee come and clean for her as well. Selma had responded furiously, but the thought had cheered Sajee. She would be glad of the change of scene, and the money.

'Can't you clean up your own filth?' Selma snarled, but Marta hadn't turned a hair.

'No more than you can,' she hissed back.

'The girl's going to be leaving in a few days, so don't come asking again,' she said firmly. Sajee stared in surprise, but Selma winked discreetly, giving her the impression that the old woman was shielding her from further demands.

When Marta's green car had gone and Selma had told her to go to her room, Sajee could hear mother and son arguing. Ísak was far from pleased that Sajee should be going over to Gröf, and said it would be as well that Thormóður didn't find out. She couldn't understand the reason for that.

The farmhouse was newer than Selma's house, but unlike at Bröttuskriður, the household appliances were worn out. The vacuum cleaner was heavy and held together with grey insulation tape. She had lunch with Karl and Marta. In the middle of the kitchen table with its vinyl cloth stood a radio, and Karl turned the sound up and down as he gave his opinions on whatever the newsreader announced, in between spoonfuls of slices of the fresh-baked bread that didn't seem to cling to his spare frame any more than Selma's pastries did. All the same, the meal was livelier than Sajee had become used to at Bröttuskriður and she enjoyed the change of atmosphere. In the afternoon Ísak appeared behind the wheel of his jeep. She quickly finished her work and put on her coat. She stood by the half-open door, waiting to be paid. The cold found its way inside and she wound her scarf tighter around her neck.

'You'd best be on your way. You're all finished here,' Marta said, clicking open the clasp of her watch and snapping it closed again.

'Do you want me to come again next week?' Sajee asked cheerfully.

'Aren't you going back south?'

'Yes, but not right away. I need to earn more money first.'

The loud blaring of a horn could be heard outside and she waved to Ísak to let him know she was coming. He impatiently sounded the horn again. Marta stood with her hand on the door handle, ready to shut it behind her.

'Anyway, I suppose we'd better not impose any more on the people at Bröttuskriður. Off you go, don't keep the man waiting.'

'I haven't been paid,' Sajee said.

'Selma will pay you,' Marta said with impatience. 'If she can afford a home help of her own, then she can pay.'

'Will she pay me for cleaning your house?' Sajee asked, pulling on her gloves. The jeep's horn blared even louder.

'That's what I said.' Marta pushed the door against her. 'Off you go. Don't let the cold in. Ísak isn't going to wait for you all day. Goodbye, my dear.'

The door banged shut, leaving Sajee standing in the yard. She pulled on her hat and watched Marta through the dark brown frosted glass until the inner hall doorway shut behind her. She felt a wave of disappointment, but as she trudged through the snow to the jeep, she convinced herself that everything would turn out to be fine.

There was a blizzard and a strong wind blew along the way from Gröf. Ísak concentrated on the road ahead, without saying a word. The engine raced and the wheels spun.

'We're not getting stuck here, surely,' he muttered, as he reversed out of the ruts in the road.

The jeep crawled ahead as he tried again.

'There. It just needs a bit of patience,' he muttered, gradually increasing the speed. 'See? That's how it's done.'

She tried to show her admiration. Ísak seemed more at ease in her company than anyone else's, but he also needed respect.

'You're a good driver,' Sajee said, trying to send a compliment his way, and a shadow of a smile flashed across his face for a moment. 'Marta said your mother would pay me for cleaning,' she added.

'Yeah, well. No problem,' he mumbled, swinging the car to avoid a patch of ice.

'Right away?' she asked.

'Soon,' he replied as he turned the jeep onto the main highway. 'That's better. A decent road at last.'

The drove in silence.

'So when?' she asked, twisting the gold ring on her finger.

'What, what?' he replied peevishly.

'When will I be paid? If I clean a house, I should be paid for it. That's how it is, isn't it?'

The snow on her boots had begun to melt, leaving pools of water on the floor of the car.

'Give it a rest, can you? It's not as if there's anything out here in the countryside to spend money on,' Ísak grumbled. 'Take a look around you, girl. The clouds are lifting. Take a look at the mountains and how beautiful it is around here.'

He gazed out of the window and saw the rusty grey handrail of a bridge, a rushing river and the endless sands beyond that stretched down to the sea as if they were fleeing the looming mountains.

'It's good,' she said, her thoughts more on payment that the landscape.

'Just a bit! It's magnificent,' Ísak said and seemed for a second to be downcast. 'I can tell you that I'll never leave this place. There's no bank or foreigner going to take my land. Never!'

'So when do I get paid for cleaning at Gröf?' she asked once again. 'And I thought you would pay me at the end of every week.'

The wheels juddered as he slowed the car down suddenly, and Sajee instinctively raised her hands to protect her face. Ísak laughed.

'You don't give up, do you?' he sneered. 'Take it easy. Not just anyone can drive in these conditions, but you're safe with me. And will you stop worrying about being paid? When we get back I'll draw up a written contract for you, setting out generous terms for payment, board and lodging. You'll be paid in full on the first of April. Is that good enough for you?'

Sajee looked at him suspiciously, and nodded in agreement.

'Or do you have a better offer?' Ísak asked, switching on the radio. He seemed pleased with the idea of a contract and sang along with the music. 'Has anyone ever offered you a contract before?'

Sajee shook her head. She was about to ask exactly what a generous payment would amount to in money, before he interrupted her before she could speak.

'No! I thought as much,' he said, and turned the radio up as a new song began and his out-of-tune voice warbled along with it.

Sajee giggled, and put her hand over her mouth. Ísak barked with laughter, and sang ever louder, even more out of tune with the music, and she couldn't help laughing, relieved to have a moment's truce. So far she hadn't been paid anything, and hoped she could expect a decent amount when it came. The thought made her feel more relaxed and she closed her eyes for a while. She seemed to be constantly tired these days, with a heaviness in her head.

'Press that button if you want to lean the seat back,' Ísak said, pointing out a switch.

The leather seat was warm, and she alternated dozing and watching the landscape through the window for the rest of the journey. There wasn't a light or a sign of life to be seen anywhere.

10

Guðgeir had been determined to sleep as long as possible, but found he was wide awake before eight in the morning. The dark brown blinds weren't enough to keep out the brightness of the day outside. Rays of sunshine leaked through the gaps, casting a sharp pattern of bars of light on the bedroom floor. He pulled the duvet up, adjusted the pillow under his head and tried to lose himself in sleep for a few more minutes.

Thoughts of his relationship with Inga had kept him awake the night before, and now he felt those doubts returning. She needed more time, understandably, and he knew he couldn't afford to allow himself to be obsessed with regret and loneliness. That would be a sure road to speculation and jealousy, as had happened the day before. This Crossfit legal guy was naturally nothing more than a decent colleague in Inga's eyes; or so he told himself.

Finnur was a helpful person who happened to have the strength to help her with the garden chores, and it didn't have to be anything more or less than that – just as Linda was for him. He fidgeted in the bed that had come with the apartment, which the couple upstairs had described as 'weekend width,' an expression he found to be dismal.

His dark thoughts returned, so he kicked off the duvet and stretched out. It would be all about patience, common sense and consideration if he wanted to win back Inga's trust. That would be his only route to regaining what had been lost.

The sunshine on the floor had almost reached the wardrobe, so it was time to be on his feet. The bathroom mirror highlighted dark bristles on his cheeks, but instead of shaving he carried a damp towel with him along the corridor and quietly opened the door to the shared utility room. His running gear was by the washing machine and there could hardly be anyone up and about on the day that Jesus had been crucified. He swung open the door, straight into Matthildur's bottom, where she was on all fours in front of him, busily cleaning out the washing machine's filter.

'Oh, I'm so sorry,' Guðgeir said, even more surprised than she was. 'Did I hurt you? I didn't think anyone else was awake.'

Matthildur stood up, the filter in her hand, and began scooping the grey gunk from it. Her eyes wandered shyly up Guðgeir's frame, which he found awkward as he stood there in nothing but his boxer shorts. He dropped the towel into his washing basket and took the few steps to the washing line where he pulled down his track suit bottoms, a singlet and a running jacket. Pegs pinged from the line.

'In top form, I see. That comes of running all the time,' she said, hands on her hips. 'Can't you persuade my Svenni to join you?' she asked, a plaintive tone in her voice.

'I'll do my best,' Guðgeir said, retrieving two of the stray clothes pegs from the floor before deciding that it might be best to first put on his clothes.

She eyed him as she wiped spilled water from the floor. The detritus from the filter went into the bin in the corner.

'Do what you can with my Svenni, won't you?' Matthildur said. 'Just do it right and drop the idea into his head a little at a time, but you have to stay with it,' she said with a mawkish smile, and he wondered what he had got himself into.

'I can invite him to come for a run with me, a couple of times. But I don't put pressure on people. Either he wants to come or he doesn't.'

She looked doubtfully at him.

'Sometimes you have to persevere,' she said with a hint of reproach. 'It seems to me that you could do with some company. You're on your own down here so much that you must be lonely,' she added and the concern in her voice was clear. 'There's plenty going on here in Höfn. There's all kinds of social activity. You just have to look for it.'

It had to happen, Guðgeir thought to himself. It went without saying that people must have noticed that he kept to himself. Matthildur stood still, expecting an answer, amicably but still insistent. He wondered if she really expected him to tell her all his secrets. He had to turn the conversation around and change the subject.

'Speaking of Svenni, did he mention to you the Asian woman who washed up here during the winter, expecting to work in a salon? Do you know if the woman got a flight back to Reykjavík? From what Svenni told me, she was broke and didn't know what to do.'

'Yes, she just had a one-way ticket because she thought there was a job waiting for her here, but I suppose she must have gone back south somehow,' Matthildur said, as she finished rinsing out the filter. She crouched down in front of the washing machine to slot it back in place. Guðgeir watched, and decided it was odd of Sveinn to refer to her as 'the old woman.'

'Well, I hope at least that someone was looking out for her.'

'I'll ask Svenni to check. He'll definitely remember when that was. About two months ago, wasn't it?' Matthildur asked, obviously anxious to do whatever she could for the lonely detective.

'More like six weeks. And yes, it would be interesting to know what became of her. I suppose she could have taken a coach to Reykjavík,' Guðgeir said, relieved that the conversation had taken a new direction. 'It goes a couple of times a week, doesn't it?'

'It does. But in the winter I think you have to book it the day before, otherwise it doesn't run all the way out here. And it doesn't help that taking the coach all that way is so expensive, and the weather this winter was dreadful,' she said, emptying the washing machine as she spoke.

'Sveinn mentioned that she had trouble reading Icelandic. So she might have had trouble finding her way,' Guðgeir said, noticing a feeling of disquiet growing inside him.

'Somebody must have helped her,' Matthildur said with conviction. 'People normally manage to sort themselves out.' She lifted the basket brimming with clean clothes and squeezed herself past him. Guðgeir quickly opened the door for her. 'But I'll ask Svenni,' she said as she disappeared up the stairs. 'Come and have dinner with us on Easter Monday if you're alone,' she said, her voice becoming fainter as he heard her open the door to the flat upstairs.

'Thank you,' Guðgeir called after her, and thought for a moment. 'I'll do that.'

In his basement flat he took a banana from the fridge and ate it as he dressed. The sun shone as he jogged towards the Nature Path.

11

'Marta said you would pay me,' she said when she got back.

'It's exhausting listening to you nagging,' Selma complained, patting her steel-grey hair. 'Stop it, will you? I can't be dealing with this endless moaning.'

'She said you would pay me, and Ísak said I would have a contract,' Sajee insisted.

There was a clear flash of anger visible on Selma's face. Her grey eyes turned cold and her cheeks with the broken veins flushed as she seemed to barely manage to control her temper.

'You work here and have no business being elsewhere. I should never have...'

'I need to know what I'm being paid so I can make plans, organise things,' Sajee tried to say, but got no further before Selma cut her off.

'You're obsessed with money,' she snapped. Her head trembled, the loose skin of her throat shook and this was followed by a peal of wild laughter. She snatched up a cloth, used it to polish the gleaming new coffee machine, and moved the old one aside. Sajee watched in astonishment as Selma went through the same movements three times before saying anything.

'There. You can go upstairs and get some rest,' she said in a tone that made it an instruction rather than a request, and her eyes flashes, at odds with the neutral words she chose with care. 'I'll go and get my boy and he'll bring the contract up to you in a little while. You ought to calm down a little,' she said, hobbling away and muttering under her breath that it was downright impertinence to be bothering a busy man with something so trivial.

Sajee hurried up the stairs.

A little later Ísak appeared with sheets of paper and handed them to her. Her hand shook as she took them. The lettering was tiny and the lines were crammed close together into black smudges on a white background.

'I'll leave one copy with you,' he said. 'Bring it with you down to the kitchen when you've read it and signed.'

'Thank you,' she said. 'I don't know how long I'll be staying here.'

Her eyes scanned the sheet of paper from top to bottom.

'It's a contract up to Easter. It's just a formality. Mother and I want everything to be correct, so we're not accused of any wrongdoing. It sets out that you get payment, board and lodging while you're here at Bröttuskriður,' Ísak said. 'It ought to answer all your questions.'

'How much will I be paid?' she asked, about to explain how much she had been paid for cleaning people's houses in Reykjavík, but Ísak raised an impatient hand and pointed at the sheet of paper.

'Don't make things difficult. Like I said, it's all in there. Just read through it all carefully. If there's anything you want to discuss, then make a note of it so we know where we stand. You know, it's sometimes harder to understand you than other foreigners because of...'

He touched his own upper lip, looking pointedly at her mouth. Then he patted her shoulder.

'You see, Sajee, it's better if you write everything down, so nothing is left in any doubt between us,' he added, his tone gentler.

'But, I can't ... I don't know how...'

The words formed on her lips, and for a second she was about to tell him the truth, but stopped short. That wouldn't be a smart move. Her clear lack of literacy would leave her even more defenceless out here in this place. She couldn't trust them to understand. No, the simplest thing would be to sign her name on this lousy piece of paper, whatever the writing on it meant, even if the payment was going to be something less than the usual rate. The main thing was to get some money and regain her independence, and a few thousand krónur either way would hardly make a difference while she wasn't paying for food or rent. She gave him a courteous smile of agreement, held up the sheet of paper and looked at it as if she were giving it her full attention.

'Fine,' Ísak said and she sighed with relief as he left the room.

Five minutes later she stood by the closed kitchen door with the paper in one hand and her phone in the other. She could hear mother and son talking.

'There's something about her, I feel a strong connection,' Selma said. 'It's not just her mouth.'

'Sure,' Ísak said, sounding distant.

'Could there be something?'

'Anything is possible.'

'But her colour?' Selma said.

'What about it?'

'A different colour … but apart from that there's such a resemblance to your sister. It was so painful to lose her.'

'Relax, mother,' Ísak said reassuringly. 'Now you have Sajee.'

'She massaged my feet yesterday and she did it wonderfully,' Selma said.

'There you are. She helps you relax and she's company for you,' Ísak replied. 'She's a real Godsend but you'll have to behave yourself, and no more lending her to those people at Gröf. I don't want to see their faces here again. You hear me?' Ísak said, his voice rising.

'It was just once, and I like to see visitors once in a while,' Selma complained. 'I don't want to be here alone. They promised to keep it to themselves if she cleans for them as well. What else was I supposed to do?'

'Well, now you have company and help, so you can stop complaining and behave.'

'Yes.'

'And if you hear from them, you can tell them that she's gone. You know we don't want visitors here. Just get rid of them all.'

'Yes.'

'Is that crystal clear?' Ísak's voice was cold and hard. 'Well?'

'You mustn't take her from me. I'm like a prisoner here.'

There was a note of desperation in Selma's voice.

'Not if you do as you're told.'

'I don't want to be alone,' she wailed again, her helplessness plain. Low sobs could be heard through the door.

'There, there. It'll be fine,' she heard Ísak say. 'You can keep her a while longer. But you can moan at her and leave me and Thormóður in peace.'

The floorboards creaked and Ísak's voice sounded closer. Sajee quickly moved away from the kitchen door. She just managed to get to the stairs as the door swung open and she shook as she sat on the steps, while his heavy footsteps receded into the distance. She tiptoed back upstairs and thought over everything she had heard. This bizarre conversation had left her agitated, and she decided it was time to tell Hirumi the whole story. The phone rang a couple of times and then she saw that the battery was practically flat, so she pulled her suitcase from under the bed and felt for the charger that she kept in the pocket. It was nowhere to be found. She emptied everything from the case, searched under the chest of drawers, hunted through the whole room – without success.

In a panic she picked up the phone and called the first number she saw. It was answered after two rings. She tried frantically to explain where she was, before the woman politely interrupted her. She recognised the voice as Hulda's, someone she had cleaned for.

'I'm sorry, Sajee,' Hulda said. 'I found another cleaner.'

12

As the pool had been closed, Guðgeir took a shower at home. Satisfied with his seven-kilometre run, he scrambled eggs, reflecting that at this rate, he could be ready for the Reykjavík marathon in August. He fetched cheese from the fridge and dropped slices of bread into the toaster. The endorphins were still coursing through him, but were slowing down, and his thoughts became more grounded. A half-marathon, at least, he decided. At the very least, a ten-kilometre run. He should be able to complete that in a respectable time, and with any luck, by then he'd be back in Reykjavík and back at work.

His outlook brighter than he remembered for a long time, he opened the local paper and scanned the pages as he ate. Just as he forked up the last mouthful, Inga called. She was in a good mood and it was good to hear her voice.

'You know, I'm looking forward to your long weekend off,' she said, and Guðgeir felt a surge of wellbeing.

'So I get to stay at home?' he quipped. A knot of concern immediately tightened in his belly and the muscles in his neck stiffened. It was a ridiculous question, and it was painful that it had to be asked.

'Well, of course. You're hardly going to get a room somewhere for a couple of days,' she replied and Guðgeir felt the tightness at the back of his neck disappear and the muscles in his back relaxed.

'I'm looking forward to being home,' he said tapping his empty plate a couple of times with his fork as he spoke. 'How's the garden looking? Was Finnur much use,' he asked, unable to hold back the question.

'Just a bit! He was brilliant and went back and forth to the dump with his trailer, and then we went for a meal at that new place that just opened along the street. Lovely food there. I had the fish and Finnur had lamb and we both decided it's worth going there again.'

Guðgeir was silent for a moment.

'Together?' he asked at last, and the hesitation in Inga's voice was almost palpable.

'No, of course not. Don't be like that. He's just helping me. He's a really decent guy and he does a great job at the office,' Inga said hurriedly.

'That's good to know,' Guðgeir said drily as he felt his mood change. It was surprising how this smooth guy who talked too much had made an impression on Inga, who normally saw right through Finnur and his type.

'How about we go there when you're home? Good idea?'

'Go where?' he asked in a hollow voice, his eyes closed. Patience, common sense and consideration, he reminded himself, the three key instincts.

'The restaurant, of course. The new one,' Inga said, with a hint of impatience. 'The one we were talking about just now.'

'Yes,' he said and felt his heart begin to race. He imagined Inga sitting at a restaurant table with flowers in a vase, opposite Finnur. He rubbed his eyes and pulled himself together. 'Yes, it would be great to go out for dinner.'

This jealousy was an unpleasant emotion, in fact, it was a terrible feeling, he thought. This was something that magnified his remoteness from everything, and made him miss his family, job and friends all the more. Now he'd have to get out of the house, as that would keep at bay the visions of his colleague and friend Andrés, the one and only Andrés.

In his worst moments, Guðgeir saw his friend's face rippled with pain and the green of his jacket soaked through with blood. Guðgeir let his plate clatter into the sink. Days off were a nightmare. He needed something to occupy him, something to keep his mind busy.

He laced up his walking boots, snatched a coat from its hook and banged the door shut behind him. A few moments later he was behind the wheel, heading for the lagoon.

13

'Let me have it,' Selma said. Sajee glanced at the sheet of paper to make sure. As far as she could make out, her signature was correct.

'Here you are,' she said, taking a seat on the kitchen bench. 'Did Ísak go out?'

'He's out in the barn,' Selma replied, her earlier sharpness gone. 'I didn't mean to be unpleasant just now, but the pain makes me short-tempered. It tires me out.'

She stretched for a bottle of pills, shook two tablets into her palm and washed them down with a gulp of coffee.

'I understand,' Sajee said softly, and held out her phone. 'Do you have a charger that fits this? I can't find mine anywhere.'

'No, we don't have that type,' Selma replied quickly, without looking. 'Would you like me to make coffee for you?'

'No, thank you,' she said in a dull voice and stared out of the window. There was nothing to be seen in the gloom outside.

'Don't worry. I'll ask Thormóður to pick up a charger for you. That's as long as something that old-fashioned can still be found.'

'I could go with Thormóður, do some shopping and come back,' Sajee suggested.

'He has better things to do than ferry you back and forth,' Selma said.

'I could stay at the hostel for one or two nights, and do some cleaning there in return. A bit of a break…'

'Anyone would think that you're wearing your fingers to the bone here at Bröttuskriður,' Selma snorted. 'You work a couple of hours a day, have a room to yourself and get healthy, home-cooked meals. There's nobody going to tell me that you were so well off back in Sri Lanka. I've seen a few things on the television,' Selma said, her voice again rising steadily.

Sajee stood up without a word and began to clear dishes from the table. Her mechanical movements evidence of her unhappiness.

'You could go outside,' Selma said after a while. 'A good walk is always good if you're feeling down.'

'Maybe I will. I seem to have a constant headache.'

'A breath of fresh air will cheer you up,' Selma said, more cheerful now. Her mood seemed to change from one moment to the next. 'But don't go far. The weather can always turn and we don't want anything to happen to you. You don't know how fierce the weather can be here in Iceland. A storm can be whipped up in the twinkling of an eye.'

'I know,' Sajee muttered.

'Take the torch that's by the window, because it's getting dark. Don't go too far from the house and don't spend too long outside. People can lose their lives and there are lots of foreigners who have died of exposure in Iceland. They get lost in the dark and simply freeze to death, and it's a dreadful way to go. Yes, and watch out for foxes. They can attack people. Once there was a man who fell and broke his leg outside in storm, and a fox chewed his foot right off.'

Selma stared doubtfully out of the kitchen window. Sajee wondered whether she was telling the truth about all the foreigners who had lost their lives in Iceland, and she felt a fondness for the little fox who looked to be such an innocent creature. She hadn't heard that there were any dangerous animals in Iceland, but Selma was right about the darkness. Even though it was now the middle of March, the daylight didn't last long.

She put on her coat and gloves, and looked longingly at Selma's padded snow boots. But they were several sizes too large for her, so she slipped her tiny feet into the rubber boots she had bought for the trip she should never have taken.

There was still some daylight and she walked briskly over the pasture below the scree. Fallen rocks lay here and there, boulders and smaller stones. She perched on one of them, pulled the hood of her anorak over her head and zipped it up tight under her chin. Then she closed her eyes and let her thoughts wander.

She skipped in thin sandals between the stallholders

as they called out across the market. She was again a little girl, tugging at Hirumi's bright green skirt, trying to draw her attention to enchanting toys and tempting sweets. She could smell the newly baked bread with coconut, hear the soothingly repetitive music, until the cold from the grey stone seeped into every one of her bones.

Home. She no longer knew what that meant.

She opened her eyes and stared up at the mountainside looming over her, as she had done on the few occasions she had gone outside the farmhouse at Bröttuskriður. The mountain resembled a vast fist with sharp nails at the ends of long claws, and she had the feeling that the fish could clench and crush her.

She tried to shake off her disquiet, switched on the torch and let the narrow beam of light travel up and down the steep mountainside. Nooks and crannies gave it the look of being pocked with scars, as if a giant sharp points had been pushed deep into the pasture. She was cold, her feet numb. It was becoming properly dark and she could hardly see anything other than what was within the beam of torchlight. All the same, she put off going back inside. Eventually she had to admit defeat, and set off.

After a few steps she sensed a presence behind her. She glanced around, but saw nothing but the all-enveloping darkness. She took a few deep breaths and resolved to remain calm, but thoughts of the hidden people in the rocks above the farm came vividly to mind. Karl had talked about the elf woman who could drive people mad, or even make then disappear.

Yesterday she had watched as Selma had hobbled up the largest of the rocks, taking with her a pot containing the remnants of a meat soup that she tipped out into the snow. Then she had spread her arms wide and yelled at the sky above. She was convinced that the old woman had been making an offering.

She herself could never use a part of an animal as an offering, and any hidden people who took meat as a sacrifice had to be truly terrible. The idea made her shudder. The grey stone around her began to take on the shapes of people and her footsteps rustled in the gloomy silence. With every step she took, her trepidation grew, alongside her inner blend of fear and conscience over having neglected her own customs the previous evening when she had rolled, exhausted, into bed.

There was snow in her boots, and the cold was eating into her shins. She tried to hurry, by the soles of her boots were too smooth for her walk fast, and she struggled to keep her balance. Without warning, she missed her footing and fell forward as she tripped. She cried out feebly, but to her relief she was unhurt and took off a glove to be able to switch on the torch. She had strayed to the fenced-off copse that they referred to as the family plot, and had tripped over a flagstone in front of the iron gate.

Sajee struggled to her feet and went closer. The narrow beam of light flickered over one grave after another; five altogether. These were all imposing gravestones, with the largest one in the centre and she guessed that under this one lay Selma's father, or even both of her parents. Illegible letters stretched out beneath large crosses. Maybe under the middle stone lay an old man with the same dark brow as Ísak and at his side an elegant old woman with steel-grey hair and blue-grey eyes beneath a low forehead. These were the eyes that Sajee sensed as she slept. It was terrifying to imagine these corpses lying beneath the frozen ground. Those poor dead people, she thought. Back home in Sri Lanka the dead were burned and their souls well looked after.

Her breath came faster, forming clouds in the cold air. Under these heavy stones had to be the souls of people caught in desperation, locked in their earthly bodies. Had the priests or the people in the district held a vigil for them, or had they been abandoned for ever, left for months on end in nature's deep freeze until the return of summer when the worms could return to their work? The terror that had fallen away for a moment gripped her again. Treating the dead like this could fill a restless soul with evil. She shivered, stepping back away from the gravestones, wanting to escape. Evil could give those souls the power to rise up into the world of men.

She took to her heels, but the slippery soles of her boots let her down, so she tumbled forward and found her fingers touching an ice-cold stone so smooth that it was almost soft. A white stone teddy bear sat atop a little gravestone. Sajee had not imagined that a child could be buried here as well. Selma had mentioned only parents and grandparents, but not a word about children. The thought of a child deep in the frozen earth was too much for her, and her eyes filled with tears. A tide of emotions rose to the surface inside her, twisting and colliding. She told herself that she mustn't lose her grip, that she had to keep herself under control and not let her imagination run away with her.

It wasn't far back to the house, but it still felt like a long trek. Just like passing time in this place, she thought, reminding herself that spring was not far away, and by then she would have enough money for a flight to Reykjavík where she could find work cleaning or washing dishes.

She stepped cautiously in her treacherous boots, taking care not to fall as she spoke calming words to herself. She saw a light in the barn as she came closer. First she would make it there, and then it would be an easy walk to the house. The fear followed behind her, as if it were breathing down her neck, but with Selma's words about people who died of exposure in mind, she didn't allow herself to run in the darkness.

Outside the barn she saw the fox as it trotted back and forth, to the limit the chain would allow. As she came closer, it stopped and watched her, its dark eyes catching hers and she felt a pang of discomfort at seeing the animal tethered there, running ceaselessly back and forth all day long as it sought to break free.

Music echoed from the barn; the same tune that Ísak had sung along with on the way back from Gröf.

14

As the door wasn't locked, she went in. A long, burgundy-red car floated above the floor, jacked up so that she could make out the deep pit beneath it. Ísak was nowhere to be seen, so she crouched on one knee and peered into the darkness.

'Hello?' There was no response and she called again, louder, but still with no answer. 'Hello?'

She stood up and looked around her. Along the walls were shelves of tools and drawers for smaller items. Every tool shone like new, and it was obvious that Ísak was tidier here than in the house that was his mother's domain. She was about to leave when hands fell on her shoulders and she felt heavy breath on the back of her neck.

'Hello, Sajee.'

Ísak stood behind her, his hands firmly on her shoulders.

'You took me by surprise,' she said. 'Where were you? I didn't see you down there.'

'Sorry. I didn't mean to alarm you,' he breathed into her ear. 'What are you doing out here in the dark?'

His meaty hands squeezed and she could feel goose pimples form on her arms at his touch.

'I went for a walk and I heard the music. Where were you? I didn't see you when I came in here,' she said, twisting out of his grip.

He stood with his feet far apart as he looked her up and down. He was broadly built but with round shoulders, dressed in a grey overall. Pieces of shiny paper, with blue letters and an image of an imposing woman wearing a hat stuck out from a pocket – banknotes.

'I was under the car. I'm fixing it up,' Ísak replied.

'I looked everywhere and couldn't see you.'

She turned and moved away from him, forcing a friendly smile.

'No,' Ísak said. 'You don't always see everything.'

He took a step towards her and she instinctively edged towards the door.

'What do you mean?' she asked, but when he didn't reply, she tried to change the subject. 'Are you going to pay me this evening?'

She looked pointedly at this pocket and he took out one of the five thousand krónur notes, let the brand-new banknote flutter between his fingers for a moment, and then stuffed it back where it had come from.

'No, not with this. It's cash for parts I ordered for the car. But don't you worry. You'll be paid according to the terms of our excellent contract.'

'When?'

'Soon. There'll be more money soon,' he said pompously, preening like a rooster with something to be proud of. 'You can bank on that.'

'That's good,' Sajee said, not troubling to hide her relief. 'Next time you go to Höfn, can you get me a charger for my phone? I don't know what happened to mine.'

'I'll see what I can do,' he said uninterestedly. 'Looks great, doesn't it?' he asked animatedly.

'The car? It does,' Sajee said quickly, remembering how much he relished praise. She went closer to it and ran numb fingers over the glistening burgundy lacquer to demonstrate her polite admiration.

'It was my Dad's,' Ísak said, with delighted pride. He stepped closer to her and whispered. 'Sajee, mother thinks that you were sent to us, that you coming here is something that's hugely symbolic, and she's terrified of losing you.' He stared at her. 'She says that we've waited a long time for you,' he said and fell silent.

'That's so strange,' she said awkwardly.

'Yeah.' He leaned against the car and grinned. 'The old lady knows a few things. She's not like other people. She sees people others can't see, and she hears voices. Some people say it's just crazy, but the truth of it is that she often knows more than the people around her.' He stood close to Sajee and reached out to touch her misshapen upper lip. 'Who knows? Maybe God himself sent you here,' he muttered, and for a second it seemed that he was about to try to kiss her mouth, but instead he pinched her cheek hard. His thumb travelled across her lip and over her cheek. 'Mother says you're just like my sister was,' he whispered, his eyes searching her like a doctor examining a patient. 'Apart from the colour of your skin, of course.'

'Just like? How?' she asked. 'I don't understand.' Sajee felt herself trembling. 'What do you mean?'

'Your mouth,' he said, relaxing his grip as a piercing cry cut through the night.

'Is the fox in pain?' she asked, concerned.

'No, he's just whining,' Ísak whispered, without taking his eyes off her.

'Where is your sister now?' she asked cautiously. She wanted to know more about this family that cold fate had brought her to.

'The Hidden People took her. That's the punishment that mother has to live with. '

The anguished cry again made its way through the walls. Ísak glanced at the window.

'He's probably a bit hungry, poor thing,' he said, going over to the workbench. It was suddenly as if nothing had happened. 'He can't go anywhere.'

'The fox?'

'Yeah, the fox,' Ísak replied absently.

'What do you give him to eat?' she asked, relieved to have something everyday to talk about.

'Raw meat,' he said, sorting through the screwdrivers on the bench. He sorted them with care, almost obsessive care, by size. 'In Sri Lanka you believe in reincarnation, don't you?' he asked. 'That people come back to this world again and again?'

'Yes…' Sajee began. 'And you?' she asked.

'Me? I don't know, but I wouldn't rule anything out. But I can tell you that there's nothing happens in this world that's a coincidence. That's my experience,' he said. The last screwdriver was in its place and he wiped his hands slowly with a clean rag. 'You arriving here at Bröttuskriður, right here … well, that's coincidence. Thormóður found you and everything he does has a reason behind it, so that makes you completely special.'

Ísak looked at her intently, his eyes somehow distant. Sajee looked away and her black hair slipped over her face, so she lifted a hand to sweep it aside and tuck it behind her ears again.

'Now I'm scaring you,' Ísak said with a lighthearted laugh. His demeanour changed suddenly as if every care had been lifted from him. 'Look at this. That's an American car, a 1969 Ford,' he said, opening a drawer. It was filled with cloths sealed in plastic packaging. Sajee had the feeling that the place was more like a showroom than a workshop. Ísak picked up a pack, bit into the plastic wrapper and extracted a clean cloth.

'Everything looks so new,' she said, relieved that the conversation had moved on from reincarnation.

'That's right,' Ísak said. 'We have good taste, mother and I. Look at the workmanship there.' A finger slid along one of the car's chromed edges. 'This is no junk, because back when these were made, things were done properly and there was a pride in people's work. They didn't make rubbish like they do today. I've put a lot of effort into restoring this. Look at that front bumper,' Ísak said, walking around to the front of the car to polish the chrome that was already so clean that it glistened. The admiration in his voice was unmistakeable. 'You don't see workmanship like this today.'

'It's a beautiful car,' Sajee said, taking a step towards the door.

'It was pretty much smashed up,' Ísak said, trailing his fingertips over the smooth lacquer. 'And of course the brakes were out of order, but now mother wants everything that had been wrong with it fixed. We finally have enough cash to bring this gem inside and restore it. Now we can give the Ford the respect it deserves.'

'It's very beautiful,' she repeated, edging away still further.

'It's unique,' Ísak said, his voice heavy. 'Because this was my father's car and he died in it. This was a magnificent car that was perfect for a magnificent couple. Mother was pregnant with us back then and she couldn't take the gossip that spread like an infection. Yank whore. Tart.' Ísak's fingers lifted and fell in time with his words, as if he were playing an imaginary keyboard. 'Whisper, whisper, whisper,' he said, leaning over her. 'Whisper, whisper, whisper. There was whispering everywhere … whispers all over. Mother heard it wherever she went, and even here at Bröttuskriður. But she was stuck. Grandad wasn't happy. No, he was furious. Mother had brought shame on the family, after all he had done to be able to own this land. She couldn't leave because of me.'

Ísak moved closer to Sajee. She felt his breath by her ear.

'Whisper, whisper, whisper, you Yank's whore,' he hissed. 'Whisper, whisper, whisper, soldier's tart. Poor mother was losing her mind. She fought and argued with Dad when he came to see her, that cold, dark winter before we were born. She had meant to have a very different life. She never meant to be stuck here, so you see I can't leave her and she can't leave me.'

Ísak opened the barn door and the cold flooded in.

'She wanted to get rid of him because he'd put her in this position. It was pure desperation, you understand?'

He took a step back and the look on his face changed.

'What the hell am I saying? Of course you don't understand, and there's nothing wrong with that.'

He laid a hand on her shoulder and pointed her towards the door.

'That'll do. Go indoors to Mother.'

15

'Get up!'

Selma prodded her hard.

'Now?' Sajee mumbled in confusion as she tried to open her eyes.

'Yes, now. Right now.' There was agitation in Selma's voice and the loose skin of her throat trembled. 'They've finished. You have to clean the cellar. Everything except the locked room.'

'Can't I sleep a little longer?' Sajee asked, huddling deeper into the duvet. The room was cold and dark.

'No,' Selma snapped back, hauling the duvet off her. 'Get up. You can sleep later.'

A car engine started outside and a beam of light flashed over the window. Sajee sat on the bed, elbows on her knees, and covered her face with her hands. For the last few nights she had slept heavily, followed by headaches that lasted well into the day, but now she felt better.

Thormóður had arrived early the previous morning, which made a change to the usual monotony of the household. He had brought with him a large rucksack that he took down to the basement that was always locked. Then he had gone back out to the car and fetched a large microwave oven that went the same way. Finally he had brought in a large TV set, placed it on the living room floor and told Selma that she could have it, handing over this gift with the same carelessness as when he dropped bags of shopping onto the kitchen table. The contents had cheered Sajee up, as he brought more vegetables than she had seen before at Bröttuskriður. On top of that, he had brought washing up gloves and avocado oil for her, but the battery charger had been forgotten. When she tried to ask if she could go with him to Höfn to buy one for herself, he pretended not to understand a word of what she said.

Ísak and Thormóður spent the whole day down in the basement. Sajee had no idea what they were doing, but it had to be something important, as they didn't even allow themselves a break to come to the kitchen for a meal. Instead, Selma had her make sandwiches for them that she left outside the basement door along with a flask of coffee. She did this twice, and both times the tray disappeared into the room beyond the door.

There were noises that came from the cellar as if something was being moved around, and upstairs nothing was as usual. Instead of spending the evening in front of the television and preparing a snack to go with the ten o'clock news, Selma had wandered to and fro, agitated, short-tempered and endlessly peering out of the windows. Sajee had gone to bed early and unusually, she had lain awake, listening out for noises from the cellar. Now she had been dragged from sleep in the middle of the night to clean up.

'Can I do it in the morning? It's the middle of the night,' she said sleepily.

'No. You have to clean the passage and the steps down to the cellar,' Selma said sharply. She took hold of Sajee's arm and hauled her to her feet.

'Yes, but…'

'None of that 'yes, but' stuff. It won't take you long, girl! The boys are exhausted and you have to clean.'

'Can't I do it in the morning?' Sajee mumbled, pulling on her clothes. 'I'm not supposed to work at night.'

'You are!' Selma hissed angrily. 'You work when we tell you to work. It's in the contract. Now get on with it. I can't do it.'

'That can't be right,' Sajee muttered as she dressed.

'Oh, yes. You signed the contract of your own free will. Nobody made you do it. If you want to make something of it, then it can go to court, girl, and you'll end up in prison. Don't imagine that anyone's going to believe that tale you spun about a salon. No, you came here to work at Bröttuskriður.'

16

Selma forked up mouthfuls in between yawns. After lunch she said she was tired and went to lie down. Over the last few days she had been tense, had nagged constantly, but now she just seemed to be tired. As usual, Ísak spent the day in the barn and Sajee glanced out of the window occasionally to see if he was on the way back to the house.

The memory of the night's cleaning was clear in her mind, and the little that she had seen made her think that Ísak and Thormóður had to be doing some kind of experiment down there. She wanted to know more and was more at ease now that she felt better than during the previous few days. There had been a heaviness to her, a weight that made her sleep deeply and heavily, accompanied by nightmare in which she was sure there was someone standing over the, staring down at her.

'You're dreaming about the Hidden Lady who lives in the rocks over there,' Selma had said when Sajee mentioned her nightmares.

'But you said that the Hidden Lady was just Karl making things up,' Sajee said in surprise.

'The man doesn't always talk complete nonsense,' Selma said with a joyless laugh. 'Unless it's my old mother, who's buried in the family plot, has taken to visiting you at night. She might not like you being here.'

Sajee shuddered. The thought of a restless spirit was deeply disquieting. In her society it was a matter of conscience to make the dead's transition to the afterlife as painless as possible. Family and friends would hold a vigil over the body, lasting at least a day and a night, and monks would bring blessings, but here in Iceland the bodies of the dead were quickly taken away and buried deep in the earth only a few days after death. That couldn't be good, and as far as she knew there were no ceremonies after the funeral, so it had to be hard for the dead person. It was important to ease the transition, or the consequences could be terrible.

'Are you sure you dreamed a woman?' Selma asked. 'My Christopher has come closer since you arrived and I think it's because our little girl was like you. But she died because there was nobody to help her, any more than you.'

Selma had a strange look in her eyes, as if she were staring at someone only she could see. Sajee looked around quickly. There was nobody to be seen, but the feeling of a presence was powerful. Selma smiled and her grey eyes shone.

'I'll put you right,' she said, putting out a finger and running it slowly over Sajee's lip. 'Don't worry. It'll soon be time for everything to be put right.'

That conversation left Sajee increasingly uncomfortable whenever she was close to Selma, and she tried to console herself with the thought that this had been just a daydream on the part of an old woman who was losing touch with reality. All the same, something strange was going on. Whatever Thormóður and Ísak had been up to the previous night in the cellar, it was suspicious. Now she knew where the key was kept, she could sneak down there and take a look when nobody was likely to notice. She felt a wave of trepidation at the thought, although she was most frightened that the secret was something connected to the hidden people and that her curiosity could trigger something bad.

Selma treated Thormóður like a saint, and maybe he was? At home in Sri Lanka there were many holy men. Selma had said that it was largely thanks to Thormóður that they could continue to live at Bröttuskriður. She also reminded Sajee that Thormóður was the one who had come to her aid. He had given her a place to stay and found her work just when circumstances had conspired against her. Naturally, Sajee was grateful. But she was still uneasy about him.

Thormóður was charming in his own self-assured way, but made no effort to connect, and she felt that he looked down on her, while Selma practically worshipped the ground he walked on. He brought her expensive gifts that she delighted in, and the house was packed with all kinds of expensive toys. All the same, Sajee felt herself constantly on the defensive towards him, and the feeling grew.

Thormóður was an enigma with vast personal charm that he turned on and off like a tap when it suited him. When the charm was turned off, he became positively hostile, although she felt ashamed of these thoughts about a man who made such efforts to help others.

She listened intently for the slightest sound and peered out of the window. There was a light in the barn, so she hoped that Ísak would be at work in the pit. Low snores carried from Selma's room. She tiptoed along the passage and hoped that what she had seen during the night was right. A large palm stood in a pot by the cellar door, and if her suspicion was correct, Selma had pushed the key into the earth. She felt for it and soon found it, the metal cold against her fingertips, with a shiver of excitement as she withdrew the key. She wiped it carefully so that none of the soil would fall to the spotless floor. Then she carefully opened the cellar door. The hinges creaked, so she stood stock still until she heard Selma's snore again.

The steps down to the basement were even steeper than those to her room upstairs. Sajee shut the door behind her, took a deep breath and fumbled her way down the stairs she had scrubbed only a few hours ago. It had been simple enough, the marks of the men's feet on the steps, but she had also wiped down the wall as a fine layer of dust lay everywhere.

The ceiling was low and there was only one small window to let in a little daylight. She groped around in the gloom, as quickly as she dared, not daring to switch on a light. Further along the corridor were two doors. One led to a small room that was of no interest as it had been open last night. The other was locked and she was sure that behind it lay the explanation for whatever Ísak and Thormóður had been up to.

As her eyes became accustomed to the darkness, she searched for a key, certain that Ísak must have taken it as there was no likely hiding place to be seen. She ran her fingers over the door frame, until she heard a sound, stopped and stood perfectly still. There was nothing but the whisper of her own breath. She took off her sweater and laid it on the floor, unwound her scarf and swept it a couple of times around the door frame. She reasoned that if the key were to fall from its hiding place, it would fall soundlessly onto her sweater. After a couple of attempts, she gave up and decided to go back upstairs. Selma could have woken up and Ísak could come in at any moment. She hurried up the stairs and was about to shut the door behind her when it occurred to her to try the key from the palm pot.

She tiptoed back down the stairs, slid the key into the lock and turned. The door swung open and she stepped into a space that in the darkness looked like a laundry room. She would have to switch on the light to see better, confident that the black plastic covering the windows would prevent anyone noticing. The smell she had noticed during the night came back to her, stronger than ever with an aroma that was reminiscent of fennel or aniseed.

She clicked on the light and saw she was in a large, white-painted room. A washing machine and dryer first attracted her attention, and she noticed a stove, fridge and a microwave oven nearby. She went to the middle of the room and looked around curiously. There were smaller appliances on the table and on the floor were plastic tubs fitted with pipes and tubes. She realised that all this was something that shouldn't be allowed to see the light of day.

During the night they had cleaned this room themselves, while she had seen to the rest.

Sajee was startled as something creaked overhead. She stood still, holding her breath. She was overwrought, she told herself, and it was the wind that made the old house creak – but she still needed to go quickly back upstairs. She made another swift sweep of the room with her eyes. In one corner stood a little set of shelves, similar to the one in her attic room. On one side hung a card showing children who looked to be in distress. Sajee had often seen such advertising cards, asking for charitable contributions. This one looked to be old, in complete contrast with everything else in the room. It reminded her of the little shrines that she remembered so well from home, and which she had tried to emulate after coming to Iceland. The lowest shelf held a brass cross, a white teddy bear with yellow eyes occupied the middle and on the top shelf was a small inlaid casket. Sajee's thoughts went to the little grave in the family plot and the carved stone bear that guarded it.

The creaking sound from upstairs was repeated. She had to go back up, but the casket attracted her curiosity like a magnet. It was unlocked and contained nothing but a tightly wound red cloth, tied with a crocheted band that she quickly loosened.

Inside was a narrow, curved bone, grey-brown in colour, so it must have been pulled from the earth. She picked it up an held it to the light bulb hanging from the ceiling to see it better. Maybe it was a bone from an animal that Ísak had been fond of and wanted to keep in this pretty casket. Perhaps this was where he kept his childhood memories like sacred relics; a bone from a favourite cat or even a fox. That had to be the explanation.

The thought had just crossed her mind when a sickening feeling gripped her and she gasped. The delicate curve put her in mind of a tiny rib, brown at each end and white in the middle. Her fingers went numb and she felt a heavy breath behind her. Coarse hands gripped her shoulders. Selma stood close behind her.

'So you've found it,' she said, her voice hoarse.

'I'm so sorry,' Sajee blurted out. 'I didn't mean to… I was just so curious…'

Selma gently turned her around, staring at her.

'No, you didn't mean to do anything, but all the same, you went where you weren't supposed to go. I reckon you're not so stupid after all.'

Sajee said nothing. She knew they thought she was far from bright and took a decision on the spur of the moment to let Selma continue in this belief. She sensed that having a secret weapon could be useful in this strange household. She forced a smile and tried to make herself come across as simple.

'It's such a smart room, so clean. What do they do here?' she asked innocently. 'Do they make wine to drink?'

Selma's laughter was cold and she glared suspiciously.

'That's right. This is where the boys make booze.'

'And what's this? Sajee asked.

Selma stared at the bone and extended a hand.

'It's from Ísak's twin sister. She was like you. So the Hidden Lady let her die,' she said in a low voice. 'She was the one who showed me what to do.'

Selma took the tiny bone from Sajee's trembling hand and stroked it gently before again wrapping it in the red cloth.

'Why do you keep this here?' Sajee asked, her voice quavering. She couldn't stop herself, and had to know.

'Because she was down here all those years, but Thormóður let me keep a little bit of her indoors. It's good to know she's here in the warmth,' she added, replacing the cloth in the casket. 'There was nothing for it after my father told me that Christopher had a wife in America. But I'll never leave her.'

Sajee stared at Selma in horror. This was too much, too terrible to comprehend.

'I understand,' she said, her voice trembling when she was finally able to speak.

'I don't know what you understand, but I'm certain that you were sent here. Thormóður is one of those chosen people who walk the Earth. Nothing he does is a coincidence, and he brought you here, my sweet little thing. Now you'll be with me for ever.'

'I don't know what you mean,' Sajee said.

'No. Of course not,' Selma said, reaching out and gently stroking her lip.

17

It was late in the evening and she had eaten nothing but an apple and a few biscuits. Selma had left her some food as offerings, a little fruit and a packet of crackers. Before eating, she had prayed, hoping that the deities would understand her situation, as she was determined to take the greatest care of everything she consumed. The heaviness in her head was not normal. Earlier in the day she had told them that she wanted to quit, but they had acted as if they couldn't understand her.

Movement could be heard in the hallway as Ísak came in from the barn. He went into the kitchen, shutting the door behind him. Sajee hurried down the stairs, ready to flee out of sight if the door were to open.

'Do you think she understood anything?' she heard him ask.

'Hardly. I crushed three sleeping tablets into her tea, so she'll be out like a light.'

This took Sajee by surprise. She had left the food, but drank the tea.

'Isn't that too much?' Ísak asked.

'No. And now I need more tablets.'

'Thormóður will deal with that. But you have to understand. She has to go. Otherwise the whole business is in danger.'

'Where?'

'Thormóður can find something for her.'

'I want her to stay longer,' Selma pleaded.

'This was temporary. You always knew that.'

'But I still need help. My hip isn't getting any better.'

'She has to go,' Ísak snapped.

'I want her here with me. Always,' Selma sighed.

Sajee could feel her empty stomach complain. She wrapped her arms around herself as if to tell her own body to be quiet, edging closer so she could hear better.

'I'm not sure that's going to work,' Ísak said. 'You've ruined it for yourself.'

'But Thormóður said she was stupid,' Selma argued.

'I'm not so sure,' Ísak said firmly, a note of anger in his voice. 'She's smarter than we suspected.'

'But Thormóður said…'

'That's enough,' Ísak interrupted impatiently. 'He could always be wrong. Do you want us to lose everything?'

'No, but I want her to stay. She's so like your poor sister who didn't live,' Selma whined.

'Stop it! You're mixing up imagination and reality when you…'

Ísak didn't get to finish his sentence before Selma broke in.

'She reminds me of your father. I dreamed of Christopher the other night. He was driving his Ford, so handsome, and so proud that you had done such a wonderful job. He wants the girl to be here to help us. I'm sure of that.'

'We'll see what we can do, mother,' Ísak said, sounding tired. His patience was clearly reaching its limits.

'We can have the girl here, my boy. We just need to make sure she doesn't talk … It's good to have someone here … I get so lonely and I'm getting old.'

'Stop it!' Ísak raised his voice. 'My nerves are bad enough as it is without your mad ideas on top!'

'Please, Ísak,' Selma wailed. 'Let me keep her.'

'Then behave yourself. Understand?'

There was a crash, as if a chair had been hurled aside. Sajee wanted to flee up the stairs and almost fell. She felt her head spin and barely managed to drag herself up the steps to her room.

18

The bed arched, twisting and stretching like thin rubber. Her body was pulled as tight as a bowstring, until the bed became a deep valley. She lost her grip and tumbled deep into the darkness that enveloped her. Sajee was held inside something beyond her understanding, a dream she couldn't escape. Unable to wake herself, she reached into the blackness, trying to claw a gap that would let the light into this chamber, but the darkness was slippery. She scratched at it, but it retreated from her and she was unable to get a grip. Suddenly the bed was upended and she slid down a slimy track that seemed to have no end, down and further down, until she crashed hard against cold rock. The slime was in her eyes, but she managed to prise them open a crack. Now she could make out a trace of brightness in the distance, a crack of light beneath a door.

'Sajee. Sajee.'

The whispering voice was soft. She tried to lift herself up, to go towards the voice that filled the room.

'Sajee. Sajee … Sajee.'

The whispering voice echoed from the rocks. Now she knew who this was. She was in her place, inside her room. The hidden lady wanted to examine her shrine in the corner, to scold her for neglecting her figurines, forgetting the offerings, for always thinking of something else.

'Sajee…'

The room lurched. Wearing a shining blue dress, the grey-haired woman approached her. Something in her hand glittered.

'It won't take long,' she whispered.

The bed gave way and Sajee felt herself falling again. Rough hands took hold of her. She felt the pain in the roots of her hair and her head was pulled back as the hidden lady held tight to her hair. She wouldn't fall as long as the hidden lady held on to her. An icy chill settled on her lips. She wanted to open her mouth, but her muscles refused to obey her. Had she tumbled out into the snow? No… she felt a finger rub her lips. As she felt herself falling again, she saw a wave of scarlet spreading over the white bed linen.

19

'I want to see a doctor,' Sajee mumbled, huddled in discomfort on the kitchen bench.

'You certainly shouldn't be going outside in the cold while you're so swollen,' Selma said firmly. 'Such bad luck to have an accident like that, but it'll heal soon.'

'Will you ask Ísak to drive me to a doctor when he comes back?'

She was in pain and tears rolled down her cheeks. The lower half of her face was bruised and swollen.

'What on earth are you talking about? I can't understand a word!' Selma sniffed. There was an undertone of accusation in her voice, as if it was Sajee's fault she couldn't get her words out.

'I want to go…' Sajee mumbled, making another attempt. 'I want to see a doctor today,' she finally managed to say in a muddle of words, but Selma patted her on the head as if she were a spoiled child demanding a treat.

'There, there, my dear. There's no need whatever to be troubling the doctor. I've put plasters on there to keep it all closed and poor Ísak has enough to do without running trivial errands. He needs to rest and then he's going to finish Christopher's car, so we we're not likely to be going anywhere without good reason. You're just a little swollen after that clumsiness and there's a bruise that's coming up. That's what comes of tripping over your own feet, but it's nowhere near as serious as it might look. It'll start to heal up in a day or two and who knows? Maybe that lip of yours will look better than before,' Selma said. 'That would be something of a silver lining, wouldn't it?' she added cheerfully. She opened the fridge and took out a jug with a lid. 'Here, I prepared something to help with the ache. I made a drink so you can sleep off the discomfort. Cold tea that soothes any pain.'

Sajee felt faint, slumped forward onto the table, but hauled herself back upright, the pain surging as the blood went to her head. She sat with her eyes closed until Selma brought her a drink.

'Isn't that what you need?' Selma said, placing a straw with blue stripes in the cup. Sajee tried to drink, but it was difficult.

'Here, hold that to where it hurts,' Selma said, handing her a damp flannel. 'Put that on there first, and then drink. Sajee obeyed, then held the straw to her mouth with trembling fingers. Slowly and carefully she sucked up a little of the liquid.

'Good girl,' Selma said, patting her shoulder.

'I can drive myself to the doctor,' Sajee mumbled. Her eyesight was fuzzy and she felt drowsy.

'Are you out of your mind? Of course you couldn't drive in the state you're in. In this weather, alone and with all those painkillers inside you. And it's that late in the day that the clinic will certainly be closed by now, even if you and Ísak could get all the way there. They shut at four and it's forbidden to call them out unless it's a real emergency. You'll just have to be strong and get a good night's sleep. Sleep does more good than any doctor.'

'Can I make a call?'

'To whom, may I ask?'

'A woman I know in Reykjavík.'

'You can forget that until that cut has healed up. Do you think anyone's going to understand you over the phone? It's hard enough as it is,' Selma snapped in disgust as she shook her head. The loose skin at her throat trembled and her grey hair swung from side to side.

'Maybe I'll lie down again,' Sajee mumbled, making an attempt to get to her feet, but struggled to keep her balance. The walls seemed to billow and the floor rocked like the deck of a ship.

'You do just that, my girl. I'll go with you so you don't tumble down the stairs like you did before, you clumsy thing.'

Sajee stumbled and she felt Selma take her arm with a firm hand, supporting her along the corridor, up the stairs and into the room under the eaves.

'And stop trying to talk. You'll pull the plasters off and then I'll have to put in more stitches.'

'No, don't do that,' Sajee said meekly, and let herself drop onto the bed. There was nothing she desired as much as to go to sleep.

'Try to sleep, my girl,' Selma said, her voice gentler than before. 'And don't let the hidden lady come after you, or whatever nonsense it was that you dreamed,' she said with a laugh and placed a hand on the duvet. 'Look at the bedclothes and tell me where the blood is, eh? This duvet's perfectly white.'

And where was the blood? Sajee wondered. Had she imagined everything? Selma's painkiller tea was clouding her thoughts again.

'But I can tell you it took me a while to clean the steps,' Selma added. 'I had to take a pill to get myself going and another to bring myself down again. Hadn't I warned you about those steps again and again? They're so worn that they're slippery. Do you think that an old woman with bad hips like me should be cleaning up after you? You know as well as I do that I don't have the strength for this kind of work and you mustn't do this to me again. You'll have to take care, my girl. Keep yourself safe so you can help the old lady.'

'I had a nightmare,' Sajee sighed. 'The grey woman…'

'Ach. That's what comes of listening to Karl from Gröf. We can blame him for this. You had a nightmare after those tales he was telling you about the hidden lady in blue on that first day you were here. Did he tell you more stories that day you went to clean for them? I should never have allowed it. That was a mistake, just like my Ísak said, and I shouldn't have done it. Other people have no business here with us, and we shouldn't interfere in their affairs.'

'No…' Sajee agreed. She was practically asleep, and had no interest in anything else.

'Well, I'm convinced it's Karl's fairy tales that frightened you. He deserves some harsh words, but you're also on the clumsy side sometimes, my dear. I heard that thump this morning and found you flat on the floor. You must have come down hard against the step and burst open your lip. At any rate, you won't be telling any tales…'

Selma's voice faded as Sajee drifted off to sleep.

20

Guðgeir reflected that it was remarkable that he hadn't taken a look at the Lagoon before, as he gazed upwards at the mountainside where the track of the old Almannaskarð road could still be seen. A conversation with an elderly man at the swimming pool was still fresh in his mind. The old man had been brought up near the Lagoon and his account of life there seemed to Guðgeir to be closer to the nineteenth century than the twenty-first. Electricity hadn't arrived until the seventies, and it was some time later that the state broadcaster's TV signals reached the area. In wintertime the place had often been isolated for months at a time when the Lónsheiði road to the east was blocked and the Almannaskarð road to the south of the Lagoon had been impassable. Vehicles had generally been poorly equipped for the conditions and the ice that formed on the pass had been terrifying.

Guðgeir pondered how life had been back then as he drove along the broad, well-lit tunnel that passed through the mountain. The tunnel beneath Almannaskarð had been a huge improvement when it opened in 2005, and as it took only a minute or two to get from one end to the other.

Amazing what a difference it makes being able to go through one mountain, Guðgeir mused as he emerged at the far end. Shafts of sunlight were reflected from the snow-white mountainside onto the grey-black sand and smooth boulders. The green moss clinging to the white-flecked basalt was the same as around Höfn, although the colours appeared to be stronger. There was also less snow here than had fallen in the town.

He drove along the road that passed through the sands and across the bridge over the glacial river, seeing a few patches of green at some of the farms. The further he drove, the scarcer the farms became. A few reindeer cropped at the grass by the road and hardly seemed to notice the car as he passed by. Higher up a hillside he could see a cluster of reindeer trekking along a track, and he drove slowly so he could watch them, before putting his foot down again and keeping it there until he was at the eastern edge of the Lagoon. For a while he sat in the car, gazing at the steep, boulder-studded screes. Wisps of fog swirled around the peaks and where the topmost band of rocks could be seen, they glittered with a green-brown-grey sheen. He switched off the engine and got out of the car. The silence was absolute, as was the attraction of the place's raw beauty. This was what he should be doing; seeing new places and thinking of something new instead of harbouring hurtful, depressing thoughts.

Bröttuskriður was a magnificent place, bleak and stark. Curtains were drawn in every one of the grey farmhouse's windows and there was no sign of life to be seen, neither outdoors nor inside. The place had the look of being inhabited by nobody but ghosts, but all the same, this had to be the right place. This was the last farm, right at the corner of the mountain, just below where the slopes began to rise. He walked briskly up the farm track, from there out over the pasture and from one stepping stone to the next as he crossed the brook. Next to the farmhouse stood a barn, with clear tyre tracks in front of it that looked fresh. He followed them until he stood in front of a handsome 4x4 parked behind the barn. A cry of anguish cut into him and he started, looking around, but nowhere able to see the source of it. Now he could hear it again, lower this time, like an echo, or a drawn-out sob. The echo made him glance instinctively up at the looming outcrop of rocks close by, pitted with fissures that a small animal could easily be caught in. A fall of small stones tumbled from one corner of the outcrop, and he jogged up the slope and squeezed between the rocks. His footsteps disturbed the grey moss and the jagged points of stone nipped at his coat. In between, the ground had been disturbed, but there was nobody there to be seen.

'Hello! Anyone there?' he called, glancing in every direction. 'Hello!' His voice echoed from the rock walls and there was no other sound. An unnerving feeling came over him as he squeezed back the way he had come. Fulmars glided silently around the mountain peaks, but there was no other life to be seen anywhere and he walked back towards the barn. A long, stifled moan cut through the silence and now it seemed to come from the barn. The door was locked, so he walked around the building until he found a narrow window under the eaves. A neatly hung towel covered most of the glass.

He lifted himself onto the toes of his heavy walking boots to peer through the slim gap the towel hadn't been broad enough to cover, and in spite of his height, he couldn't see more than a narrow strip of concrete floor. The sound wailed again, a pained, muffled cry that put him in mind of the cries of exposed infants that the old tales recounted. A newborn lamb calling for its mother? Surely not this early in the spring?

Or was someone there?

'Hello!' he called out and listened intently before circling the building again as he searched for a stone large enough to stand on. There were enough rocks and just a few inches more would be enough to let him see inside. So far all he had been able to make out was that there was a claret-coloured car inside, some old model.

'Can I help you?'

Guðgeir almost missed his footing at the sound of the gruff voice and almost fell. A black-browed scowling man with a mop of tousled hair had made a sudden appearance behind him. The man held an iron chain in the firm grip of one hand.

'Just taking a look around,' Guðgeir said quickly, hopping down from the stone. 'I couldn't see anyone about and thought I heard a strange noise coming from inside your barn. A cry or something like that.'

'Really?'

'That's right,' Guðgeir said. Now he could see that on the end of a lead the man had a fox that was muzzled like a dog that bites or barks too much. The man's working clothes were filthy, he clearly hadn't shaved for many days and his fair hair was wild. He fastened the chain to an iron ring that had been drilled and bolted to a rock beside the barn, and the animal instantly leapt to its feet in a hopeless break for freedom, until the chain brought it up short. Guðgeir thought it was a sorry sight.

'Are you the farmer here at Bröttuskriður?' he asked, assuming that this was the son, the anti-social type Linda had mentioned to him the other day in the café. The man's name was Ísak, he recalled.

'Call me what you like,' the man said drily, stuffing his hands into his pockets.

'In that case, good morning,' Guðgeir said, making an attempt to come across as friendly. 'It's a beautiful place.'

The man nodded but said nothing.

'My name's Guðgeir and I'm from Reykjavík. But I'm working over in Höfn for a while. I heard that this was something special about this place, so I decided to go for a drive and take a look for myself,' he said, looking around to give his words some emphasis. 'I can't say I'm disappointed. It's a magnificent place, especially down at the Lagoon. Are there always that many swans there?'

The man watched him suspiciously, still without making a reply.

'Are you fixing up a car in there?' Guðgeir asked.

'Do you make a habit of looking through strangers' windows?' Ísak asked coldly.

'No, far from it,' Guðgeir said. 'Not at all, but I thought I heard something. Like a cry or a howl. That's why I was looking through the window.'

He extended a hand and Ísak took it gingerly.

'You must have heard the fox. This one makes a noise,' he said, kicking the stone away from beneath the window.

'Why's the fox muzzled?' Guðgeir asked. 'He doesn't seem happy.'

'He's used to it,' Ísak said. 'There were five cubs in a lair I dug up last spring. I didn't have the heart to kill them all, so this one's become something of a pet here at Bröttuskriður. Mother spoils him and gives him scraps.'

Guðgeir looked at the bony animal that was probably a metre long from snout to the tip of its tail. The beast looked wretched.

There was something that jarred – both the place and the man. He had an intuition that something was wrong. Ísak obviously hadn't looked after himself for some time, but still had a clean towel covering the window of this down-at-heel barn. The grey farmhouse had a shabby look to it, contrasting against the smart 4x4 parked outside. On top of this, there was the fox that Ísak said himself was a wild animal, now muzzled and tethered to a length of chain. All these things taken together added up to something that thirty years of police experience told him had to be suspicious. Besides, Ísak acted as if Guðgeir was a peeping Tom looking through bedroom windows, rather than being curious about an old barn being used to fix a car. There was a chance that the root of this feeling was the man's hostile attitude, which seemed to have become increasingly unfriendly with the passing years. He might well have been through childhood traumas, leading to fear and suspicion having a formative effect on his nature, Guðgeir thought, recalling Linda's recollections of her old schoolmate.

Ísak's expression changed suddenly and a friendly look appeared on his face.

'Why don't you come with me and say hello to mother?' he asked, a new eagerness in his tone. 'We see so few visitors at this time of year.' He placed a hand on Guðgeir's back, and set off towards the farmhouse. 'Come on in, coffee and fresh doughnuts.'

'I was going to be on my way…' Guðgeir protested weakly. 'I just came out here to stretch my legs and enjoy the view.'

'You'd best come and have a cup with us. The old lady wouldn't forgive you if you didn't,' Ísak said in a loud voice.

'All right. Thanks,' Guðgeir agreed, grudgingly. He cursed himself, and hurried after Ísak. Then he heard the sound again, a long, drawn out sob. He stopped in his tracks.

'Did you hear that?' he called out. 'That's the sound I meant.'

'What?' Ísak asked without showing any interest and without turning. 'I didn't hear anything.'

'It sounds like someone crying,' Guðgeir said, slowing his pace.

'That's just the fox howling. Come on.'

'But the fox is muzzled.'

'Then it must have been a swan calling. You city types don't know anything,' Ísak said dismissively.

'No. It came from somewhere there,' Guðgeir said, looking back. He listened. The fox seemed quiet, lying on the ground. It was the only sign of life to be seen other than the fulmars high above in their endless flight.

'You're mistaken,' Ísak said. 'It must have been the poor old fox, or the birds up there on the cliffs. The gulls are ready to start nesting,' he said with a laugh. 'Unless you're hearing the exposed infant that's supposed to be around here somewhere.'

'Exposure?'

'That's right. Haven't you read the old tales?' Ísak asked. 'Unwanted newborn infants that were left outside to die?'

'Well, yes,' Guðgeir replied. 'Of course. For a moment I thought you were serious.'

The door of the farmhouse swung open and he saw a woman standing in the doorway, an older woman with grey hair. She stood still for a moment, and then disappeared back inside.

'Mother's seen you now. So now there's no way you'll get away without coffee and doughnuts,' Ísak said, affable once again. 'She loves having guests and doesn't like to let them go,' he said, accompanying his words with a heavy pat on the visitor's back.

They went along a dim corridor and Guðgeir sensed a familiar smell that put him in mind of his daughter Ólöf. But as Ísak opened the kitchen door, the aroma was overpowered by the smell of freshly made doughnuts.

He looked around curiously, and it occurred to him that so much had changed since his own childhood in the west as he took in the sparkling appliances in the shabby kitchen. A pair of yellow washing-up gloves that would have been just the right size for Inga lay on the draining board. Guðgeir noticed Selma's swollen hands, and that Ísak's hands were even bigger.

The gloves would fit neither of them, so maybe they had someone who came in to help. He would have to tell Linda about this, and also about the smart 4x4. She had been convinced that they had to be struggling badly, but that certainly didn't appear to be the case judging by what he could see around him, although there was also things that looked down-at-heel and poorly looked after. Then he noticed one more stark contrast. A smart coffee machine occupied part of the kitchen worktop, while Selma boiled water in a kettle and brewed coffee the old-fashioned way. She looked to be a powerful woman, who had all the hallmarks of having toiled hard for much of her life. She was dressed in grey, and with a blue apron tied around her middle.

'Thanks,' Guðgeir said as Ísak pulled a chair for him from under the table. The place wasn't sparkling clean, with the table top sticky and dust in the corners. Selma greeted him shortly, handed him a cup and placed a couple of doughnuts on a plate. Then she leaned back against the stove and a string of questions flooded out of her, wanting to know who he was and what brought him to Bröttuskriður, and how long he had been wandering around outside without coming indoors for a cup of coffee?

'He'd been out there so long he thought the fox whining was an exposed infant's ghost,' Ísak said with cold delight. 'I saw him peering through the barn window and asked if it was the custom where he comes from to sneak a look through strangers' windows.'

Selma echoed her son's laughter. She was as heavily built as her son, but it was obvious that one hip was causing her pain.

'Well, no. Not at all,' Guðgeir said, unsure how he should react. These people seemed decidedly odd.

'I was just taking a walk, enjoying the landscape,' he said.

'That's fine. Just as well foxy didn't give you a nip. He's not fond of snoopers. Here you go, have another doughnut.' She held out the plate, and waited until he had taken a large bite. Ísak sat and drummed the table with his fingertips.

'It's not often you see these home-made,' Guðgeir said, taking another bite. He could feel the fat ooze out of it. 'They're good.'

'They are,' Selma and Ísak replied, practically in unison. They stared at him, almost as if they were waiting for something. Maybe they were waiting for him to leave. At intervals Ísak's finger tapping the table could be heard. Guðgeir chewed his doughnut and drank his coffee unhurriedly. It tasted fine, but there was something uncomfortable about the place. He decided to let fly and ask about Sajee.

'Did you happen to see a young foreign woman around these parts last winter? She could have been travelling through around the end of February. The twenty-seventh and twenty-eighth, to be exact,' he said as Selma and Ísak looked at him blankly. 'Her name's Sajee, originally from Sri Lanka. She has long black hair and a cleft palate,' he said, drawing a finger along his own upper lip for emphasis, but there was no reaction.

'No,' Selma said after a long pause. 'We haven't seen this person. You're the first stranger to call at Bröttuskriður this winter.

'Really? I hadn't realised that so few people came this way. The main highway passes right along here below the slopes,' Guðgeir said. 'Have you seen Thormóður who runs the Hostel by the Sea in Höfn drive past with a dark-skinned woman? The weather was pretty bad that day.'

Selma and Ísak exchanged glances.

'Thormóður? No,' Selma said at last. She reached for the coffee pot and refilled Guðgeir's cup. Then she pushed another doughnut towards him. 'Help yourself,' she insisted. 'They're freshly made.'

'Thanks, but I'm full. It would have been the twenty-eighth, or so I reckon.'

'Don't you like the doughnuts?' Selma asked plaintively.

'Of course I do,' Guðgeir said. 'Everything in moderation.'

He tried to give the woman standing tight against the table with a look of accusation on her face a polite smile.

'You don't think they're good enough,' Selma wailed, the hurt plain in her voice. 'My great-grandmother's recipe and nobody has ever turned up their nose at our doughnuts before.'

'Maybe one more,' Guðgeir said, reaching for the plate. 'They're wonderful. Crisp on the outside and soft inside.' He took a bite and sipped his coffee while Selma and Ísak watched his every movement. 'So you haven't seen Thormóður or a foreign woman passing by?'

'We're not that far from the beaten track here that we remember every car that goes past. What we said was that nobody had come up here to the farm,' Ísak said. 'Who's this woman you're looking for, and what does she have to do with you?'

'Nothing at all. She's just a young woman who came here thinking she had a job to go to, but that turned out to be a misunderstanding. I've been wondering if she went back south, and if so, how,' Guðgeir said, taking another bite of his doughnut. Now he felt there was a rancid taste to it and he wanted to spit it out, but the woman's steel-grey eyes stared at him unwaveringly. Her gaze was as cold as ice.

'Well, she would have taken a flight, of course,' Ísak said, raising an eyebrow at Guðgeir's ridiculous curiosity.

'Or by car,' Selma said. 'You're a strange one, asking about strangers who are none of your business, and imagining you can hear an exposed infant crying.'

'Those are your words, not mine,' Guðgeir said.

'All the same, you seem to be thinking along old-fashioned lines. Times have changed and people travel fast these days so there's no keeping up with them,' Selma said, pushing the dish of doughnuts at him again. 'Go on, help yourself,' she said with an intensity that was almost discourteous.

'Thank you, but no, I'm stuffed,' Guðgeir said getting to his feet.

They followed him like a pair of shadows along the corridor. A patterned scarf hung on a hook by the door and its bright colours were in stark contrast to the grey of the walls. He took a deep breath and realised that the smell was of nail polish remover, something that had put him in mind of his teenaged daughter who spent so much time on her nails. The smell triggered darker thoughts and he tried to linger as long as he could in the corridor, but there was nothing more to be seen. Selma and Ísak went out into the yard with him and he deliberately took his time before going on his way. Black plastic had been taped over all of the basement windows, and Ísak could see where he was looking.

'We're doing up the cellar,' he volunteered. 'Painting and whatnot.'

'Well, so I see. So you're not giving up living out here?' Guðgeir said.

'No,' Ísak replied. 'Why on earth would we want to do that?'

'True. Why would you?' Guðgeir said, looking around at the harshness of the surroundings. There wasn't much evidence of any farming activity going on. 'Yeah, why would you want to do that?' he muttered to himself as he sat behind the wheel.

As he drove past the barn he could see the fox running futilely back and forth, as far as the chain would allow.

21

She knew that she would feel more pain. Her hair was coming out and before long her scalp would give way as well. Now her eyes opened by themselves… Her body refused to obey, but she snatched at the thoughts that swirled around her. She was aware of the Hidden Lady there, somewhere down in the dark depths. She was back. The blue-grey woman was beside her. Sajee felt her heart hammer in her chest, but sensed it as no more than a distant, weak beat. She knew she was afraid, but felt no fear. The Hidden Lady let go and Sajee fell to the soft grass and her eyes closed again. She could hear the woman speaking and tried to open her eyes again, so see, hear and understand. She saw grey-blue fabric and something held between two fingers glittered. The chill settled on her lips and she could feel the touch of rough fingers.

'You silly little thing. There was me letting you get away with sneaking down to the cellar, but I can't be having that,' the hoarse voice said. It seemed both distant and familiar. 'You had no business touching my bone with your filthy fingers. So now I'll see that you don't go anywhere. My boys don't need to have anything to be worried about.'

The glittering flashed again in front of her eyes and she felt her mouth fill with hot fluid.

22

In the cold light of morning Sajee huddled on the bench in the kitchen and stared into the distance with dazed eyes. Selma sponged her back and shoulders.

'There, my dear. Isn't that better?' she asked gently, laying the flannel aside to help her into a clean shirt.

Ísak was away and there had been only the two of them there since the second accident. This was the second time Sajee had fallen so badly on the stairs. She had been terrified after yet another nightmare. This time she seemed to have practically thrown herself into the darkness, as this fall had been harder and the consequences much more serious. As before, she had landed on her face, leaving it damaged and bruised. The old injuries had torn themselves open, and new ones had been added to them. The only explanation for her dangerous sleepwalking were nightmare memories of something glittering and the woman in blue who loomed over her. Then there was a vague recollection of a red flood, and that had to be the steps.

Selma pulled up a chair and sat in front of her. A towel, a blood-spotted nightdress and a hairbrush lay on the table.

She inspected Sajee's face, placing a broad thumb under her chin and pulling her forward.

'Let me see how it looks today,' she said. 'The stitches look fine. The swelling has increased, but that's only to be expected. I'll put some antiseptic cream on there.'

She hummed a tune as she took a tube of ointment from the pocket of her apron, unscrewed the lid and squeezed some of the contents onto two fingers.

'There, there. I'll be as gentle as I can so it doesn't hurt,' she said softly. 'You'll have to be strong.'

A shudder of pain crossed Sajee's face.

'It hurts and I feel terrible,' she groaned. Her words were unclear and she struggled to move her swollen lips.

'Stop that moaning. It'll all be over soon,' Selma said as she screwed the top back on the tube. 'Now I just have to made sure there's no infection in those cuts. I'll make you a healthy drink every day and before you know it, you'll be as good as new. If you behave, the Hidden Lady will leave you in peace.'

'But you said the Hidden Lady was nonsense I had dreamed up,' Sajee whispered, shivering. She was chilled after being washed and didn't know what to believe. Selma's words and deeds could change direction as easily as the wind in this cold place.

'Nonsense, and not nonsense,' Selma said seriously. Frown lines formed around her grey eyes, her lips pursed and her breathing came more heavily. 'There's nothing we can be sure of in these matters and I've often noticed things that seem unearthly here at Bröttuskriður, without saying too much about it. I just know that it's best not to pry into things that aren't your business, and to leave the dead in peace.'

'But I...' she began, before Selma quickly cut her short.

'To think that you disobeyed me by sneaking down into the basement, snooping into what's no business of yours.'

'I...'

'With my bone in your grubby fingers. That's like going up to our family plot and putting your feet all over one resting place after another. That was a dreadful thing you did. Haven't you heard that ill fortune follows those who disrespect the graves of the dead? I don't doubt you know the anger of the spirits back in your own country? Well?'

Selma's breath was coming in fast, deep gasps.

'I'm frightened.'

'You know what I mean?'

'Yes,' Sajee whispered.

'You should have left our little girl be, because my Hulda was angry. She talks to me all the time these days...'

23

The sound of a car could be heard outside and Selma shut her mouth with a snap and hurried over to the kitchen window.

'They're here. I thought we'd have more time, just the two of us,' she said quickly. 'Come on. Upstairs and behave. That's the best thing.'

Selma took hold of her arms and tried to pull her to her feet. The front door banged.

'I don't want to be alone up there,' Sajee moaned, sinking back onto the bench.

'Yes. You need to lie down and rest. Come on!'

'Fucking hell… What have you done?'

With Ísak behind him, Thormóður stood in the doorway, glaring at them. Selma stepped back from Sajee and looked up at the two men.

'She fell again. Tumbled down the stairs like a bale of hay,' Selma said and began clearing crockery from the table with fast, troubled movements.

'Do you expect me to believe that?' Thormóður snarled. His agitation was obvious and he ran a hand repeatedly through the thick, fair fringe that repeatedly fell back over his forehead. 'No broken teeth this time?'

'No, but of course I had to put in some stitches myself. I couldn't be taking her to town, and we're used to dealing with things for ourselves.'

'If mother says she fell down the stairs, then she fell down the stairs,' Ísak said heavily, fidgeting nervously as he stood behind his companion.

'I told you, Ísak,' Selma said defensively. 'She had another nightmare.'

'Let me take a look,' Thormóður said, taking a seat in front of Sajee. He took hold of her chin and inspected her injuries carefully. There was no mistaking his distaste as he scowled and swore.

'Sajee, it looks like you cut yourself on something. Now, open your eyes properly,' he said in a loud voice. 'Sajee, tell me, did you have something in your hands when you fell?'

'No,' she groaned.

'How did this happen?'

'The Hidden Lady,' Sajee mumbled.

'What did you say?' Thormóður demanded.

'The Hidden Lady cut my face,' she sighed and looked directly into his eyes. 'She's an evil spirit.'

Thormóður let go of her as if his hand as if he had been scorched. He stared at her swollen face.

'So the Hidden Lady cut your face,' he said as he got to his feet. 'Is that the one who lives in the rocks up there, or one of these wretched Bröttuskriður ghosts?'

'The Hidden Lady,' Sajee repeated.

'Is that so?' Thormóður said. 'And what do you two have to say for yourselves?' he snapped furiously at Selma and Ísak. 'What the hell is going on here?'

'Don't be so foolish. I told you what happened,' Selma told him, arranging doughnuts on a tray in a precise pattern. 'The silly girl tumbled down the stairs. You know yourself how steep they are and the steps arc so worn that they slope in all directions. You really need to get them fixed up,' she said, running fingers through her grey hair, closing the tin of doughnuts and placing it in a cupboard. 'I can tell you, Thormóður, that I had to clean up the blood myself and you know what an invalid I am.' She took a damp cloth and wiped down the yellowed cupboard doors. 'But I did it anyway.'

'Is that so, Selma? That's a burden for you, considering I brought her here to ease the load for you and give you a little company,' Thormóður sneered, staring first at Selma and then at the clumsy stitches in Sajee's face.

'You mustn't think I'm not grateful,' Selma whined, like a cat looking for attention.

'Haven't I done enough for you? Well? Do you want to wreck everything?'

Thormóður glared at Selma in despair and resignation.

'It'll be fine,' Ísak said, awkwardly patting Sajee's shoulder. She was huddled against the wall, her eyes closed and appeared to not be taking any notice of what was going on around her. The minutes ticked past.

'Don't you want coffee, boys?' Selma said, breaking the silence, and went into the pantry. They watched her leave the room.

'A word,' Thormóður said. Sajee heard the kitchen stools scrape across the floor and when she opened her eyes, she was alone in the kitchen. They had gone out into the corridor.

'You'll have to stop the old woman,' she heard Thormóður say.

'I'll keep an eye on mother,' Ísak said meekly.

'You can't keep her in order! Do you think I can't see what's going on?' Thormóður grated. 'The old bitch is mistreating the girl. What the hell do we do now?'

'What are you trying to say? She'd never... I know she gets confused but ... she...' Ísak hesitated. There was no conviction in his protests. 'Mother was upset when she found her down in the basement with the bone in her hands.'

'Fuck! The old woman's completely mad.'

Thormóður's voice was as sharp as a scalpel.

'Leave it to me,' Ísak repeated. 'I can look after my own people.'

'You're sure about that? There's no knowing what she'll get up to next. She's getting worse by the day, going on about ghosts, elves and all sorts,' Thormóður said in a voice as hard as steel. 'That's not to mention the obsession the pair of you have with that car and all the rest of it! I've heard her going on about fixing the girl's face, and I've heard her say that she'll make sure Sajee never leaves this place.'

'You'll never understand what Mother has been through,' Ísak hissed. 'And you were the one who brought the girl here. You and your brilliant ideas.'

'Hold on. Let's take it easy for a moment,' Thormóður said, dropping his voice almost to a whisper. 'All this chaos jeopardises the work we've been doing, and we can't let anything wreck that. All the same, good of you to stick up for the old lady.'

'It's for her and for Bröttuskriður that I'm in this business with you,' Ísak said, the bitterness spilling over into his voice. 'I'm not so thick-headed that I can't tell you're using us. You leave a trail of misery behind you. Poor Kristín spent pretty much two years in a mental ward and I'll tell you right now that mother's never going there. Leaving this place would be the death of her.'

'Ísak, Kristín Kjarr was just a drama queen who wanted nothing more than to be all over the newspapers,' Thormóður said with all the authority of the one with the upper hand. 'She had more problems than you could possibly imagine.'

'Yes, but…'

'Hey, calm down, will you? There's no need to make even more of a drama out of this. To my mind the two of you are soul mates. Ísak, think of everything we've been through together,' he said, his tone softer but firm. 'So I reckon you'd better keep any knives away from the old woman while the girl gets better. After that I'll find her work somewhere else. End of story.'

'Where?'

There was a note of concern in Ísak's voice.

'She can be put to work somewhere, but your mother's efforts at plastic surgery haven't exactly helped there. Who's going to pay for a girl who looks like that?' Thormóður asked. 'But you don't need to worry. I'll sort this out, like everything else.'

The mixer could be heard whirring in the kitchen. Selma stood in a cloud of flour, smiling at the young woman who tried to fight her way through the drugged haze as she tried to make sense of what she had heard. A nightmare vision of the grey Hidden Lady appeared before her eyes. Her worst fears were becoming a reality.

Sajee's hopes had all but faded when finally a thick envelope arrived, one that required a signature. An Icelandic family Hirumi knew were prepared to take her in as an au pair. The letter contained money and precise instructions of what she needed to do, and a month later she left. The last few days had been difficult, but the journey to the airport was hardest of all. She sat rigidly in the bus. Her feelings almost overcame her as she left her own country behind, unsure if she would ever see it again. At the airport she needed all her energy to follow the instructions and go to the right place. She had never been on an aircraft before and now there were to be more than ten hours in the air to London. While she trembled with fright during takeoff, she managed to stay awake until a meal was put before her. Overcome by exhaustion and weeks of tension, she slept until a steward gently prodded her awake to offer her breakfast.

At the airport in London there were armed men everywhere, so she tried to be unobtrusive. People hurried past, some of them jostling her on their way. When a young woman with a child in her arms stopped, Sajee plucked up courage to speak to her and was relieved when she answered in the same language.

'Can you tell me why there are so many soldiers here?' Sajee asked.

'Because of the terrorists,' the woman replied. 'There was a bomb in one of the underground trains. Many people died and many more were hurt.'

'Is there a war here?' she asked. 'I don't know much about Europe.'

'Yes, the war on terror,' the woman answered. 'Be careful what you say and don't leave anything lying around or you could find yourself in trouble.'

The woman's words frightened her so much that she was consumed with nerves during the flight to Iceland. She was no less apprehensive about what might be waiting for her in this new world ahead of her, but as she took her first steps she immediately felt a very different atmosphere to the tension of the airport in London. Hirumi was waiting for her and she had changed. She was plump, her hair brushing her shoulders, dressed in trousers and a fleece. Crying and laughing, they fell into each other's arms. Sajee asked after her husband, but Hirumi told her to forget him – he was history.

24

'No,' Sajee said thickly, her eyesight flickering as she looked at the soup dish in front of her.

'You're so difficult to please. Then go up to bed,' Selma said, putting her spoon down. 'I'll bring you a vitamin drink.'

The two men hardly looked up as she stumbled from the room.

In her room she found her bottle of oil and rubbed some on her injuries to soften them. She took a gulp of it and retched. But she was determined that this would be the only nourishment that would pass her swollen lips. She lay on the bed.

The wind battered the roof and whined, and the electricity cables flapped against the wall outside. She listened for a sound, and by now she had become adept at working out what noises were due to the weather and which originated with the four walls of the building. She heard footsteps in the hallway, the sound of the toilet flushing and Ísak calling for his woollen socks to be fetched. Finally she heard the outside door slam and peered out of the window. Flakes of snow stuck to the top of the pane before sliding down to form a layer on the window sill. There was mist on the glass, but she clearly saw three people as they trudged along the track that lay down to the barn.

Ísak went first, holding his mother's hand as she followed close behind him. Thormóður followed and Sajee quickly drew back from the window as he suddenly glanced behind him and up. She felt faint, but she was fairly sure he hadn't seen her. A moment later she saw the lights come on in the barn. She waited a few minutes before making her way down the stairs.

There was no phone at Bröttuskriður, only the mobile phone that Ísak used, and that was what she was looking for. Or Thormóður could have left his phone behind as they three of them went down to the barn. She knew how to call the emergency number, and that was her plan, to call for help even though it was difficult for her to speak. She hoped that whoever took the call would be able to trace it, even though she had only one vital word ready to use. She would have to put her faith in that. This was her only hope.

There was no sign of Ísak's phone in the kitchen, and Thormóður had obviously also taken his with him. She searched high and low without success and her desperation grew with every passing minute. There was no phone to be found in the house. Looking around in despair, she noticed Thormóður's car keys lying on the chest of drawers in the hall. For a moment it occurred to her to sneak out unseen. She could hide in the back of Thormóður's car, aware that people left them unlocked. The she realised that Thormóður might well stay long enough for her disappearance to be discovered.

She decided to prepare to flee. On the way upstairs she picked up gloves and a hat, but didn't dare move her coat and boots, knowing that Selma noticed everything and would see straight away that her things were missing from their usual hook.

She suddenly felt an aching pain in her belly and hurried back down the stairs, where she retched, bent over the toilet. Although the bile burned her throat, it was nothing compared to the agony of opening her mouth. She struggled to her feet and caught sight of herself in the mirror. Her face was covered in scratches. Two deep cuts running from upper lip to nose had been amateurishly patched together with a few stitches. Her face was swollen and she could see as she leaned close to the mirror that the cuts were infected. She rooted through the bathroom cupboard and found surgical spirit in a plastic bottle and some cotton wool. She splashed spirit onto a ball of it, and cleaned her injuries with hands that trembled. The pain ate deep into every nerve. She held tight to the sink with both hands while the shock rippled like fire through her face. When the worst had passed she cleaned the cuts again with greater care. She felt dizzy, but fought it off. On the way up to her room she took a pair of scissors from the kitchen drawer.

She collected everything she dared take and put it all in a bag. Warm clothes were vital. Anything else missing would trigger suspicion and the room had to look as it usually did. She still had the torch Selma had lent her and that went into the bag. She paused by the shelf in the corner where Buddha sat. After a moment's thought she squatted on her haunches and poured a little oil into the saucer on the lowest shelf. Before lighting an incense stick and praying, she held her mother's ring tight in her hand to bring herself strength. As she rose to her feet again, her composure had returned, along with a certainty that she would escape this terrible place.

She had escaped before. When every door had slammed shut in her face back home in Sri Lanka, new hope had appeared and she had overcome all the obstacles. Sajee twisted the fine gold ring around her finger. She'd do this again.

The door banging and voices downstairs told her that they had returned. Selma was clearly cheerful as she laughed long and loud. She seemed happier than Sajee had ever imagined she could be. They appeared to be celebrating the repairs to the burgundy-red Ford being finished, and their conversation revolved around the car.

Her intentions changed with the weather and the goings-on in the house. At one point she was determined to go outside and hide in Thormóður's car, and a minute later she changed her mind, deciding to wait a little longer. She heard the blows of a hammer, and laughter. Then there was the smell of meat cooking and she heard Ísak say he'd go down to the basement to fetch a bottle and a decent smoke. As the evening passed, she realised that Thormóður was going nowhere. The company downstairs seemed to be enjoying themselves, or else the reason for his extended stay was that the weather worsened with every passing hour. The wind's strength grew and out of the window she could see a furious sea battering the rocks.

She pulled a nightdress over her head and hurried to get in to bed as she heard the howl of the juicer, a bulky machine that Thormóður had heaved on to the table a few days ago. Then she heard the creak of footsteps on the stairs. She had kept a warm shirt and tights on under the nightdress. If Selma were to say anything, she would explain that she had felt a chill. The old woman would surely believe that.

The door opened and Thormóður came in, a glass in one hand and a straw in the other. There was something green in the glass and Sajee was sure that something to knock her out had been mixed in with it.

'I've brought you a spinach smoothie to keep your strength up, made with celery and all sorts of good stuff. Thought I'd bring it up myself so we don't have to worry about any hidden ladies, especially when they've had a glass or two!' He laughed at his own joke and bumped against the door frame. 'Whoops! This place really is a dump…'

Sajee shifted a little and mumbled as if she had been asleep. She sensed that he hesitated before taking a seat on the bed.

'Or are you out for the count?' he asked without expecting a reply. 'Drink this anyway.'

He put a hand on her shoulder. She moaned in pain and turned over. She could smell the strong reek of alcohol and something else.

'Can you help me sit up?' she mumbled, pretending to struggle to open her eyes. He placed a hand under one arm to lift her up and she took care to let her hair fall clear of her face so he could see how she had been treated. As she felt the hand of the man she had thought of as her saviour, she knew that now she was back where she had been and she promised herself that in future she would never again use her hair to hide her face. If she were to survive, she would no longer hesitate to look the world in the eye exactly as she was. After this, no person or thing would be able to harm her.

'Fucking hell, the state of you,' he grunted, handing her the glass. 'Here. Drink this. It'll do you good.'

'You are a good man,' she tried to say, appealing to his conscience. This time he seemed to understand her and grinned.

'I sure am. You've no idea how good I am. I've helped heaps of people, helped them on their way out of this miserable life. There you go, drink up.'

Sajee swallowed a little and pretended to take another sip. He failed to notice as she spat it back into the glass. He had never been in this room before and was too occupied with looking around him to notice the liquid going back down the striped straw.

'Fairy lights and all sorts,' he said, smirking as he inspected the shrine in the corner. 'You people are so weird... Now, finish that drink and you'll feel better.

Your face'll be better than it ever was after all this vegetable shit mixes up and you'll sleep like a baby.'

He put glass down on the table, got to his feet and looked ready to be on his way, bored with her company already.

'You understand what I'm saying? Well?'

She pretended to be too drowsy to keep her eyes open, muttering agreement. Her heart beat fast and she could hardly draw a breath until the door had closed behind him. She felt her inner strength grow now that she had managed to deceive him, and she would have to take the next step before it was too late. For long minutes she lay as still as stone in bed, listening to the loud argument that broke out in the kitchen over a TV programme, until peace returned, punctuated by gurgles of laughter. Sajee slipped from the bed. The pain in her stomach had abated, her mind was fairly clear and now she would have to work fast. She poured what was left of the green drink into a bag and put it in the cupboard. She rolled up the bed cover and pushed it under the duvet, shaping it to resemble a sleeping body. The nightdress went into the same place, with a little cloth showing here and there from under the bedclothes.

She looked up as a shower of hail battered the roof and felt that it was giving her strength as the unpredictable weather was working with her. Without any hesitation she cut a couple of long locks of her own hair. The scissors were blunt and she had to saw at her hair until she had enough of a handful. She arrayed the hair on the pillow, making it look as if she had pulled the duvet up over her head. A few stray hairs fell to the floor and she picked them up before she pulled on her outdoor clothes, picked up the bag from under the bed and made her way unsteadily down the stairs. The key to the car was still in the bowl on the chest of drawers. She held it tight in her grasp and opened the door that would lead to freedom, out into the darkness and the howling wind. The hail greeted her, battering her already damaged face, but she didn't care.

The 4x4 stood behind the barn and she walked the track towards it with confidence in her slippery-soled boots. The dim light high on the wall of the barn showed her the way to the car. She gripped the handle and squeezed the key as she put it where she thought it should go, but nothing happened. She felt along the curved metal in the gloom, but found nothing that looked like a lock. The key was a strange shape, she had noticed that earlier in the day.

It had been years since the last time she had driven a car. Back then she had been working as an au pair, looking after the children for Ragnhildur, who had let her practise when the family spent time in their summer cottage. Sajee had enjoyed driving along the potholed country roads and had easily kept control of the car.

But that was then, and it had been a terribly long time ago. She squeezed the key in her hand and tried again. A button inside popped up and she realised that the locking mechanism had to be remotely controlled. By chance she had managed to open it.

SÓLVEIG PÁLSDÓTTIR

Now she recalled that when Thormóður had driven her to Bröttuskriður, he had just dropped the key into a compartment on the dashboard. There had been no need to use it to start the car. She sat behind the wheel, dropped the key into the compartment and pressed the button on the steering wheel. The car's engine started instantly and she could see the road ahead of her before she managed to switch off the lights. Then she drove carefully into the darkness.

25

The wind battered the jeep as its wheels fought to keep a grip on the road's surface. On one side was the mountain slope, on the other a sheer cliff above the sea far below. It was dark and the snow was driven by the wind. Sajee held tight to the steering wheel and tears streamed down her cheeks. She could see only the white flakes spinning towards her out of the darkness and for a moment it occurred to her that it was time to give up, walk out into the teeth of the storm and leave the snow to pile up and cover her. She could let herself drift into unconsciousness before they could catch up with her. She could fall asleep in the cold and dream her way to the warmth of home. She glanced into the mirror and moaned at the sight of her face, swollen, the cuts turning septic and the clumsy stitches.

'I will,' she whispered to herself, feeling the old determination return. 'I will go home,' she told herself, out loud this time as a gust of wind made the car bounce. She gripped the wheel so tightly that her knuckles turned white as she cautiously put her foot on the accelerator.

Eventually, she realised that she had taken the wrong road.

She must have passed out, as she wasn't aware they had reached her until she was shaken roughly. They tried to pull her clear, but she held tight to the steering wheel and only relaxed her grip when Thormóður bit one of her fingers until it bled. Her cries could hardly be heard over the howling of the wind as they dragged her along the road. She had a hazy memory of being violently shaken and was sure she must have lost consciousness on the way back. When she awoke, she was on a mattress in an unfamiliar place, and it was pitch dark.

She slept and dozed without any idea of the passing of time. Ísak brought her a bucket so she could relieve herself, and water and food. She begged him to allow her out, but he acted as if he hadn't heard her. A little later he came back with the torch that she had taken with her in her unsuccessful attempt to escape.

It was obvious that this hole had been used to store goods. When she found a banknote on the floor, she remembered the five thousand krónur notes she had seen in Ísak's pocket, and realised that he had been down here that night when she had been so frightened and had gone into the barn. Thormóður and Ísak had locked her away in a storeroom that was hidden behind the pit. The storeroom was no more than a few square metres with a ventilation pipe above her head. It was in this cold, dark place that she had been left alone to cope with her own suffering.

There was a blanket, a quilt and a pillow on the mattress, and after a while Ísak also brought her things, so she hoped there must be some concern for her. She could sense his discomfort as he stood wordlessly in the doorway and shone a light as she tried to line up the statues she prayed to with trembling hands.

26

'Dad, when are you going to stop working there?' Pétur Andri asked, a demanding note in the fifteen-year-old's loud voice.

'My contract is until June,' Guðgeir replied slowly. 'I can extend it, but probably won't if I can find something to keep me busy in Reykjavík.'

'Are you moving back home?'

There was an innocent earnestness to his question that was clear, even through the poor internet connection.

'Yes…' Guðgeir hesitated. 'If your mother and I have sorted things out between us by then. You know we were going to spend a year apart and then see how things look.'

'I think you should go back to the police after the summer holiday,' Pétur said.

'That's not certain, and it's not my decision,' Guðgeir said, trying not to be irritated that the boy always came back to the same thing. After all the explanations, he ought to have known better, but it seemed that he had difficulty facing facts.

Sometimes he felt that Pétur Andri found it hard to accept that his father was no longer a senior police officer. The lad had always looked up to him, putting him on a pedestal, and it hurts to find one's hero wanting. This appeared to be harder for him to bear than his parents' separation.

'I ought to be able to find a job of some kind when I've finished in Höfn,' he said, trying to sound encouraging.

'I think you've been punished enough, Dad. You're a great cop. You're the man they need. Særós came here and talked to Mum. I heard her say it.'

The picture on the screen faded into a mess of pixellated colours.

Lousy internet, and a lousy flat, Guðgeir sighed to himself.

'I'll call you right back,' he said quickly, closed the connection and took the computer into the living room. So, Særós, his former colleague and assistant, had been to see Inga. The thought pleased him. She was now the acting detective inspector in his place, and if things didn't go his way, then her appointment would be confirmed as permanent within a year. Guðgeir reflected that it wouldn't be a bad outcome and he could see himself working as her subordinate, but decided it wouldn't be likely to turn out that way. A former senior officer working under a former subordinate went against all the usual management rules, although Guðgeir knew that they could easily switch roles and work together. He had appointed Særós himself. She was smart, outstandingly precise and had never been inclined to spare herself. For the first couple of years she had occasionally messed things up, as she tended to take things too literally. But she was eager to learn, and snapped up every potentially useful training course on offer. He suspected that she had even taken a sense of humour course; maybe more than one and with some success. Særós was also a devotee of healthy living and every week brought something new, generally something that would take her closer to her latest goal.

'Pétur? Are you there?' Guðgeir called into the computer. The connection seemed stronger, and both sound and picture had improved.

'Yeah, I'm here.'

'Did Særós say she wanted me back at the station?' Guðgeir asked.

'That's what she said, that you're the best one to work with, and that you're the best detective and the best boss.'

Guðgeir felt a warm buzz, even though he wasn't sure that those would have been Særós's exact words. All the same, this was the smart reliable Særós he knew.

'And your Mum?' he asked. 'Do you think she's missing me?'

'Dad, you should know better than to ask me that kind of leading question,' Pétur Andri said, sounding very grown-up. It wasn't for nothing that he was the son of a lawyer and a police officer.

'Well, you're quite right,' Guðgeir admitted.

'But I think she misses you,' Pétur Andri said. 'She's in tears sometimes. How could you do this to us?'

The accusation was plain in both his expression and the tone of his voice.

'Pétur, we've been through this again and again. Life isn't simple, and it's never black and white. There are reasons behind everything to do with peoples' relationships.'

'Pack it in, please? Just come home and talk to Mum properly,' Pétur said through clenched teeth.

'It's not that simple,' his father explained patiently. 'You'll understand better when you're older.'

'I hate it when you say that! It is simple!' Pétur yelped through the screen, his temper rising. Guðgeir had been increasingly aware of this tendency, even though his son had always been a quiet boy up to now. He decided to end the conversation before Pétur became too upset.

'Hey, I have to go to work, do my rounds and check on a couple of buildings. Enjoy the Easter egg I sent, and give Ólöf a kiss from me.'

'Ólöf? You have to be joking!'

Guðgeir laughed, relieved that he had managed to steer the conversation away from his and Inga's marital problems.

His phone pinged and a moment later a message appeared on the screen.

'Pétur, I have to be on my way to the school. There's a water leak I need to deal with. I'll speak to you again soon.'

'A water leak? Dad, come on… You're going to fix a leaking pipe? And you were a senior detective in the murder squad.'

'It's not called a murder squad in Iceland. You've been watching too many cop shows, my boy,' Guðgeir said as he stood up. 'I have to run. See you later.'

During her first few days in Iceland Sajee was sure that it was winter, as she was constantly cold, until she realised that this was what summer was like over here. It was also a shock to discover that she understood only a few letters of this new language's script. The streets seemed to be practically empty and she wondered where all the people were. She could see no animals. The silence was unsettling and the scarcity of people was terrifying.

Now she had largely adapted to the environment she had found herself in, and understood much of the language, although she spoke little. There were still things that she found strange, in particular how gloomy people were and how they complained about everything. She found it difficult to understand if this habit had something to do with the religion, or some other reason, but she was thankful that she had managed to tame her own restlessness and impatience. This was something that had often served her well, not only after Lakmal's death, but also during the difficult times in Iceland. It had been hard once the family she had been with no longer needed her. Hirumi found her work cleaning people's homes, although that was not easy as so many people cut back on their spending following the financial crash.

After a while Iceland began to recover and there were households that needed her again. Of course, she

*was sometimes unhappy and her thoughts would take
her home to Sri Lanka. But in spite of the long spells of
homesickness, she knew there was little future for her
there. At least in Iceland she had work and somewhere
to live. To make an effort to do better, Sajee enrolled
in a language course for foreigners, but lasted only a
few weeks. The people in the group were varied and
those with similar educational backgrounds kept to
themselves. There was one woman from Sri Lanka
who only appeared a couple of times and then never
came again. Sajee missed having someone to talk to
and tried to maintain contact with the woman, but she
was too occupied with her husband and children for
friendship. It wasn't as if they had much in common
other than being from the same country.*

*It was not only for this reason that she gave up on
the language course, but also because the Icelandic
letters were so confusing, angular and stiff, unlike
the script she was familiar with. She was not aware
that she had ever struggled to learn to read and write
back in Sri Lanka, but here it had become a constant
battle. The Icelandic she had picked up came from
the children she had looked after, or from Hirumi,
who had now departed on her longed-for trip home.
Sajee was not even sure when, or even if, she would
return as she had only sent one postcard describing
a banquet she had held for the district's Buddhist
monks, and telling her that she had paid for repairs
to a large shrine. Hirumi must be a respected person,
she decided. One day she would also travel back to
her old district, showing people how well she had*

done for herself in Iceland. The thought gave her a warm feeling inside and she opened her eyes.

Guðgeir mulled over the conversation with his son several times over the day as he listened to the plumber and the caretaker trying between them to identify the source of the leak in the primary school's boiler room. Then he drove his usual security route around the town and as everything seemed to be absolutely fine, he pulled up outside the Coffee Corner and peered through the windscreen. If Linda were here, they could have something to eat together and he could tell her about the trip to Bröttuskriður. He picked up his phone and got out of the car. Outside the café a group of tourists shivered in the cool spring weather and looked lost.

The café was packed with people and at the entrance he stopped by a large table stacked high with beautifully wrapped presents. There was another table by the bar, laid out with nibbles and cakes, with a large, pink marzipan cake decorated with the face of a young girl at the centre of the display. It took him a moment to assess in the situation. He glanced around at the roomful of guests dressed in their best, the complete opposite of the travellers who usually occupied every corner. The tall girl from the marzipan cake picture came towards him, a flower in her long hair.

'I'm sorry,' Guðgeir said. 'I didn't realise there was a confirmation reception in here. I was just looking for a bite to eat, and it looks like there are other people with the same idea,' he said, nodding towards the group in the car park outside. The confirmation girl smiled and a tanned woman with inky eyebrows approached.

'It's closed.'

'Sure. When's it open again?'

'Don't know. If the reception goes on for a while then it won't open today,' the woman said, and he realised that she had to be the confirmation girl's mother.

'Fair enough. Congratulations,' Guðgeir said and went outside, squeezing past the group of tourists and gave them the message that they'd have to look for somewhere else.

Next, he tried the restaurant in the old building down by the quay, and found himself walking in on yet another confirmation reception. A boy in a suit came over to him, just as Guðgeir noticed another marzipan cake. The wording on this one read 'Alex Breki' but this time there was no picture. He apologised and backed out. There were a dozen hire cars and a minibus by the harbour. A variety of faces peered out, expectant that the restaurant would open once the reception was over. Cheers could be heard from one of the cars every time someone left the celebrations going on inside. There was only one other place that was open, albeit with a good two-hour wait for a table.

Guðgeir had just about decided that he'd have to settle for the scanty contents of the fridge in the rented flat, when he remembered that Matthildur upstairs had invited him for dinner. How on earth had he been so absent-minded as to forget? It wasn't as if invitations came his way every day. He hurried home to change.

'You look very stylish,' Matthildur said with admiration as she opened the door for him. 'Svenni! Come and see how smart Guðgeir is!'

'Suited and booted,' Sveinn observed, followed by his characteristic bark of laughter. 'Come on in.'

'It is Easter, after all,' Guðgeir said apologetically, realising that he had probably overdone it. 'Sorry I'm late.'

A heavy vase stood in one corner of the living room with a spray of birch branches extending from it. Colourful wooden eggs – blue, yellow and green – hung from every branch, along with a yellow chick pushing up the lid of a chocolate Easter egg. Flowering daffodils stood in a vase on the window sill.

'He runs and he swims,' Matthildur said. 'Svenni, look at Guðgeir's lovely tie. You'll have to find out where he shops for clothes.'

'The old lady's comparing us, and not exactly in my favour,' Sveinn laughed, clapping a hand on Guðgeir's back. 'Good to see you!'

Matthildur and Sveinn were excellent hosts. The amiable companionship dampened his longing to be at home and it turned out to be a relief to spend some time upstairs with its high ceiling and wide rooms. Existence downstairs could be depressing for a tall man.

Sveinn and Matthildur had sons of eighteen and twenty. The elder boy was at sea on a ship from

Vopnafjörður, while his younger brother was at technical college in Reykjavík. Photographs of them charting their growth from babies to teenagers could be seen on walls and tables, and Guðgeir looked around curiously. He hadn't been upstairs since they had signed the rental contract in the autumn. He recalled that had been a bittersweet occasion for him, confirming that he wouldn't be going back home for months to come.

They had a warm and welcoming home, bearing all the hallmarks of their fondness for it. A sofa that looked deep and comfortable, decked with cushions, occupied part of the living room, opposite a large TV on the wall. The dining table was covered in a sparkling white cloth, with daffodils in a vase and matching yellow candles.

The slow-cooked leg of lamb was done to perfection and after a while Guðgeir brought up the mystery woman from Sri Lanka. She had been on his mind and he was curious to know what had happened to her, as this woman must have been through a great deal before she had washed up here. As far as he himself was concerned, he had certainly been through a lot before he had landed this job, far from his family.

'Ach, I'm sorry, Guðgeir. I completely forgot to mention it to Svenni,' Matthildur said.

'What was that?' Sveinn asked.

'About the foreign woman who turned up here in the winter. He was wondering if you could check if she had taken a flight back south. Can I offer you some more?' She said, cutting a thick slice from the joint of meat. Guðgeir shook his head. His belly was full and although he would have liked a little more, good sense told him to stop, even though the meat was exceptionally good. You couldn't beat home cooking.

'Sure you won't have a little more?' Sveinn asked, helping himself to another slice of lamb.

'Didn't you hear him, Svenni? Guðgeir doesn't like to gorge himself,' Matthildur said. 'That's no good for people who are on the move all the time, like he is. Maybe you ought to go for a run with him some time…'

'Or maybe we ought to start by going out to the airport and I'll see if I can get into the passenger lists,' Sveinn said quickly. There was no mistaking his eagerness to escape any discussion of eating habits or fitness. 'We can go out there and see if the poor girl made it back south. I don't recall seeing her taking a flight,' he said with a sidelong glance at his wife. 'But I'm only human.'

'She could have taken a coach to Reykjavík,' Matthildur suggested.

'If I can't get into the passenger lists, then we'll check any other possibilities,' Sveinn said and got to his feet. 'We can stop off for a chat at the police station as well. So when we get back, we'll be hungry enough for dessert. Don't worry about the dishes. We'll deal with those later.'

'There's no need to trouble the police,' Guðgeir said quickly, reluctant to involve his colleagues with something so vague. That wouldn't do him any favours. Sveinn appeared to understand his position.

'I'll talk to them,' he said slipping into his coat.

'Fine,' Guðgeir said. 'Otherwise we ought to keep quiet about this, keep it to ourselves for the moment, at any rate. Rumours can travel fast.'

At the airport Sveinn started by going through the arrivals at the end of February.

'Here she is. Sajee Gunawardena. That has to be her,' he said after searching through the list. He hardly looked up as he continued to click the mouse. 'I'm looking to see if Sajee Gunawa.. Gunawar-something took a flight south.'

He hunched over the computer, but his search returned no results. There were no unusual names to be seen on the list until well into March, and none that were even close to Sajee's name.

'And the coach?' Guðgeir asked.

'I'll check,' Sveinn said, reaching for the phone and punching in a number. A few moments later he had confirmation that nobody of that name had travelled by coach to Reykjavík.

Sveinn went back to the 27th February passenger list and they read out Sajee's name, as if to convince themselves that there could be no similar name that could have slipped past them. They sat in silence, engrossed in the computer screen.

'Thormóður from *Hostel by the Sea* was on the same flight,' Sveinn said. 'You remember? That's where I took her.'

Guðgeir nodded.

'You're sure she was able to stay there?'

'I'm fairly sure of it. She came out again and waved to me. She had the man's card, and come to think of it, I don't recall having seen that one before,' he said, reaching for a plastic rack on the desk. 'No. Nothing like that here.'

'I had a meal at the café a while ago and was chatting to Linda. You know her?'

'Yes, sure.'

'Linda said she had seen Thormóður at the Ólís filling station with a woman who could be Sajee, and that they had been on the way up to the Lagoon,' Guðgeir said.

'How can she be sure who it was?' Sveinn asked.

'Her appearance was striking,' Guðgeir replied. 'Her mouth, and her hair. And that day there was exceptionally bad weather and very few people about.'

'Understood.'

'Since we're checking this out, it wouldn't do any harm to give Thormóður a call and ask him about all this,' Guðgeir said, and Sveinn needed no encouragement. The familiar tingle ran through him as he listened to the conversation. This was something that called for further investigation.

'That's weird,' Sveinn said as he put the phone down. 'The man says he's never seen this woman in his life and acted as if he had no idea what I was taking about. Said I was losing my marbles when I asked about the flight.'

27

Practically the only sound that carried to her was the fox and she wondered if the animal got better treatment from Ísak than she did. The fox was able to run and breathe the fresh spring air while she suffocated in this hole. The huge American car that had been Ísak's father's was over the pit. Sometimes she could hear the radio playing while Ísak pottered in the barn and she once heard him in a conversation with Thormóður.

That had been while she still had the energy to shout out and batter the door. Ísak had told Thormóður that he would have to sort out the problem. Thormóður had snapped back that Ísak acted like a spoilt boy, and why should he have to clear up the unholy mess Selma had created?

Their argument had echoed through the barn and Ísak yelled back at Thormóður. Then she heard a car start up outside.

28

The Hostel by the Sea was an old workshop that had been partly renovated. A wooden portico that had been built around the door was out of character for the district, as were the two big tubs, intended for flowers. Guðgeir sat in the security company's car and watched from a distance as a muscular man stacked things in the back of a Land Rover. First there was a box that looked to be some kind of kitchen appliance, then a black plastic bag that looked heavy, followed by a large backpack.

Guðgeir thought that this was providing a backpacker with some exceptional service, and waited for the backpack's owner to appear. But no other person appeared and the man, who Guðgeir assumed had to be Thormóður, occupied himself with the contents of the car's boot before locking it and going back inside.

When there had been no sign of him for ten minutes, Guðgeir set out to look for him. The narrow entrance hall was overstuffed with junk and furniture. The man stood at an old, renovated desk that served as the reception, where he tapped with two fingers at a computer keyboard. He looked to be around middle age, unremarkable and neatly turned out in a white shirt under an expensive outdoor sweater. His fair hair had had been clippered close at the sides, leaving a thick mop on top.

A lobster-pink heap occupied a space in the middle of the floor. It appeared to be intended as a place to sit, although anyone using it would struggle to stand up with any dignity. A couple of chairs and little table stood against a wall, scattered with leaflets detailing relaxation opportunities in Eastern Iceland. A magnificent set of reindeer antlers had been fixed to the wall, next to a framed print of the Vatnajökull ice cap taken on a bright summer's day.

A narrow corridor led from the entrance hall to numbered rooms on either side. There looked to be no more than five or six. The end of the corridor opened out into a space guests and a long window providing a view over the harbour. This looked to be a place for taking meals while also taking in the scenery, with a small fridge and an electric hob on the table.

'Good morning,' Guðgeir said and the man returned his greeting. 'Cool place. Just the retro feel that my wife's so fond of,' Guðgeir said cheerfully as he introduced himself.

Describing the place as cool was maybe an exaggeration. He could see that it wouldn't take much to make it more attractive for travellers, but he needed to make a connection with the man, and that had been the first thing that had entered his head.

'Sure,' the man said with a clear lack of interest.

'I like to see old stuff being given a new life,' Guðgeir said, glancing around the crowded reception area.

'Can I help you?' the man asked.

'Yes. I'm…' Guðgeir said and suddenly had the feeling of no longer being what he had been. This role-playing felt uncomfortable.

'You're looking for a room?' the man asked and there was a touch of an accent in his voice.

'No, not exactly,' he said and paused, deciding how to pursue this. 'I'm looking for a woman who came here to Höfn this winter. She's dark, Asian.'

The man looked at him suspiciously.

'There are so many people who pass through here,' he said with a sarcastic laugh. 'Do you think I remember every single dark-haired woman? I run a hostel and there are guests of all shapes, sizes and colours.'

'Her name's Sajee Gunawardena and she's from Sri Lanka,' Guðgeir said, nodding towards the computer. 'Couldn't you..?'

'Who are you?'

'You're Thormóður, aren't you?' Guðgeir said, replying with a question of his own.

The man raised an eyebrow and nodded slowly.

'Sveinn out at the airport said he brought this woman here on the twenty-seventh of February,' Guðgeir said.

'Right. He was asking something like that a day or two ago. I don't remember anything like that,' Thormóður mumbled, his attention on the screen.

'Sveinn is very sure.'

Thormóður glanced at him uninterestedly, pushing his hair back from his forehead. Guðgeir noticed the red birthmark that ran from the roots of his hair like an icicle. His hair dropped back forward as he hunched again over the computer.

'So what's the problem?' Thormóður asked as his fingers tapped rapidly at the keyboard.

'We're wondering if you might know what happened to her,' Guðgeir said.

'Who?'

'Sajee. The woman from Sri Lanka.'

'Why?'

'Sveinn is concerned about her,' Guðgeir said, changing tack. 'She came to Höfn due to some misunderstanding, as far as we can make out. As far as he was aware, she was practically penniless. He said she was certain she would be able to stay here, otherwise he wouldn't have left her at your place.'

He decided against mentioning that he had been through the passenger lists, as that could put Sveinn in an awkward position.

'And why are you poking your nose into all this?' Thormóður asked. 'There are foreigners on the move everywhere. They get lost here and there, but they always seem to turn up sooner or later.'

'I don't recall seeing tourists here before the middle of March,' Guðgeir said. 'So you must have some recollection of this woman.'

'Are you a cop, or something?' Thormóður demanded in obvious irritation. 'I don't recall this at all.'

'I… Well, no. Not exactly. I'm just asking a few questions,' Guðgeir said, to Thormóður's clear relief.

'Look, I run a company and I work long hours. We're overbooked and surely you can appreciate that I don't have every minor detail at my fingertips. I'm rushed off my feet the whole time here,' he said, as if asking a child to grasp something beyond its understanding.

'Yes, but this was the end of February,' Guðgeir repeated. 'The woman came to Höfn in the belief that there was a job waiting for her, which turned out to not be the case. She needed somewhere to stay and according to Sveinn, she stayed here in your hostel.'

Thormóður glared at him.

'Listen, I don't remember everything. Back in the day I wasn't all together, if you know what I mean. Memory plays tricks. Understand?'

He grinned, winked, as if asking for his colourful past to be excused.

The door opened, and a young woman with short black hair, a wool scarf around her neck and a backpack on one shoulder appeared. Thormóður waited until she had gone along the corridor before continuing. Guðgeir made no reply, making it clear that this excuse wasn't one he was prepared to accept.

'I'm in no hurry,' he said. 'I'm sure it'll all come back to you, but you ought to take a look in that computer of yours.'

'What?'

'Don't you register all your guests?'

'Sure I do, but take it easy…' Thormóður said, as if registering guests was an unnecessary formality. 'You said the twenty-seventh of February?'

'That's right, and her name's Sajee, with two Es at the end.'

'Nothing that day and nothing the day after,' Thormóður said, finally appearing to show some interest. Guðgeir noticed a gleam of sweat on his forehead, quickly wiped away with the back of his hand, exposing a birthmark.

'Aren't you supposed to register all guests? For the overnight tax?' Guðgeir asked. He wanted to step around the sideboard and take a look at the screen for himself.

'Well, of course. But not if I don't charge people,' Thormóður said with a laugh that indicated Guðgeir's question has been an exceptionally stupid one.

'You do that often?'

'Do what?'

'Let people stay in your hostel for free,' Guðgeir said.

Thormóður scratched the back of his neck as he looked slightly awkward, clearly looking for a way out.

'You're right!' he said with unexpected emphasis. 'A tiny woman with a lot of hair. She was here one night and then left, flew back south again as far as I know. I let her stay so she'd be able to afford the flight.'

'Is that so?' Guðgeir said, his voice laden with doubt.

'Yep. Sure,' Thormóður said. 'What's the problem, anyway? Has she gone missing, or broken in somewhere? Hey, don't you work for Hornafjörður Security? I'm sure I've seen you about.'

'Yes, that's me. And no, she's not suspected of having committed any crime. I'm just asking around about her.'

'Small-town life makes you curious,' Thormóður said, visibly more relaxed. 'And more susceptible to gossip. It must be as boring as hell being a security guard in a place where nothing ever happens.' He laughed, clearly relieved that he had managed to turn the conversation around, but continued in the same vein. 'I think someone told me you had a shock and lost your job in some scandal or other. Did you have a nervous breakdown, or what?'

'So you didn't drive this woman up to the Lagoon during the winter? There's an individual who reported having seen you,' Guðgeir said, staying cool. It would need something more than that kind of talk to upset him and the man's impertinence disgusted him.

'How the hell should I remember if I gave someone a lift or not?' The question had obviously left Thormóður rattled, as he fell silent, apparently trying to figure out what tack to take next, before he burst out angrily. 'How nosy can you be? I'm always giving people lifts here and there. The place is constantly busy and and I'm pretty flexible. Now, I don't have time for this,' he said, fidgeting impatiently. He stooped and lifted a box of leaflets that he placed on the sideboard.

'Were you busy during the winter, what with the weather as bad as it was?'

There was an undertone of doubt in Guðgeir's voice as he leaned forward over the sideboard.

'I'm always busy, and you must be as bored as hell. I have better things to be doing, and you'll have to find somewhere else to stick your nose because I have more than enough on my plate,' Thormóður said, a stiffly artificial smile on his face as he started to arrange the leaflets into stacks. But Guðgeir wasn't inclined to give up.

'This woman has a cleft palate, so she's pretty conspicuous.'

Thormóður sighed, rolled his eyes and his memory suddenly improved.

'Listen, I remember now. I gave her a lift out to the airport. She took a flight south.'

'Quite sure? Guðgeir asked.

'A hundred per cent,' Thormóður said with a clap of his hands. 'End of story.'

'When was that?' Guðgeir asked. His feeling for what had become of Sajee was getting stronger by the minute.

'The next day. Or the day after that,'Thormóður said. 'I don't recall if she was here for one night or two. Look, I fucked my head years ago and my memory's shot. Drugs and all sorts, like I told you. Anyway, I drove her out to the airport, and if she didn't get the flight, then I've no idea where she could have gone and it's not my business to keep tabs on everyone who washes up out here.'

'No, of course not,' Guðgeir said, his tone ice cold as he drummed his fingers on a stack of leaflets. 'Sorry to have troubled you, and I can see you're busy,' he said and sensed Thormóður relax. 'Since I'm here, could I take a look round? I have some guests coming soon and there isn't room for them at my place...'

Thormóður cut him off short.

'No. That's not possible. We're booked up solid.'

29

Guðgeir rested the back of his head against the windowsill as he sat on the sofa in his rented flat with his phone in his hand, his attention flitting between the number on the screen and the sofa's colourful upholstery. He rubbed his chin thoughtfully before taking his decision, and tapped the screen. Særós answered almost instantly.

'Haven't heard from you for a while,' she said. 'How are you doing out there at the edge of the world?'

'Struggling along,' Guðgeir said, standing up. He looked out of the window and saw Sveinn and Matthildur walk out to the car. 'There's not long to go, and I don't know what happens in June. The inquiry panel will have to reach a decision soon. It's the waiting that wears you down. To be honest, I've had enough.'

'We miss you at the station and we all hope it goes the right way,' Særós said, and her words gave him a warm glow deep inside. There were occasions when he had the feeling that his blameless thirty-year police career meant nothing. All that made no difference when everything could be wrecked by a single error of judgement. Admittedly, it had been a big one.

'And you? How are you getting on?' Guðgeir asked, imagining his office with Særós, dark-haired and sharp-eyed, in his chair and the week's fitness plan pinned to the wall behind her. Her hair always looked as if she had just stepped out of a salon, regardless of whether she ran, swam, cycled or pursued some other sport, which she did every single day. The shirt under her fitted jacket would be carefully pressed and she had a taste for elegant clothes that never showed a crease or a stain. Særós's appearance would make anyone think that she had been born with a silver spoon in her mouth but that wasn't the case; far from it. Her childhood home had been plagued with alcoholism and neglect, of both physical and mental varieties. She had taken charge of her younger siblings from a young age, and more often than not had also looked after their parents. None of this was common knowledge, and Guðgeir had often heard suspects and even colleagues grumble about Særós purely on the basis of her looks.

'Just fine! I'm relieved that Easter's over because that weekend's crazy, like it always is,' she said. 'There are cases piling up…' She dropped her voice. 'Plenty of interesting stuff going on, as you can imagine. A shooting in Grafarvogur, the body in the Nordic House bin, and dope everywhere…'

'I can imagine,' Guðgeir said. He badly wanted to know more about these cases, but decided not to ask. He didn't want to sound desperate. It would be better not to waste time, and to get to business, although he had the sudden intuition that his errand was trivial in comparison. This was just a waste of time compared to these big cases going on in Reykjavík.

'I was going to ask if you could check out someone's movements for me. It's a woman who took a flight to Höfn on the twenty-seventh of February. The woman's name is Sajee Gunawardena and she's from Sri Lanka. Age thirty to thirty-five. She flew here and definitely didn't get a flight back. The weather was terrible at the time and it's uncertain how or if she got back to Reykjavík. She was pretty broke and not dressed for those conditions,' he said, rapidly reeling off information. It was as well to get it out, now that he had begun.

'OK. Picture?'

'No pic.'

'Description?'

Guðgeir hesitated.

'Petite, with long black hair. She has a conspicuous cleft palate and uneven teeth. The airport supervisor drove her to a hostel here in the town and chatted to her on the way. He can't remember exactly how she was dressed, other than that she was wearing jeans and there was something colourful about her that he can't put his finger on. She had one case, which was a fairly large black suitcase that she couldn't easily lift on her own.'

'Is she missing?' Særós asked.

'Not exactly,' her former boss said, sitting down again on the blue-and-pink sofa. 'I'd like to be sure of her whereabouts.'

'What's the problem?'

'The woman came out here believing she had a job to go to at a beauty salon on Höfn, and she showed Sveinn – that's the airport supervisor – all the text messages she had received from something called *Höfn Hair and Beauty* and thought she'd be working for some big company,' Guðgeir said, and paused, waiting for a chuckle that never came. 'With all due respect to Höfn, that's not a description that could be applied to any salon around here.'

'Is this woman literate? Særós asked, quick as always.

'Yes, at least, she can manage western letters.'

'And the text messages? They tried to call the number?'

'Repeatedly, but it's out of service.'

'Did he make a note of it?'

'No. Sveinn said it hadn't crossed his mind, and he found it weird, to start with. Anyway, he found her a place to stay. People are good like that out here.'

'Sweet,' Særós said in a neutral tone.

'He dropped her off at a hostel here.'

'Ah, and?'

'Sveinn and I have been wondering if and how Sajee could have travelled south. She didn't fly and she didn't travel by coach.'

'Then she must have hitched a ride,' Særós suggested, and Guðgeir could sense that there were more pressing things on her mind than this vague request. Her tone changed, becoming distant. He knew the job himself and the pressures that came with it.

'That's unlikely,' he said. 'Hadn't I mentioned that the weather was terrible just then? We've been asking around and nobody seems to know anything.'

'Are you bored, Guðgeir?' Særós asked suddenly, straight to the point as always. 'You won't have long to wait,' she added encouragingly.

'No, not at all. I'm fine,' he said, against his better judgement. 'What's bugging us is that at the time the roads were as good as impassable and Sajee didn't have any decent outdoor clothing. She was struggling to get around with this big black case and of course there's the possibility that someone could have offered her a lift south,' Guðgeir said, determined not to let any hint of loneliness upset him. 'The strangest thing is nobody other than Sveinn appears to have been aware of this woman actually having been here.'

He stood up from the sofa, and shifted it to one side with his foot so that he could rest an elbow on the windowsill. Sometimes he felt like an animal in a cage in this flat, but by looking up, out of the window he could see the café across the street.

'With one exception,' he added. 'There's a woman called Linda working at a café here who reckons she saw Sajee one day when the weather was really bad, on the way up to the Lagoon with a man called Thormóður, who runs the hostel where Sveinn dropped her off. That's quite a journey in foul weather. Well, I paid him a visit and at first he said he had no recollection of ever having laid eyes on Sajee, and did his best to wriggle out of it. When I pushed him a bit harder, he claimed to have driven her out to the airport. But there was no flight on the twenty-eighth, and she's not on the passenger list for the following day.'

'Has this Sajee committed any crime?' Særós asked.

'Not as far as I know,'

'How did she get here?'

'No idea. But I understand she speaks reasonable Icelandic so she must have lived here for a few years,' he said. 'It's as if she's just disappeared into thin air. It shouldn't be possible to just vanish in a little community like this. This man she was seen with has links to an isolated farm called Bröttuskriður. I went over there and had a very strong feeling that there's something about the place that's not quite right.'

'Do you want us to put out a public request for information about her?' Særós said, and he sensed that her interest was growing.

'Not right away, at any rate. Let's wait and see.'

'Any suspicion that she might have been trafficked?'

'Who knows?' Guðgeir said. 'I'm going to check on this Thormóður, the guy who runs the Hostel by the Sea. It's pretty small and I'm wondering if it might be a front for something else...'

'Yes. Looks like he'd be worth checking out more closely,' Særós agreed. 'But how are you going to get close, considering you're on indefinite leave from the police?'

'I'll find a way, and I'll take care.'

'Can you give me a more detailed description of Sajee, or more info?'

'Unfortunately, Sveinn just remembered she said she had rented a place with some Chinese women in Reykjavík.'

'Names? Address?'

'Nothing precise but somewhere central,' Guðgeir said. 'That's what Sveinn recalled, and I'm sorry I don't have more details.'

'Very helpful,' Særós said, a little coldly. 'But as we have a name we should be able to find something out.'

'It seems most likely she had worked as a cleaner. Svenni said she had mentioned cleaning houses.'

'All on the black, then?'

'Probably,' Guðgeir said. 'That's the way it usually works, isn't it?'

'I'll look into it. Probably best to start with the Directorate of Immigration,' she said. 'I'll ask around in Asian shops and restaurants.'

'Thanks, Særós,' Guðgeir said gratefully. 'You're a true friend.'

'There's not much I wouldn't do for you,' Særós said, ready to end the conversation. 'I'll give you a call as soon as I have anything for you.'

'Hold on a moment. I heard you dropped in over at Fossvogur.'

'I did. Everything's fine. But I reckon you ought to sell that place. It would relieve the tension for you and Inga, and for the children. I could feel it the moment I walked through the door, and I've never been the over-sensitive type, as you well know. So my advice is, sell it and start fresh somewhere else.

You two belong together, and you belong here at the station with us. A security guard, Guðgeir. Really?' Særós sniffed. 'You working as a security guard is just completely off the stupid scale.'

'There's nothing wrong with being a security guard,' he said, suddenly defensive.

'No,' she said seriously. 'There's nothing wrong at all with that. Except that Guðgeir Fransson shouldn't be doing a job like that. You could just as well be at home trying to become a poet.'

He laughed at the thought.

'It's great to talk to you, Særós,' he said with warmth. 'It's done me no end of good. And would you be up for asking around online? Maybe pretend to be looking for a cleaner, you've heard of a girl from Sri Lanka who's supposed to be good at that kind of work. Not sure of her name except that it starts with an S?'

'Why don't you do it yourself?'

'Well, I thought it would be more convincing coming from a woman,' Guðgeir stammered, and Særós snorted.

'All right. I'll put something up on Facebook and a few other places. I'll ask people to send me a PM and we'll see if anything comes of it.'

'Thanks for helping me out. And please say hello to everyone at the station, especially Leifur in the tech department,' Guðgeir said.

He realised as he ended the call that this was the first time he had sent his former colleagues his regards.

THE FOX

Guðgeir sat for a while with his phone in his hand before he went to the kitchen to switch on the kettle, standing over it until the water had boiled and he could fill the big mug that held almost half a litre. It had been a present from his daughter Ólöf, who said that a smaller mug was no use for a man with such big hands. He felt the heat seep into his hands as he held the mug with the tea bag in it. He took it with him to the computer and started searching.

Thormóður seemed to be more common a name than he had expected. He was able to exclude some people quickly as there were sometimes numerous references to the same individual. He had scrolled through sixteen pages of search results and had almost emptied his mug when he chanced on an article from a magazine that had folded a few years ago. The name of the interviewee, Kristín Kjarr, who had been prominent for a while in the art world, caught his eye. Guðgeir hadn't heard mention of her for a while and told himself as he hunched over the screen that this was most likely because he hadn't paid attention. The name he was looking for didn't appear until some way into the article, but it sparked his interest. Kristín recounted a pivotal course she had attended a few years previously, run by a man who called himself Thor. He had claimed to be Canadian, although she later found out that he was from Iceland but had been brought up in Canada. Her opinion was that his real name was Thormóður Emilsson, and that he had a rare talent for persuasion. She said that back when she had first heard of him, she had been searching for something after struggling to find her way in both life and art.

She had been plagued by self-doubt, battling to set her own internal rhythm and to follow her own intuition. On top of that were the financial headaches. Despite the fact that she worked shifts at a hostel for the disabled and spent every Saturday mopping floors in a block of flats, she found it hard to make ends meet. Kristín first heard of Thor at a college party where a lecturer and a well-known critic discussed him approvingly in low voices. A month or so later she heard more tales of the man's unbelievable spiritual energy. Wild, exciting rumours circulated everywhere. Those in the know spoke in muted tones of their experience, so that Kristín felt even more strongly that she was out of the loop. Then a young actress, who had enjoyed a great deal of early success, invited Kristín to join one of Thor's seminars, and from that point on there was no turning back.

The man's personal magnetism and the vibe around him fascinated her, enough for her to persuade her parents to guarantee a loan for her so she could join a twenty-day retreat held in a remote rural location. The subsequent months were expensive ones, but she lived in the hope that her life was about to change for the better.

In the interview Kristín described how those taking part would sit in a circle, except for one who occupied a chair in the centre to be cross-examined by Thor as he stopped at nothing to drag their deepest secrets out into the daylight. If there was any resistance, the rest of the group would join in to pile on the pressure, backing up the leader. These sincerity circles, as he liked to call them, could last for hours, and everyone took part, in the innocent belief that they were liberating the individual at the centre by relieving them of their inner burdens.

Kristín said that she had confessed to things that she wasn't sure had ever occurred or that had any basis in her emotional life, but the whole time she had been at the retreat she had been starved of sleep, hungry and her nerves in tatters, in addition to the pressure to make confessions. The rationale behind the process had been to achieve spiritual purification, because Thor decreed that this would be the fundamental step in the individual being able to make a fresh start in beginning a new life. Although the retreat was expensive, everyone slept on thin mattresses and there was little to eat. They hardly stepped outside the whole time, but were encouraged to work off inner anger by beating their mattresses. According to Kristín, the atmosphere had become highly charged in a few days. Undoubtedly some of them had harboured doubts, but had been reluctant to call the Emperor out for having no clothes.

Kristín admitted that she had been quickly drawn into the groupthink that smothered any doubts. In spite of a number of shortcomings, their group ethic had been strong, and afterwards she realised that Thor had fostered a 'them and us' attitude, a recognised method of bringing a group together by identifying a shared enemy. She concluded that this would be the one and only time that she would agree to speak about this experience, because two years on, she had barely regained her mental and physical stability. The retreat had affected her badly, leading to a breakdown and a spell in psychiatric care.

The interview covered three pages, and in a separate column at one side of the page was all the information the journalist had been able to find about Thor. The man had an unbelievable career behind him and Guðgeir cursed when he saw there wasn't more information there. The interview opened with a large portrait of Kristín, and further down was a grainy image of man who sat like a teacher facing a group of people.

He enlarged the picture but the man's face remained indistinct. Guðgeir dropped the computer onto the sofa and hurried to the bedroom, where he found the magnifying glass on the shelf above the bed.

Staring through it at the man's forehead, there was no doubt in his mind. Just below the roots of his hair was the dark patch of a birthmark. Guðgeir took a deep breath and enlarged the picture still further. At Thormóður's side sat a young man, fair-haired and with dark eyebrows, who looked remarkably like Ísak at Bröttuskriður.

30

Spring was in the air as Særós stepped out into the stillness of the morning. Along the garden wall lay a wafer-thin layer of snow which would melt later in the day. A few daffodils had flowered and stretched towards the morning sun as heralds of the coming summer. They could have flowered yesterday, or the day before that, but it was only on this bright, warm morning that Særós had noticed them.

She was in a good mood. After all the pressure she had been under, she was ready to get to grips with reality again. The last few months had not been easy ones, as not all of her colleagues had been supportive when she had stepped at short notice into Guðgeir's role. It had been a difficult time for the police, but things had improved and she was looking forward to a little stability.

Særós hummed to herself as she dumped her sports bag on the back seat. As she drove through the city, she noticed that pedestrians, people waiting for buses and others heading for their cars seemed more upright. The chill of winter seemed to be leaving people's bones at last, and straight backs had returned now that nobody needed to lean into the wind. There was hope as well as spring in the air.

She felt full of optimism, and as a woman who liked to have clear aims, she told herself that she ought to smile more in the next few days. That ought to put a few things right at the station. She strode into the building, cheerfully greeting everyone she met along the way and handing out a few compliments as she passed. She left a few puzzled looks behind her. Pleased with herself for making a positive start to the day, she shut her door after asking for no disturbances unless absolutely necessary.

She didn't take a break until she had spent three hours reducing the swamp of emails almost down to zero. She stood up, took a few paces, stretched and checked her phone. Her request for the renowned Sri Lankan cleaner whose name began with an S had come to nothing, even though she had been through plenty of groups on Facebook that had some kind of domestic connection. There had been a number of responses, she'd been pointed towards foreign women who cleaned houses for a living, but all had turned out to be false trails. She dropped to the floor and took a few press-ups, telling herself that this was the kind of trouble she would put herself through for Guðgeir alone. His hunches were normally on the right track.

Back at her desk, she saw a new message from someone called Ragnhildur who had employed an au pair called Sajee who had come from Sri Lanka. Her message included her phone number and an invitation to call for more information. Særós tapped the number into her phone immediately, but the line was busy. Særós tried to go back to her work before calling again, but found herself unable to concentrate.

31

It was a weekend at home in Reykjavík for Guðgeir and he had dropped by to see her the night before. Særós had gone over everything with him and they compared notes. She agreed with him that something was wrong, but it was difficult to pin down exactly what was happening. Now they knew that Thormóður had a dubious past, and after unsuccessfully trying to reach Kristín Kjarr, they managed to track down the journalist who had written the article Guðgeir had come across online. The man had lost his job when the magazine had gone bust, and instead turned to making a living as a gardener, which he described as being better for both his wallet and his mental health.

The former journalist remembered the Thormóður angle clearly as the story had sparked his interest, and he was willing to share what he knew. He had even put together a detailed dossier of information, intending to write a series of articles that were supposed to have appeared in the weeks following the interview with Kristín. The magazine's bankruptcy ended those plans, but he described for them how Thormóður had been brought up in the Westman Islands, but at the age of eleven had moved to Canada with his mother. There he had had come under the influence of a stepfather who was a member of a religious cult that clung to a set of beliefs not far removed from scientology.

Thormóður, or Thor as he called himself, joined the cult along with his mother. At seventeen he was arrested arriving from Morocco with a serious amount of hashish in his luggage. He was also prosecuted for smuggling ancient artefacts, although he protested that he had no idea of the provenance of the items, and thought it had been no more than old junk picked up at a street market that he could sell on. His story was that the hashish was intended to finance his escape from the cult his mother and step-father belonged to. He spent fourteen months in prison, and set up his own religious group when he was released, claiming to have experienced a divine revelation while in prison. A few years later he was prosecuted for abducting a young woman, but without any further proof, charges were dropped.

Guðgeir had found one of Thormóður's relatives in the Westman Islands, who referred to his cousin as a wastrel constantly hustling for money.

'That bastard can charm the birds out of the trees,' said Thormóður's relative, who wanted nothing to do with him. That was all the man in the Westman Islands had been prepared to say.

Ragnhildur's number was still engaged, and Særós did her best to concentrate on her work. To begin with she had looked on this as a way of doing Guðgeir a favour, out of support for him but a waste of her own time. However, she was finding herself increasingly intrigued. On top of that, she and Guðgeir had got on better the evening before than they had when he had been her boss. In spite of their concerns over the fate of the young woman from Sri Lanka, puzzling their way together through the mystery had been highly enjoyable. Guðgeir had stayed at his old home in Fossvogur, and Særós sensed that things there were moving in the right direction, which she welcomed. In the past she had occasionally imagined herself in Inga's place, but those days were long gone. Now her only wish was for Guðgeir and Inga to be back together and for things to be back the way they had been before their colleague Andrés had lost his life.

Her phone buzzed and a message appeared on the screen.

I'll be in touch later.

No, Særós thought as she called the number again. That's not good enough. Ragnhildur answered on the third ring, and Særós explained quickly, without going into detail.

'And you think Sajee has disappeared?' Ragnhildur asked, clearly shocked.

'We have reason to believe so, but no evidence to back it up. This isn't a police matter yet, but my colleague is looking into this informally, if you see what I mean.'

'Yes, well. I got to know Sajee when her aunt who cleaned for me for a while asked if I could help the family out... Listen, can we meet? I don't want to go into this over the phone. Two-thirty?'

32

Time ticked slowly past. Sometimes she called out for help when she had the energy, but mostly she dozed on the mattress, thankful for the soporific effects of the drink Ísak brought her every day. It was increasingly rare that she asked him to release her, because, if she was quiet, he would sometimes sit and talk to her. It was comforting to hear another voice. Anything was better than solitude in the darkness. Normally he would talk about himself and the hard life his mother had led, and sometimes he would mention Thormóður, who was supposed to be fixing things up but hadn't shown his face for days. Sajee felt that the quieter she was, the more his anxiety grew.

'What am I going to do?' he groaned, hunched over the hatch in the narrow beam of light from his phone.

'Let me out,' she gasped, hoping her words wouldn't drive him away. She longed for the energy to attack him and snatch the phone from him, but by now the slightest movement had become a struggle.

He sniffed.

'No, I can't do that. But I won't let the old lady touch you. I'll make sure of that.'

'Just take me somewhere far away and leave me. If someone finds me I won't say anything. I swear.'

He blew his nose onto the floor and coughed.

'Thormóður's looking for a way to get you to Reykjavík. He normally knows what's best and you can't go anywhere looking like that.'

'Bring a doctor. I won't say anything.'

'Stop this bullshit,' he snarled, making to shut the hatch and leave.

'Ísak, you're not a bad man.'

'Stop!' he snapped and banged the hatch. 'Thormóður will fix everything. We just need to be patient.'

Drained of energy, she watched as he backed out of the pit and she was in darkness again.

Was it Thormóður's intention to kill her? The thought flashed into her mind. The easiest way out would be to bundle her body into the back of the car and dump her in the sea somewhere, preferably somewhere near Reykjavík. If the sea were eventually to wash her remains ashore, there wouldn't be much left of her. Depressed foreigner drowns herself. *End of story*, as Thormóður liked to put it.

'Help me,' she moaned, her voice weak.

33

Særós waited in the lobby of the solid, respectable building in the centre of Reykjavík. She had vague memories of it having once been a library with numerous small rooms, every wall lined with books of different shapes and sizes, and more bookcases in the middle of the floor. As a little girl she had stayed with her grandmother when her father had been on an unusually long bender, and there had been a daily visit to the library; something that had had a deep and lasting effect on her. Ever since, a library had been a place of calm and safety for her.

The building's exterior had hardly changed, but inside it was no longer a wonderland of books but the offices of a financial company with irons in numerous fires. A glance at her phone told her that she had been hanging around for twenty minutes. She would have loved to speed things up by letting drop a mention of her job title, but she held back. Instead, she paced the floor to quell her impatience, inspecting the artworks on the walls and the prominent sculpture on a pedestal in the corner. There was fruit in one bowl, chocolates in another and a selection of drinks lined up in a bright orange fridge.

'Can I get you something while you're waiting?' asked the young woman behind the reception desk. Særós's impatience seemed to worry her.

'No, thanks.'

'Won't you take a seat? I'm sure Ragnhildur will be along shortly.'

Ragnhildur Tryggvadóttir had turned out to have a role in something called specialist investment. Her diary must be full, the same as mine, Særós thought, again examining the artwork that occupied part of the room. It was a whitish, semi-transparent lump, and a closer look showed that a human face could be made out in there. She discovered that the sculpture came with its own soundtrack as she pressed a button and calls and shouts could be heard, backed by familiar voices discussing the Central Bank's financial situation. That faded into a new voice claiming to be from the analysis department as it reeled off figures. The sounds and voices came together and ended in a babble of noise. The artwork's name and what she took to be the artist's were inscribed on a small plaque: *The Pots and Pans Revolution – Ógíla.*

'That thing's driving me crazy. I can't wait for them to get rid of it,' the receptionist grumbled.

The woman who strode towards her looked to be approaching sixty, and a far cry from the placid older women Særós recalled seeing in this building. Ragnhildur looked fit and glamorous, dressed in casual but expensive jeans and a fitted jacket. Glasses with red and black frames complemented heavy silver earrings, but the long fair hair seemed somehow out of keeping.

'Good morning,' she said, offering a hand. 'It's a fantastic piece, isn't it? Brutal and striking.'

Her handshake was firm and confident.

'Thanks for finding time to talk,' Særós said.

'Of course. I hope I can help,' Ragnhildur said. 'We'll go to the meeting room. We won't be disturbed there.'

There was no need to prompt her to talk. Ragnhildur was confident and concise, and Særós found herself liking this woman. Sajee's aunt, Hirumi, had cleaned for her, and the connection had come through an old school friend.

'She stopped me going mad, and saved my marriage as well … for a few years, at least,' Ragnhildur said. 'It was just as well we didn't get divorced when the children were small, and with help in the right places it all worked out. No arguments, no trouble, and we could both concentrate on what we needed to do.'

She explained that there was only a short gap between the two older children after she and her husband had returned to Iceland after years of study abroad. Both of them had immersed themselves in work as they embarked on buying a house as soon as they were back, as well as establishing social lives and networking, all of which was time-consuming. Once a week Hirumi had cleaned the house, and had in fact done so much more than that, as she had made beds, washed and ironed, and even cooked meals, preparing Sri Lankan vegetable casseroles and curries, and the children had loved her food.

'She did so much more than local cleaners, who work to some ridiculous rules, and they're always in a hurry. Hirumi came to us every week and I was rarely at home, so I just left money in the hall for her. I don't know how she came to be in Iceland, or where she lived. To be honest, I never asked her about her personal circumstances,' Ragnhildur said apologetically, fiddling with one earring. 'Hirumi's Icelandic was very limited, plus there was so much pressure on us back then, and it always got heavier. When I was pregnant with our third child, Hirumi asked if her niece could be an au pair for us for a while. She wouldn't need to live with us because she could stay with Hirumi, and nobody would need to know. All I would need to do would be to fill in the paperwork. So Sajee came to us a couple of months after our youngest was born and she was a Godsend, except it could be difficult to have a conversation with her because of her mouth … you know about that, don't you?'

'Yes,' Særós said. 'I know.'

'Well, Sajee picked up Icelandic remarkably quickly, even though it could be a problem to understand her sometimes, especially on the phone. Just think, if she had been born in Iceland, she'd have been just fine. Hardly anyone would ever have known that she had been born with a cleft palate.'

'Exactly,' Særós agreed.

'That's the way it is in some parts of the world. That's life, as my old father always said.'

'True. The luck of the draw,' Særós agreed. She knew from her own experience how that worked out.

'It was wonderfully convenient. Sajee came five days a week and sometimes on a Saturday as well if the children had kept her busy, and it was always clear that the children took priority. I helped her with work and residence permits, so she's here legally, but after a while we lost touch. She cleaned for us once a week for a few months, but by then the marriage was falling apart and we had enough to worry about. After that she used to bring us food sometimes, which I found awkward, but I understand that's the custom from where she's from, people constantly bringing each other food. After I became single again I wasn't able to afford a cleaner, so I haven't been in touch with her. It's only now that I'm back on my feet financially.'

Ragnhildur fell silent and there was a perplexed expression on her face. She picked up the phone she had put on the table and quickly scrolled through her messages. It was obvious that she felt she had said more than was necessary about her personal circumstances.

'Have you seen either of them recently?' Særós asked, crossing her legs as she sat back on the thick leather of the chair. The company's stylised name was artistically presented on the wall opposite, with large white letters in relief on a white wall. A plump green plant stood on the broad window sill. Særós missed the books.

'No,' Ragnhildur said, putting the phone down. 'Sorry, checking on meetings,' she added. 'When was Sajee last seen?'

'The twenty-seventh or eighth of February. Do you have a phone number we could check out?'

'Unfortunately, no,' she said. 'I lost both their numbers. Lost my phone, had to move twice after the divorce … you know. And I have to admit that they haven't crossed my mind for a long time. I'm so busy all the time and can't be everywhere,' she said with as a sigh as she looked at Særós, as if expecting a sympathetic response.

'Surname?'

'That's… If I can remember.' Ragnhildur said and picked up a pen from the table. 'I have to write it to be able to get it right.'

She wrote a few letters, crossed them out and corrected them, and handed Særós the slip of paper.

'I think that's right,' she said.

'We're definitely talking about the same person,' Særós confirmed. 'Do you recall if Sajee had any friends or acquaintances here in Iceland?'

'That's what I've been trying to remember since you called, and recall her mentioning someone who found a job cleaning or washing up in Ikea. For whatever reason, she hadn't wanted to work there herself. She was used to working cash-in-hand, and the salary they were offering there wasn't anything special,' Ragnhildur said, catching Særós's eye. 'We'll keep this to ourselves, but that's the way it is. Cleaning houses, it's all like that. You just have to live with it, whatever your opinion is of working on the black. Everyone does it, otherwise you'd never find a cleaner.'

Særós nodded, indicating that she wasn't inclined to take this any further. Ragnhildur smiled and rubbed her hands together.

'It's not the black work that comes to mind when I think of her, but her hands. She was so careful with them and maybe that's why she didn't want to be splashing in water all day long,' Ragnhildur said with a smile of recollection. 'Sajee took such care of her hands that it was almost an obsession. You'd have imagined she was a concert pianist. Never bare-handed, and she always wore strong rubber gloves. There was no point trying to get her to use disposable latex gloves and she said they were rubbish, so I was constantly buying rubber gloves ... and cloths,' she laughed. 'She didn't make big demands, but she had principles stuck to them. A lovely girl, and very bright.'

'Do you have a picture of her?' Særós asked.

'I'm not sure,' Ragnhildur said thoughtfully. 'Maybe, I'll see what I can find when I get home. The children absolutely loved her and there could be a picture of her with them. There's just so much to do that I haven't had time to look. I'll check tonight or tomorrow, as soon as I have a spare minute.'

'Thanks. Do you remember anything else that might help us?'

There was always a particular smell about Sajee,' Ragnhildur said after a moment's thought. 'She worked oil into her hands to keep them soft. She had worked as a masseuse in Sri Lanka, and she was proud of that. I think that's why she took such good care of her hands.'

'What sort of oil did she use?' Særós asked, and Ragnhildur stared at her. 'You said there was a particular smell about her.'

'I see. I just thought it was odd you should ask about that. Sajee always used avocado oil, and I remember that because seeing her use it was the first time I saw it. She rubbed it into her hands a couple of times a day to keep them soft. The smell of this oil is quite heavy and unusual, and that's why it stuck in my mind. The thing with her hands was ingrained in Sajee ... like a ballet dancer looking after her feet. She was a lovely girl,' Ragnhildur said, and corrected herself. 'Is a lovely girl, I mean, and I hope she's safe and well. But I have to go. I have to go a meeting in town in a few minutes. I'll go outside with you.'

They parted outside the building and Særós watched as Ragnhildur walked away along the street. Then she took out her phone to make sure that the recording was good. Her voice came through clear and strong.

After the narrow streets of Reykjavík's Thingholt district, Særós's next call took her to Garðabær where Ikea's car park stretched out in front of her. It was almost four in the afternoon, so she called the station to let them know she wouldn't be back that day. She wrapped her woollen coat tight around herself to keep the sharp wind at bay as she marched smartly past the fenced-off outside area. Staff in thick gloves were hard at work setting up displays of garden furniture and summer plants.

She slipped through the heavy swing doors and took the steps two at a time up the escalator. There was a special offer on candlesticks in the showroom. Særós rarely went to Ikea. Living alone, she had little time for mass-produced Nordic design and she found the rambling families that normally filled the place exhausting. With relief, she saw that she wouldn't have to go through the whole store, as an opening beside the escalator provided a quick detour taking her straight to the cafeteria. Holding her bag behind her, she squeezed nimbly between tables, on the lookout for staff who could be from Sri Lanka. The simplest and easiest option would have been to find a supervisor, but she was reluctant to involve too many people in this private investigation that was so far between her and Guðgeir.

She took a tray and put a glass of carrot juice on it. At the food counter she asked for salmon. The staff were cheerful and most looked to have origins far from these northern latitudes.

'Not quite so much sauce, please, Særós said, giving the man behind the counter a smile as he served up boiled potatoes, green beans and the light-coloured sauce that came with the salmon. He stopped pouring.

'Is that enough?' he asked, the ladle poised over her plate.

Særós nodded and leaned closer.

'Listen, the thing is, I'm looking for people from Sri Lanka, or of Sri Lankan origin, but living here. I'm writing a thesis, and need to talk to some people from there,' she stammered and immediately felt mortified at her own clumsiness. She would always be a poor actress.

'Thesis?'

The man clearly hadn't understood, so she decided to try another tack. Maybe it would be worth hinting at market research? No, research or a thesis would be better.

'It doesn't matter. Research…' she began, and abandoned Plan B for honesty. 'I'm looking for people from Sri Lanka to talk to.'

The man grinned, and then laughed.

'No problem. I'm from Sri Lanka.'

'Really?' Særós looked around, and saw that there was fortunately no queue behind her. An older couple who seemed to have decided to make do with sandwiches from the self-service counter took a detour around the hot food counter and headed for the checkout. 'You're from there? That's fantastic. Do you know a woman called Sajee? There can't be many in Iceland, surely? I mean, from Sri Lanka?'

The man didn't reply straight away, but handed her the plate with a quizzical look on his face. He seemed to be wondering if Særós was who she claimed to be.

'Her name's Sajee Gunawardena,' she said, taking care to pronounce the name as clearly as she could.

'What did you say?' he asked, and Særós tried again.

He laughed, and repeated the name, the stresses on different syllables so that it sounded completely different.

'Well…' he said, wiping up pools of sauce that had fallen to the steel table. It looked like he was playing for a little time as he didn't reply right away.

'I've been told that Sajee is the person who can tell me so much,' Særós said, certain that she was sounding ridiculous, but there was nothing else for it as she could hardly wave her warrant card in the man's face. 'Or a woman called Hirumi? Do you know her? They're related.'

'Hirumi?' the man echoed, and Særós had to recognise that her pronunciation was certainly askew. She thought of writing the name down, but realised that she would write it just as she said it, which would hardly help. 'I'm probably not saying it properly,' she said apologetically. 'Hirumi is a few years older. But Sajee is young, like you.'

'I know Sajee,' the man said. The name sounded so different the way the man said it. 'He does too,' he added, nodding towards a slim man who pushed a trolley as he cleared tables.

'Do you know where I can find her?' she asked, trying to hide her eagerness.

'My wife tries to call her all the time, but her phone's switched off. Maybe Sajee has gone to be married.'

'Gone to Sri Lanka?'

'Maybe,' the man replied. 'I don't know.'

'Did she work here?' Særós asked.

'Sajee can't work here,' he replied and it was clear he wasn't inclined to explain why.

'All right. But Hirumi? Do you know where she is?'

'Hirumi is home in Sri Lanka,' the man said, his agitation growing as in a couple of minutes a queue for food had formed behind her. 'Talk to him,' he said, pointing at the man with the trolley.

'Thank you,' Særós said, taking her tray. As she paid, she watched the man clearing and wiping tables. He was a young guy, who worked well and quickly. She carried her tray over to him.

'Can I sit here?' She asked. 'Are you finished?'

'Better there,' he said, waving at the clean, empty tables all around.

'Of course,' Særós said. 'Could I have a word with you?'

He paused and looked at her uncertainly. She realised that he was expecting her to complain that the place hadn't been cleaned properly.

'You're doing a good job. What's your name?'

'Amal,' he said shortly. 'Can I get you anything? There's salt, pepper, sauces. It's all there,' he said, ready to fetch whatever she needed.

'No, no. Amal, my name is Særós and I'm looking for a woman called Sajee. I just want to ask you about her. He... The guy...' said, nodding towards the man at the counter now filling a plate with Swedish meatballs. 'He said you know Sajee.'

She watched his expression and this time she knew she had pronounced the name correctly.

'I know her,' he said. 'Sajee went away.'

'Away?' Særós repeated. 'Do you know where?'

'No. Just away. My wife has been calling her and so has Nuwan's wife,' Amal said, jerking his head in his colleague's direction. 'Sajee has turned off her phone. Maybe Hirumi took her home to Sri Lanka.'

'Do you know where I can find Hirumi?'

He shook his head and she could see he was becoming increasingly suspicious.

'Do you know where Sajee lived in Iceland?'

'Yes,' he said. 'On Snorrabraut. We have been there but the women said that Sajee had gone away on an aeroplane.'

'Where on Snorrabraut? Do you know the house number?' Særós asked earnestly.

'No. It's near Hlemmur,' Amal said, taking a spray bottle from the trolley and squirting liquid on the table. Særós watched his dark hands wipe the surface with smooth movements.

'Could you try to remember? I could drive you home after your shift and you could show me the house?'

He stared at her and moved to another table.

'No, thank you,' he muttered. He was clearly uncomfortable with her presence. She knew that she was often too direct, too quick. She would have to learn to be more guarded in her approach.

'It won't take long,' she said, all the same. 'I just need to know where the house is.'

'Enjoy your meal before it gets cold,' Amal said, indicating the salmon on her plate.

He pushed his trolley away and didn't stop until there was a good distance between them. For a moment it occurred to her to follow him, but instead she dropped into a chair and stirred the pale sauce and the salmon into little mouthfuls, but left the string beans. She had managed to frighten Amal and now he wanted to tell her nothing. She would have to learn to rein herself in.

Særós dug her fork into the mixture on her plate and took a mouthful, deciding as she did so that it was idiotic to be working under a false flag. Now she would sit here for a while before telling them the truth to get the two phone numbers she needed.

34

Today she felt better. Ísak had brought a first aid kit and a bucket of water, washed most of the filth off her and disinfected her injuries. Then he helped her out of her dirty clothes and into clean garments, gazing at her lean body as he dressed her. She was sure that there were tears in his eyes as he looked away.

'I found this,' he said gruffly, crumbling a large tablet into her green drink. 'It's supposed to be for animals, but it should kill off the worst of the infection. I have three of these so I'll bring you another tomorrow.'

'Ísak,' she begged, holding his hand tight. 'Help me get away from here.'

He tried to disengage from her grip, but she held tight to him, her fingers locked around his hand.

He pushed her away abruptly, and quickly put everything back in the first aid box. He crawled out the way he had come in. The hatch banged shut and she felt she was no longer alone while she still had hope.

35

'Sajee's phone is switched off and there's just some incomprehensible message when I call Hirumi's number. I can't find any trace of either of them online, but the good news is I have a register of everyone living on Snorrabraut and have already eliminated more than a third of them based on what information we already have. I've made a few calls and that's narrowed it down to ten apartments that I'm sure are rented out.'

'That's great,' Guðgeir said, his phone at his ear while Inga looked at him enquiringly.

'Who is it?' she mouthed, and Guðgeir mouthed Særós's name in reply.

'If we're in luck, we should be able to pin down these Chinese women this evening,' Særós said. 'What do you say? Shall we do it?'

Reluctant to leave Inga, Guðgeir didn't reply right away. They had been able to discuss things calmly and that had brightened his hopes of a better future. There was nothing he longed for more than for things to be the way they had been before he had shattered her faith in him. They both knew that they were happier together than apart, but it seemed that Inga was still unable to swallow her pride and admit it. She had the idea fixed in her mind that they needed to be apart for a whole year before looking to the future. Even though she said that she missed him, she had remained inflexible – until now. Her resolve seemed to be softening. They had chatted pleasantly with the children over dinner and now they were able to relax together. Everything was the way it had been, and then Særós had to call.

'What about around nine in the morning?' he suggested, settling deeper into the sofa. It was so good to be home. 'I don't have to travel east until the afternoon and I'm back at work the day after.'

'I have a meeting in the morning, and I need to be prepared,' Særós said. 'You know there's always a better chance of catching people at home in the evenings, so we ought to get to work.'

'All right,' Guðgeir said, his eyes on his wife as he spoke. 'I'll be outside your place at eight.'

'We have to be prepared to accept that Sajee may have left the country,' Særós said as she sat in his car half an hour later. There was no need for a greeting. She was now too caught up in this case to be bothered with pleasantries. He knew her well enough to be aware that once she had the bit between her teeth, she didn't waste energy on anything else. Særós clicked her seat belt into place and took her notes from her bag.

'I printed all this out and I've already eliminated a few of the names. Let's get on with this before it gets too late and we'll start close to Hlemmur.'

He listened as she read out the list of names of the registered owners of apartments in the district as they drove along Bústaðavegur towards Snorrabraut. They agreed that their attention should be on an old building containing a number of flats, of which several were registered as being owned by one individual, Ísleifur Árnason. Apart from that, nothing stood out as being suspicious, except that one flat in the building was registered to a charity.

'*Children in Crisis,*' Særós read out. 'Have you heard of this organisation? Is it normal for them to put money into property instead of spending it?'

'It could be an inheritance, or a gift from a someone with a kind heart who wanted their property to go to a good cause. But this Ísleifur? I reckon I've heard the name before. I'm not sure where or in what connection, but I think he's come to our attention before now,' Guðgeir said thoughtfully and Særós agreed.

'I looked him up and he seems to have property all over, mostly out in the suburbs, and some of them are real shitholes, to put it mildly. I hear he rents them out at extortionate rates. He's been renting to foreign construction workers ever since the boom got under way and there was something about this on the news a few days ago. Lousy conditions, mould, and all the classic stuff, while Ísleifur's adamant that everything is absolutely fine.'

The lightbulb in the lobby was dead, so Guðgeir used the torch in his phone to examine the poorly marked postboxes and unmarked doorbell buttons. As someone leaving the building opened the door, they took the opportunity to slip inside. An old man opened the door of a flat on the top floor, the door swinging open while Guðgeir's finger was still on the doorbell button. The man wore a suit that, like him, was long past its prime. His hair was thick but tousled, and there was a fine layer of dandruff around his collar.

'Come on in,' he said cheerfully, and held the door open wide. 'Are you the taxman?'

'No.'

'Police?'

'Yes,' they both said. 'But keep quiet about that,' Særós added.

'Well, yes, of course. Come in, please. Lovely to have visitors. I can't go out often. The stairs … you understand? I've a duff knee.'

They followed him into a dark living room where he ushered them to a high-backed, mustard-yellow sofa. They perched on the edge. The man vanished into the kitchen, returning with a kettle that he placed on the table, plugged in and switched on. Then he disappeared again, returned with a carton of milk and was gone once more. Særós rolled her eyes, and Guðgeir gave her a gentle smile.

'We're looking for a woman, originally from Sri Lanka, who lives, or lived, here on Snorrabraut. We don't know exactly where, but we need to speak to her. It's important.'

'I've been waiting for a knee operation for ages. They did the other one a few years ago, and that was wonderful, but I had to wait for that as well,' came the man's voice from the kitchen.

'Good grief,' Særós sighed and scowled while Guðgeir raised his eyebrows. They sat close together on the sofa and listened as the man rummaged in the kitchen, opening cupboards and running the tap. Særós glanced at her watch and Guðgeir rubbed the stubble on his chin.

'Are you going to deport her?' The man stood in the doorway holding a tray of cups and a jar of instant coffee. He seemed to doubt whether or not to offer them anything after all. 'If that's your game, then I want nothing to do with you. I'll have nothing to do with that kind of dirty business.'

'That's not what we're here for,' Guðgeir said gently. 'I assure you of that. We suspect that this woman, Sajee, may have disappeared. To be honest, we're concerned that she may be the victim of some dirty business, as you call it.'

'Really?' He placed the tray on the inlaid table and spooned coffee into cups. 'You mean trafficking? There was something on the radio about that yesterday.'

'We can't be sure yet,' Særós added, smoothing down the collar of her pressed shirt and fiddling with the fine chain that lay over her collarbone.

'Is that strong enough?' the man asked.

'Two spoonfuls for me,' Guðgeir replied and Særós shrugged. She preferred to avoid coffee, but accepted a cup to humour the man. He poured boiling water onto the granules in the cups and stirred slowly and carefully. He took his time before handing them their cups and taking a seat opposite them.

'Ísleifur Árnason, the landlord here. Is he a decent sort of guy?' Særós asked, crossing her legs. She wore high boots with heels, made in brown leather and one foot rocked back and forth, with the occasional tap as her toe connected with the table.

'Why do you ask?' the old man said and settled himself into his chair. A spasm passed over his face, indicating that every movement brought him discomfort.

'Just curious,' Guðgeir said, raising a palm to show his innocent intentions, and the man understood what he was driving at.

'There's nothing special about this place, as you can see.'

'No,' Guðgeir agreed. 'Not exactly.'

'I guess it would be cheaper to rent rooms at Amalienborg than here,' he continued.

'It's that bad?' Guðgeir asked, glancing around. The walls were grubby and the window frames were starting to rot.

'On my pension, yes. It's bad. But I suppose one should be grateful for having a roof over one's head,' he said. 'Would you like milk in your coffee?'

They both shook their heads.

'Amalienborg? Where's that?' Særós asked, her foot stopping its movement.

'The Queen of Denmark's palace, of course,' the man replied, clearly surprised at her ignorance.

Særós rolled her eyes again.

'I don't see how that's relevant.'

'You say you're searching for a woman from Sri Lanka. That used to be called Ceylon when I was a younger man,' he said, as if vouchsafing a valuable nugget of knowledge, and without answering her question.

'Really?'

'Ceylon, like the tea,' he continued, undaunted.

'Sure,' Særós said, ready to get to her feet. Her patience was running out. She shot a meaningful glance at the clock on the wall, and then at Guðgeir. Time was running away from them and this old man had nothing to tell them. He was clearly lonely and wanted company.

'Is he in this dirty business you mentioned earlier? Ísleifur, I mean,' the man said.

'We're investigating the circumstances, but it's too early to say much,' Guðgeir said stirring his ink-black coffee as if he had all the time in the world. 'We're just checking out a few places to try and locate this woman.'

The man's mouth clamped shut and he was silent, clearly trying to reconcile some inner doubt. Guðgeir sat solidly on the sofa without saying anything more. Særós got to her feet, took a couple of steps, then gave up and sat back down, taking a sip of coffee for show. She found the long silence deeply disconcerting, but suspected that Guðgeir was onto something. He had a knack of figuring people out and often used conversational techniques that she had always struggled to master. That included silence, sometimes for a surprisingly long time.

'It's not complicated. Just be patient, even if your question's left hanging and it doesn't seem like the person you're questioning is going to say anything. Be patient, because almost everyone will eventually say something, and something's better than nothing,' was what Guðgeir had tried to drill into Særós when she had joined, and she realised it would be worth remembering his words.

The man examined them in turn, apparently unsure of his ground. Særós took a seat on the sofa again, and made herself comfortable.

'Do you mind?' Guðgeir said, unscrewing the cap of the coffee jar.

'Be my guest. Help yourself,' the man said, deep in thought and clearly ill at ease as he watched Guðgeir put two spoonfuls of coffee in his mug and pour water that was no longer at boiling point into it. The granules dissolved reluctantly.

'The young woman we are looking for originally came here to work as a domestic help for an Icelandic family and after she left them, she worked mainly as a domestic cleaner. Sajee is a little over thirty, petite, and with long black hair. It seems she was born with a cleft palate. She speaks reasonably good Icelandic, as far as we're aware, but her pronunciation could be not entirely clear,' Guðgeir said.

The man remained silent and Guðgeir sipped his lukewarm coffee. An undissolved granule caught between his teeth, and his picked it out with a fingernail, before leaning back on the lumpy sofa, making it plain that he was in no hurry. He glanced out of the window, and at the clock on the wall. It was getting late, but he decided that a few more minutes would be worthwhile. Maybe the old man had nothing to say, but had dragged out his answers to keep them there. Solitude could be painful and a visit from the police was better than nothing. They would have to be on their way before long. Guðgeir leaned forward to place the cup on the table in front of him.

'And you're trying to find out where this Sajee has disappeared to?' the man asked, enunciating her name clearly.

'That's right. We believe that something may have happened to her,' Guðgeir said.

The man got stiffly to his feet. To their surprise, his manner made it clear that their visit was over. His expression changed and he appeared anxious to be rid of them as soon as possible.

'Take a look at the flat in the basement,' he said in a low voice as he limped towards the door.

'Who lives there?' Særós asked.

'That miser Ísleifur knocked together a flat out of a storeroom and a laundry room. It's completely illegal, but he has those women under his thumb,' he said quickly, as he mimed zipping his lips shut. 'But you didn't hear it from me.'

36

The visit to the old man and Sajee's whereabouts had been in Guðgeir's thoughts through the whole of the day-long drive from Reykjavík back to Höfn, and now he felt restless, anxious to again pick up the trail.

There was an upside-down 'welcome' woven into the mat as he pushed open the *Hostel by the Sea's* door and stepped inside. The last time he had been here he hadn't noticed the doormat, so maybe it was new. The reception area was deserted, but on the reception desk stood a heavy copper bell with a long wooden handle. He picked it up and rang. There was no immediate response, so he rang again, sending the bell's tones echoing through the building. After a while a dark-haired young woman appeared in the corridor, in no obvious hurry and more interested in her phone than in the customer waiting at the reception desk.

'Good morning, is Thormóður here?' Guðgeir asked.

'I don't speak Icelandic,' the woman replied. 'You speak English?'

'Sure. Is the owner here?'

'You can speak to me.'

'I'd prefer to speak to the owner,' Guðgeir said courteously. 'His name's Thormóður, isn't it?'

'He's not here,' she said sharply, apparently satisfied that she had done everything required. Her attention went back to the phone in her hand.

'Do you know where he is?' Guðgeir asked. 'Or when he'll be back?'

'No,' she replied, running fingers through her spiky hair.

'You're sure?'

'Of course? Do I look like some sort of idiot?' she snapped, clearly in no mood to hide her annoyance.

'No, of course not, and no offence intended,' Guðgeir said with an apologetic smile. It was obvious that she had little time for customer service and wanted to be rid of him as quickly as possible.

'Any rooms available?'

The woman shook her head, eyes on the screen of her phone as she swiped it quickly with her thumb.

'No.'

'I'm asking for a friend,' he added, in case the woman had taken a personal dislike to him.

'Fully booked,' she said, glancing at him. He noticed that she didn't trouble to ask when his friend would be needing a place to stay.

'Sure?' he asked.

'Yes!'

'In about ten days' time?' he said, acting as if her display of ill temper had gone unnoticed.

'Full up,' she said.

'Ach. That's a shame. But don't you need staff, considering the place is so busy? My daughter's looking for work here in Höfn,' he lied. 'How many rooms are there here?'

She finally put the phone aside and gave this awkward man who asked endless questions her full attention. Her expression was one of deep fatigue and irritation, but all the same, she managed an artificial smile. He had seen this young woman before, with her cropped hair and sleepy eyes. That time there had been a rucksack hanging from her shoulder.

'I'm so sorry but we have no rooms available and we don't need any more staff,' she said in a mechanical voice. 'Is there anything else I can help you with?'

'No,' he said, and left.

With his shift almost over, Guðgeir drove slowly up to the top of the town and parked outside the old workshop that was the Hornafjörður Security's home. The sign on the building was a big one, reaching from wall to wall, as the twenty letters of the company's name required space. His opposite number, Helgi, hadn't arrived yet, and had already let Guðgeir know that today he would be late. They had agreed that there would be no harm in the later security round being delayed an hour. Guðgeir walked along Hafnarbraut to where his own car was parked once his shift had finished, and at the shopping centre he picked up a cheese roll and a coffee before driving back down towards the hostel. He stopped along the street, switching off the engine with the car parked next to a hay binder parked outside a workshop, and started on his sandwich. His phone buzzed, Særós's name appearing on the screen.

'Did you try the place on Snorrabraut again?' he asked right away, not bothering with a greeting.

'Twice today. Rang the bell and banged on the door. I could hear movement inside the second time, so I'm certain there's someone in there. But if those women are there, then they might be scared.'

'More than likely,' Guðgeir agreed. He sipped his coffee and eyed the hostel. They would have to find another way to get in touch with the women in the cellar flat.

'Where are you?'

'I'm sitting in the car and if this cheese roll was a doughnut, then I'd be a perfect American cop show cliché,' he said with a sarcastic laugh. 'But all the same, I'm doing what I can to keep tabs on Thormóður's hostel. It feels like I've reached peak ridiculous right now. You've no idea how difficult it is to be inconspicuous in a little place like this.'

'You could try a false beard,' Særós said, giggling at the thought.

'One joke after another,' he said with a grin. 'That tells me you're onto something.'

'Just a bit. Leifur in crime scene has been a big help .'

'Let's hear it,' Guðgeir said, chewing quickly as Særós – in her usual meticulous manner – went over what she knew; no long descriptions, just the key points in strictly chronological order.

Leifur had found that Thormóður was not only the individual registered for the *Hostel by the Sea* in Höfn, but also something similar in Reykjavík, *Hostel by the Shore*, with both places apparently letting rooms. When Leifur had taken a look at the place, he found it suspiciously quiet, considering the number of tourists in the city. Further checks told him that Thormóður Emilsson was also the individual registered for a charity called *Children in Crisis*, which boasted a magnificent website with grand claims about its achievements, which as far as Leifur and Særós had been able to ascertain had in fact amounted to very little. The site also had links for donations, two phone numbers and an email address, but next to nothing about what the charity actually did. Nobody replied to repeated calls to one number and the other turned out to have been disconnected, as did the site's mailbox. All the same, making a donation to *Children in Crisis* was not a problem.

Thormóður also had a chequered career behind him, and had been charged once, but this had been dropped. After that, nothing about him had attracted police attention until eighteen months ago.

'For what?' Guðgeir asked.

'A tip-off about dope being sold at the hostel in Reykjavík, but no evidence was found. But you know who the directors of *Children in Crisis* are?' Særós asked, palpable excitement in her voice.

'Go on. Tell me,' Guðgeir said, although he already had a suspicion.

'Thormóður Emilsson, Ísak Kristoferson and Selma Ísaksdóttir. The unholy trinity.'

'That's quite something. Very interesting,' Guðgeir said, scratching at the stubble on his chin. He could feel the familiar buzz of excitement well up inside him.

'I'm going to dig deeper into this,' Særós said, her voice distant. 'Hold on a moment,' she added and Guðgeir took the opportunity to look up the charity's web page. It offered three levels of sponsorship, all of them fairly low, and with only a small amount separating them.

'Yes, the personal ID numbers match the mother and son at Bröttuskriður,' Særós said.

'There's definitely something spooky going on there. Can you ask Leifur to check out the sponsorship on the web page? It looks all wrong to me, as if this is a front for something else. Those sponsorship buttons could be a way of sending messages, some kind of system of alerts. It would be interesting to see the payments going into that account to see if they tie up with the sponsorship tabs.'

'Exactly. We'll do everything we can to get to the bottom of this right away,' Særós said. 'It's suspicious that this charity has no profile and doesn't seem to have done any kind of fund-raising. At least, Leifur said that he's found nothing at all, and he mentioned just now that *Hostel by the Shore* doesn't have a valid trading permit, so that gives us a reason to take a look. I'm wondering if we could bring Environmental Health in on this with us.'

'You're doing a great job,' Guðgeir said. He was back on a roll, and waved to Linda who was crossing the road. He pointed at his phone, indicating that he couldn't speak to her right now. She waved back, gesturing that she was also in a hurry.

'What was that?' Særós asked. There wasn't much that escaped her notice, even over the phone with half the country separating them.

'The woman who works in the café right opposite the flat I'm staying in. Linda, you remember? The one who told me she had seen Thormóður with Sajee,' Guðgeir explained, brushing breadcrumbs from his front. 'How about *Hostel by the Sea's* trading permit? Is that in order?'

'It seems to be,' Særós said. 'I see the place in Höfn opened two months after the one in Reykjavík was raided. It looks like Thormóður made tracks out east, presumably to avoid attention.'

'Interesting timing, or a coincidence? It's a shame his trading permit in Höfn is in order. I was hoping we'd be able to trip him up on that,' Guðgeir said with clear disappointment.

'Hold on, though,' Særós said. 'There's more. The farm at Bröttuskriður was drowning in debt. The bank pretty much had the place in its pocket. All that was left was the legal repossession process. Then the whole lot was paid off a year ago, in a single payment, and the place is now mortgage-free.'

'An inheritance?' Guðgeir suggested.

'Hardly.'

'Drugs, money laundering or…'

'That seems most likely,' Særós replied.

'You remember I told you about all the kitchen appliances out there, and how that didn't add up.'

'Yes, it's clear there's a flow of cash going in that direction.'

'I'm half-certain I could smell acetone when I went into the house there, and it reminded me of Ólöf because she's constantly painting her nails. The it slipped my mind, but now it's starting to fit together...'

'And where does Sajee fit into all this?' Særós interrupted.

'That's what I can't quite figure out,' Guðgeir said, kneading his temples. There was a vague memory just beneath the surface of his mind, something about the basement windows at Bröttuskriður. 'Listen, I'm going to ask a few questions about Selma and Ísak. Linda, the one I mentioned just now, knows the people at the next farm. I'll ask her to go with me up to the Lagoon.'

37

There were only two tablets. Her condition was again deteriorating. Ísak was at a loss, while any pity he had was reserved for himself. He suspected that Thormóður was planning to leave the country as soon as their work was done. Sajee tried to make sense of his disjointed grumbling, but she had little strength and most of the time she was in a daze. Ísak retreated into a world of his own, and the hopes she had harboured that he would come to her help were vanishing.

In the fleeting moments when she came to her senses, her thoughts turned increasingly to the little girl who had been born, as she had been, with a cleft palate. It couldn't have been that long ago, as she had been interred in the family plot, the tiny rib kept in the cellar. Would it be her fate to lose her life in a filthy pit? Once again, Ísak sat by the hatch, yet again telling her that if only she and Selma had been able to keep calm and stay at home, then none of this would have happened.

38

The backdrop to the farm at Gröf aspect was nowhere near as spectacular as at Bröttuskriður. Instead of high, jagged peaks, Gröf stood by a hill not far from the glacial river's banks. There was a wider spread of open land here, although Guðgeir quickly noticed that there wasn't a great deal of usable land around the farm. All the same, it was a pretty place, like most of the farmsteads in this sparsely populated region, and the figures on the car's dashboard told him that from here to Bröttuskriður would take no more than twenty minutes.

Linda jumped at the idea of going with him once he had explained that his reasons for wanting to visit Gröf were to follow the trail of the mysterious Asian woman, and spun a tale that the woman's story had touched him. He mentioned Thormóður a few times, but took care not to make him too central a figure in his narrative. Linda made herself comfortable in the passenger seat and listened patiently to his hypothesis. It was all a little far-fetched, he felt as he listened to himself talking, but there was also so much that he couldn't tell her for the moment.

'It helps that your grandmother knows these people,' Guðgeir said.

'Yeah, whatever. It just makes a change to get away, and I need it,' she said, gazing out of the window and Guðgeir saw her smile. 'Why don't you go up to Bröttuskriður?' she asked, turning to look at him.

'I went there the other day and now I want to take a look at Gröf.' To change the subject, he pointed at the mountainside above. 'I saw a reindeer when I was here last. A magnificent stag. That's special, isn't it?'

'Not really,' Linda replied. 'There are reindeer everywhere and they come down to the lowlands after a hard winter, like this one was. You can see whole herds of them, plus a few lone stags that don't have a place in the herds.'

'So that explains why I felt we had something in common,' Guðgeir said with a smile, and noticed that Linda looked back at him with sympathy in her eyes. Hell, he thought. She feels sorry for me... Why had he mentioned that lone stag? He wanted to bite his own tongue.

'Very poetic,' she said. 'But I thought you had been in the police?'

'Just thinking out loud,' Guðgeir said, switching off the engine. 'We can walk up to the farm from here?'

'Sure,' Linda said. 'Speaking of herds, I wouldn't mind moving away from here and studying down south. For a couple of years, at least. But it's not easy to stand on your own feet with a child and without the family support.'

She wrapped a mustard yellow scarf around her neck, but left her coat unzipped. They took the rutted path towards the farmhouse. Their feet squelched in the mud, splashing their calves.

'It helps to have the herd behind you, and I don't like the thought of being in some flat that costs a fortune to rent in a block in Reykjavík, where I know hardly anyone,' she said.

'And the Dad?' Guðgeir asked. 'Where's he?'

'That's a long and unpleasant story that I can't be bothered to go into. Let's say he's not as lovely as you,' she said cheerfully, hooking her hand into the crook of his arm and he felt an inner warmth as she did so. 'Come on, let's go inside, talk about my grandmother and pretend to be secret agents.'

Over the next couple of hours Guðgeir had no regrets over having asked Linda to go with him to visit Gröf, as she had an easy relationship with Karl and Marta. Without her presence, this could easily have become an awkward solo visit, instead of a relaxed chat over coffee. Linda had a knack of putting people at their ease to draw information effortlessly out of them, and Karl talked almost non-stop. Marta appeared more reserved, sitting at the kitchen table and laying one hand of patience after another, and interrupting her garrulous husband with an occasional comment.

Before long Linda was telling the tale of the trip she and her brother had made during the worst of February's weather to check on the family's summer cottage. Guðgeir took a large bite of a chocolate biscuit and sipped his coffee so as to not appear to be paying too much attention.

'The alarm system went off and I went rushing off up there with Jói because we thought the place would have been wrecked. You know what happened to Gurrý's and Siggi's cottage up by the Jökull river? Anyway, whatever. The weather was absolutely atrocious that day,' she said.

'It's been a hard winter, especially after Christmas,' Marta muttered, shuffling the cards. 'Tell me about it…'

'February was just horrendous,' Linda said. 'The main road was closed both ways sometimes.'

'And this went on well into April!' Karl added, rubbing his bald head. 'It's not always easy living out here, I can tell you. Not like for you people who get the roads cleared. We don't get that kind of luxury out here in the countryside.'

'No, of course not,' Linda said with a touch of guilt in her voice. 'But that day was particularly bad, the last day of February.'

'You've a good memory,' Marta said. 'Was the cottage damaged at all?'

'No, fortunately we got there in good time,' Linda said. 'I saw that Thormóður was out that day as well, and there was an Asian woman with him. I can't imagine where he might have been taking her.'

Karl and Marta quickly exchanged glances.

'She could be working at Bröttuskriður,' Guðgeir said, hoping to keep the conversation alive, startling Karl and Marta into looks of surprise.

'The old lady there is getting on in years, isn't she?' Linda asked. 'Selma, isn't that her name? I remember her son Ísak from school. I think he went to university down south… What was he studying?'

'Chemistry,' Karl answered. 'I couldn't work out why the lad didn't go to agricultural college at Hvanneyri. He'd have learned something useful there and might have been able to do better than that handful of old ewes.'

'People should study what interests them,' Marta said. 'But it was a shock for that nervous boy to leave home.'

'Agricultural science,' Karl said. 'That would have been some use to him, and the farm wouldn't be the mess it is now. Absolutely ridiculous!'

'You don't know what you're talking about, Karl. What school did you go to? Life leads people in different directions.'

'Well, he should have stuck it out more than just two years, considering he was studying what he was supposed to have an interest in.'

'He didn't give up! Karl you shouldn't be going on about things you know nothing about,' Marta said, raising her voice and shuffling the cards with a new intensity. She still hadn't won a hand of patience.

'He gave up!' Karl shot back angrily, banging the table. 'People don't dare tell it like it is these days now there's this endless tiptoeing around uncomfortable truths. The reality is that his mother ruined him with all those endless mad ideas of her. He's never been allowed a chance to stand on his own two feet.'

'You mean he's insecure?' Linda asked, glancing at Marta, who seemed to pay not the slightest attention to her husband's outburst.

'I've no idea, but he comes across as the big man. More than likely that arrogance is just a facade,' Karl added, self-satisfied with his diagnosis.

'Ísak also struggled in the city,' Marta said, laying yet another hand of cards. 'The poor boy was almost dead before Thormóður saved his life.'

'Who's Thormóður?' Guðgeir asked, trying to sound off-handed, as if trying to show a polite interest in something that was in fact no business of his. 'A psychologist?'

'Who knows? At any rate, Selma says he can look deep into a person's soul and is in touch with his own higher consciousness!' Marta said.

'If only,' Karl snorted, before Marta carried on.

'Apparently he's involved in some charitable work. They think a lot of him and Ísak hadn't seen him for a few years. Then he turned up at Bröttuskriður and stayed there for a few weeks. A spiritual replenishment, they call it.'

Karl laughed coldly and sat back in his chair.

'That's something of a luxury! The man was so enchanted with the place that he bought himself a guest house in Höfn. He helps them out with money, I reckon. I can't see how else they manage to hang on there, up to their ears in debt. Since Thormóður turned up they've become too good to talk to the likes of us, and we're the only people in the district who have had anything to do with them, so good luck to them,

I say,' Karl said, planting a forefinger on a seven of clubs. 'Aren't you going to put this one on the eight?' he suggested.

'You mind your own business, Karl!' Marta replied, snatching up the card.

'He's rolling in it, this Thormóður,' Karl said sharply, as if sniping back at his wife. 'We dropped by there during the winter and as far as we could see, every smart new appliance you see advertised in the papers has found its way to Bröttuskriður. Typical greed.'

'Jealousy's going to be the death of you, Karl Baldvinsson,' Marta said, shuffling the cards yet again.

Guðgeir and Linda glanced at each other. The tension between the couple seemed almost habitual, rather than a genuine argument.

'This is the same Thormóður I mentioned earlier,' Linda said to Guðgeir, as if all this was new to him. He nodded, taking care to show not too much interest while he digested what he was hearing. To his thinking, the man's presence at Bröttuskriður was more likely to be a strategy to keep a low profile rather than a spiritual replenishment – and the timing seemed to fit.

'He brought that over here the other day. Thormóður, I mean. A television in the kitchen!' Karl said, as if trying to outdo his wife. 'Is that acceptable? To just show up with a TV set and drop it on the table? We hardly know the man...'

'Stop your bullshit, Karl. What do you know?' Marta broke in. 'Thormóður's a good man who has helped a lot of people. It's a second-hand telly, and it's not as if it's a big one.'

'Second-hand, good as new,' Karl muttered. 'You ought to see how he charms the old girls. You ought to see them drooling over him.'

'Karl! Enough of this crap!' Marta said, her anger showing through.

'How long have they lived alone, the two of them?' Guðgeir asked, as if making a ploy to defuse the tension between Karl and Marta. Much as it was unpleasant to listen to a couple squabbling, this time it was playing into his hands. He and Linda hardly needed to ask a question as everything they wanted to know bubbled up from them. He didn't even have to probe, and it was obvious they had no idea who he was, which was just as well.

'Always, apart from the two years Ísak was at university in Reykjavík,' Karl said quickly. 'Poor Selma can't be left alone as she went a little crazy after that American of hers went off the Almannaskarð road. He managed to kill himself just as she was pregnant and ready to pop. She was supposed to be carrying twins, but in the end there was just the one. I suppose the twins' story was because she was a big as a barrel all the time she was pregnant with Ísak. Not unless the Hidden Lady in the rocks took the other child and exposed the infant for her. After all, "vengeance follows those who betray the hidden…"' Karl said, pausing to let the poetic quotation sink in and watched them with a meaningful look in his eye.

'She's not had an easy life, that's for sure,' Guðgeir said mildly, trying to smother the distaste he was starting to feel for this man. He made an effort to maintain a warmth in his voice and to laugh at the right moments, hoping to encourage the man's eagerness to tell tales.

'It's true,' Marta said. 'The old man, her father, was a brute. He was terribly strict and of course he couldn't stand the sight of Yank, so you can imagine… And he was a nightmare when his temper was up.'

'Why did Thormóður bring you a TV?' Linda asked. 'Do you know him?'

'They must have sent him,' Marta sniffed, unable to disguise her disgust. 'Now they don't want us to call round. Karl went over there at the beginning of March to discuss the pastures and a few other things, and they didn't even ask him in for a cup of coffee. That's downright rude and unneighbourly, I say. And that's towards the only people around here who are prepared to be friendly towards them.'

'Ach. I reckon it's just Selma's temper getting the better of her again. She's always struggled with it, the poor old thing,' Karl said.

'And did you see the Asian girl?' Guðgeir asked, dropping the question in as if by chance and giving his voice a tone that could indicate this could be something the two of them could share an interest in. To his surprise, it was Marta who answered instantly.

'They said she had already moved on.'

Guðgeir took a deep breath. Sajee had been at Bröttuskriður.

39

'So who's this Linda?'

Inga's voice was as dry as sandpaper.

'Nobody,' Guðgeir replied.

'Surely nobody's name can't be Linda?' she said, ice-cold.

'I mean nobody important. She works at the café where I go for a meal sometimes. I can't be sitting here on my own in this apartment the whole time,' he said, already wishing he hadn't mentioned the visit to Gröf to Inga. But the habit was ingrained in him and he had always shared with her anything that troubled him. He had told her about what he and Linda had discovered, and how he was wondering what the next step could be. There wasn't a great deal of investigation needed to tie up the remaining loose ends and he was itching to bring things to a conclusion. But it would be as well to be on sure legal ground, and everything had to be correct as his position – or rather, his lack of a position – made things complex. Every legal loophole would have to be plugged, otherwise the whole thing could fall apart.

Then, in a moment's forgetfulness, he had mentioned Linda's name in connection with the trip up to the Lagoon and the cat was out of the bag. This was no longer a conversation about what Sajee's fate might be, but about a possible relationship between Guðgeir and Linda. It hurt him deeply that Linda still didn't trust him.

'Why did she go with you?'

'Like I told you just now, to open doors. Her family knows the people at Gröf. I didn't want to be caught up in the same situation as at Bröttuskriður.'

'Have you been meeting this woman?'

'No, not at all. She's just someone I know, that's all… Hell, Inga, what do you expect?' he snapped, his temper getting the better of him. It was hard enough being exiled from home without this on top. 'You want me to lock myself away while you go out to dinner with your Crossfit pal from work? Didn't you try out a new restaurant the other day? Don't you think I'm sick of this as well?' he said, and immediately regretted his words.

There was a heavy silence down the line and the distance between them grew increasingly far as the seconds ticked past. It was remarkable that Inga's silence rippled through every nerve in his body, through to his soul. They had a shared history going back a quarter of a century that had twisted and braided their lives together; and now they were acting like sulky teenagers. This couldn't continue.

'We shouldn't be arguing,' Guðgeir sighed, a hand on his forehead.

'No.'

'It's not something we've ever been good at.'

'No.'

'Inga, my love,' he whispered hoarsely. 'I miss you so much.'

'I miss you too. This isn't right.'

'No.'

'Isn't the best thing that I come home as soon as my contract's up?' he said.

'Yes,' she said after a pause. 'That would be best.'

He felt the first tears he had shed since the death of his colleague Andrés, but this time these were tears of delight. He felt himself float on air, and now he'd be out of this gloomy basement flat. He hardly gave himself time to change into his running gear and was still adjusting his track suit trousers as the door banged shut behind him. He put the buds into his ears and the trainer app immediately began to pump a beat, urging him to greater efforts.

The door upstairs was open and Matthildur stood on the steps, with Sveinn behind her. Guðgeir waved cheerfully and set off, running too fast, as he didn't have time to stop and chat now. The disappeared into the distance like a hazy memory. He soon developed a stitch, but struggled on until he was forced to stop to re-tie a shoelace. In his hurry, he hadn't bothered with a double bow. He was panting with exertion. The app on his phone didn't take any kind of a break into account, so he switched it off, as all of a sudden he had no use for the phone's automated encouragement. He sat on a rock and stared out to sea. He longed to go home to Inga, Ólöf and Pétur Andri. Home to Fossvogur.

He stood up and strolled along the Nature Trail.
The tide was out and he noticed a black plastic bag
lying in the yellow foam left on the beach by the
falling tide. Stepping closer, he saw that a corner of
it had been caught under a stone. Guðgeir carefully
freed it and carried it back up to the trail, looking
around for a bin, but none was to be seen. A pair of
ducks squawked out of the spring sunshine towards
him and it struck him as something symbolic as he
stood still with the bag in his hands. There was a new
brightness in his life and things were going to be
better from now on.

He set off, the bag still in his hand, sure that he had
seen a litter bin by the bench a little further along. An
image of the black plastic that covered the basement
windows at Bröttuskriður flashed through his mind.
How could he have forgotten that? His thoughts
jumped from the beauty of nature around him to the
darkest side of human nature. Ísak and Selma had
something to hide, that was certain. Was the woman
being held in the cellar?

He saw in his mind the rubber gloves by the sink at
Bröttuskriður and Selma's heavy hands. Ragnhildur,
the woman Sajee had worked for as an au-pair, had
told Særós that Sajee took exceptionally good care
of her hands. Everything suddenly took on a new
significance – the avocado rotting in a bowl, the
brightly-coloured scarf on the hook among all the
dark clothes. His thoughts went into overdrive as he
searched for other parts of the puzzle.

The key point was that Karl and Marta at Gröf
had confirmed that Sajee had been at Bröttuskriður,

without admitting to having seen her. Thormóður had certainly been on the same flight as Sajee and had offered her a place to stay, while claiming at first to have never seen her. In addition, there were the two hostels that didn't seem to need any guests and the inactive charity with the weird web page. Then there was the strange history that Ísak and Thormóður shared, and also Selma's story, plus the unexplained flow of cash that had somehow made it possible to pay off the farm's overwhelming debts.

He scrolled through his contacts to find Særós's number and paced in circles as he waited for her to answer. It didn't take him long to convince her.

'We have to nail them,' he said. 'There's something going on there that really stinks.'

'We ought to co-ordinate this. We take the hostels in Reykjavík and Höfn at the same time, preferably just as we go in at Bröttuskriður?' Særós suggested. She seemed to feel there would be no problem in getting any warrants they might need.

'You have enough officers for this?' Guðgeir asked. 'This is pretty big.'

'I'll arrange that,' Særós replied.

'There had better be something to all this,' Guðgeir said. 'If it all goes wrong, I'm in no position to back you up.'

40

The torch was dead and Ísak ignored her when she asked for fresh batteries. He seemed relieved not to have to look at the septic injuries to her face. The faint brightness that shone through the gap as he opened the hatch was enough light for him.

She could sense that he felt ill at ease.

While the torch had worked, she had noticed that he no longer paid attention, said nothing more than a few necessary words to avoid having to look at her. Now there was the smell as well, a strong stench of putrefaction. He no longer came inside, just hooked the bucket out when there was something in it, and passed the drink in to her – Selma's green concoction.

41

At the airport Guðgeir watched as Sveinn checked in passengers for the next flight. He chatted cheerfully with everyone and Guðgeir reflected that once he had moved back to Reykjavík he would miss the personal touch he had become accustomed to in Höfn. He could hardly step inside the local shop without a greeting from someone coming his way and he was already regretting not having taken a more active part in the local social life during the long, lonely winter. He glanced at the large clock on the wall behind the check-in desk and decided that the flight from Reykjavík must be about to land.

Særós was coming and she would manage the operation in Höfn, while their colleague Víðir Jón would handle the search in Reykjavík. The two of them had managed to tactfully avoid the usual administrative obstacles to organise this co-ordinated operation. Guðgeir sighed, stood up and paced back and forth, unable to sit still. The anticipation was becoming overwhelming. He was also concerned that too many police vehicles on the move in such a small place would be noticeable and that Thormóður might suspect something. Manpower had been brought in from Reykjavík and the Seyðisfjörður force was sending officers direct to the operation and they would be there in three hours.

Guðgeir noticed Sveinn waving him over.

'Won't you sit inside and have a cup of coffee? There are some doughnuts in a bag on the table.'

'Not for me, thanks,' Guðgeir replied quickly. 'When's this flight supposed to land?'

Sveinn looked at him, intrigued. His curiosity to know what his tenant was planning was clear.

'There's a short delay. It'll be here within fifteen minutes,' he said. 'What can I do for you?' he said, addressing the next passenger in the queue.

'Really? I thought it should have been about to land,' Guðgeir said in exasperation.

'Is anything wrong?'

'What? No, everything's fine,' Guðgeir assured him, and again declined the offer of coffee.

He tried to make himself comfortable on the bench, stretched out his long legs and yawned. It was remarkable that stress always made him drowsy. To have something to do, he took his glasses from their case and polished them, before checking the news on his phone and it wasn't long before he ran out of patience and went outside. There was a clear sky and the signs of spring cheered him. He found it even more cheering to see the aircraft approaching low over the fjord.

Now things were about to happen and every step of the operation would have to be correct. At the same time, over the next few hours he would have to be satisfied with taking a back seat as an uninvolved observer. It was an uncomfortable thought that he would have to keep himself on the sidelines, but he could do nothing that might prejudice the outcome. Just a single false step could ruin everything.

The aircraft roared to a halt and he sighed even more deeply, watching as the steps were wheeled into place. As the first passengers emerged he went back into the terminal and before long he saw Særós approach, tall and elegant. Guðgeir was so pleased to see her that he planted a kiss on each cheek, something he had never done when he had been her boss.

'That's quite a welcome!' she said, taking a step back, while Sveinn, who had been watching, gave Guðgeir an exaggerated wink.

'Good to see you've sorted things out,' he said, giving them a thumbs-up. 'Good on you, my friend,' he added cheerfully, with the customary bark of laughter.

'What was that all about?' Særós asked in astonishment.

Guðgeir put an arm around her shoulders, and returned Sveinn's gesture. He saw no reason to disabuse him of his misunderstanding. It was just fine that Sveinn had no idea who Særós really was, as for the next few hours it would be essential that people around the town would remain unaware of anything out of the ordinary. A word out of place or a remark on social media could wreck everything.

'We'll go direct to the Lagoon. The police will be right behind us,' Særós said when they were in the car. 'The operation by the harbour starts in fifteen minutes. I hope they find something there, but the key element is to keep Thormóður away from the phone so he can't let anyone at Bröttuskriður know what's happening. Did I tell you that Leifur persuaded the janitor to open the office for him?'

'The office at the hostel in Reykjavík?' Guðgeir asked.

'No, the *Children in Crisis* office,' Særós said. 'There's not a thing in there apart from an old desk. Nothing else. Not even a chair. If that web page of theirs is a front for something, then there's good chance it's drugs-related. The drug squad is already following up some leads.'

'Interesting,' Guðgeir mused. The whole case was becoming much more complex than they had imagined at the start. His concern was that things could turn out badly if the case turned out to be legally weak.

'If this turns out to be about narcotics, what's Sajee's role in all this?'

'All sorts of possibilities, drugs mule, human trafficking. Who knows?' Særós said, and lapsed into silence until they reached the turnoff for Gröf. This was their point to wait for police backup, and Særós hurried up to the farm to give Karl and Marta clear instructions that they were not to warn their neighbours about this traffic, making it plain that hindering a police operation was an indictable offence.

'Weird guy in there,' Særós said as she took her seat in the car again. 'He promised not to say a word, and then started going on about hidden people and the enchantment that hangs over Bröttuskriður. A very strange man.'

'And the woman? Marta?' Guðgeir asked. 'What was her reaction?'

'She just said that it had been bound to happen sooner or later.'

'Did she, now? That's remarkable,' Guðgeir said, but Særós was no longer listening to him, engrossed in her phone to start the co-ordinated operation.

42

She was startled, lying there in the darkness. She felt the ground shake and heard the rumble of engines. It seemed that there were many cars and as she closed her eyes, she could visualise herself in front of Bröttuskriður. With shaking hands, she poured a little water into her mouth and managed to swallow a few drops. Then she crawled to the hatch and started to call for help, her voice weak.

43

Særós had thoughtfully left a radio in the car for him. The sound distorted, and he struggled to make out the voices he could hear, interspersed with crashes and bangs. Then he saw the front door open and Selma was escorted out. A blue scarf covered most of her grey hair and she appeared to be furious, holding on tight to the female police officer at her side and yelling curses into the air. She was helped into a car, which then drove away in a cloud of dust. Guðgeir watched its progress until it vanished as the road curled around the foot of the mountain.

Nothing seemed to be happening at the house, although he could make out odd words that he tried to make sense of. He couldn't figure out exactly what was going on, and his excitement grew as he made out movement behind the kitchen windows. There was a heavy thud that came over the airwaves, and he heard Særós mention the basement.

He picked up his phone and called, but gave up when she hadn't replied after it had rung a few times. She would take the right decisions, and he couldn't allow himself to prejudice the whole operation by interfering. The banging stopped, and two officers appeared, went to their vehicle and fetched a toolbox. Then they worked to free the narrow basement window at the front of the house, trying to find another route in. After they had levered the window with a jemmy, Særós appeared and the pair followed her back inside. Silence fell again.

Guðgeir sighed out loud. His own impatience was stretching his nerves. It was almost unbearable being so close to the action but having to stay away, not even able to leave the car while everything was happening inside. He sat hunched forward with his nose against the windscreen, the radio at his ear. He felt an ache in his chest and so much condensation formed on the glass that he opened a window. There wasn't a sound outside other than the cries of the fulmars in the rocks above Bröttuskriður. He opened the window all the way and leaned out, craning his neck to see the distant jagged peaks. Life continuing as usual on the cliffs was in perfect contrast to the situation at the farm itself. The walls hadn't seen a coat of paint for years and no animals were to be seen other than wild birds.

Now a female police officer appeared, ran to the car, and then back to the house. Something was happening, at last. He heard a low whine and looked over towards the barn, catching sight of a bushy tail vanishing around the corner. The unfortunate fox was still held by the iron links of the chain. Two police officers hauled a downcast and noticeably dishevelled Ísak through the door, struggling every step of the way. They marched him between them, handcuffed him and had just put him in the patrol car when Særós hurried from the house.

'Everyone out, right now!'

There was so much noise that it was difficult to make out what was being said.

'Watch out … don't touch any switches … the place could go up. Out!'

Guðgeir was out of the car and running towards the farmhouse, slowing his pace and stopping when he saw that everyone was clear. He waited as he watched from a distance to see how things turned out at this desolate spot beneath the sharp grey crags. His nerves were stretched so tight that he felt himself shiver with the tension. He forced himself to walk slowly back to the car and sit inside again. It was as well to stay clear, as it would take them a while to cordon off the area. The extent of the cordon would tell him exactly how dangerous whatever they had found inside to be. Særós issued instructions, with her phone to her ear. He stayed away until he was sure that everything was being done before he went over to her.

'What happened?' he asked, trying to appear more at ease than he felt.

'There's a whole chemical factory down there in the basement. Ísak managed to set fire to some junk in his room before we got hold of him. We managed to put the fire out, but it was touch and go,' Særós panted. 'The wretched man could have killed all of us. You can imagine what could have happened with all that stuff in there. I've called them all out, the Coast Guard and the fire service. Nobody's going near the place until the technical team has been in there.'

'What was in there?' Guðgeir asked.

'All sorts. Chemical drums. Hydrochloric acid and caustic soda, I guess…' she said, about to continue until he stopped her.

'And Sajee?'

'No sign of her in there. We'll go through the place thoroughly, but not before that chemical factory's been dealt with.'

'You remember I mentioned the smell of acetone when I was there before?'

'Yes,' she said, hesitating for a moment. 'Of course. Right by the door to the cellar.'

'And with all my experience, I didn't put two and two together, and there's all that stuff down there,' Guðgeir said in frustration at his own shortcomings. 'Did you go down there yourself?'

'Just for a moment, and that was enough,' she said quickly. 'There's a brand-new tablet press, temperature gauges, a timer, gas… Everything. And the smell.' Særós's voice dropped and she looked seriously into Guðgeir's eyes. 'I'd have never taken a team in there if I had the slightest suspicion it was such a big factory. It's the first time I've had this kind of responsibility…'

'And you did everything exactly right,' Guðgeir said. 'How could you have suspected there could be a whole drugs laboratory in a farmhouse? It's completely insane. We suspected there was something fishy going on, but nothing on this scale.'

Her phone rang and Særós took a few steps as she answered. He fidgeted nervously. He felt increasingly sick. Ísak had done his best to set fire to the place, endangering the lives of everyone present. After thirty years as a police officer, it still took him by surprise how desperation could lead people to horrifying extremes.

'That was Víðir Jón,' Særós said, finally putting the phone down. 'They've found backpacks at both the hostels, in Höfn and in Reykjavík. All the same brand and he said it's pretty certain there are traces of narcotics in them. That's what the initial scans show. It looks like production was here at the farm and we suspect the network is nationwide, with the hostels as distribution points.'

'So that's how it all fits together,' Guðgeir muttered, and the image of Thormóður carrying a couple of backpacks and other things out to his 4x4 came to mind. 'And all that messing around with household goods…'

'The drug squad's overjoyed. You know there has been a flood of amphetamines, MDMA and all kinds of crap, especially over the last year,' Særós said happily, the shock wearing off and being replaced by triumph.

'So we know about Thormóður, Ísak and Selma,' Guðgeir counted up. 'Check the young woman who works at the *Hostel by the Sea* as well.'

'We'll do that,' Særós said, working her shoulders to release the tension that ran all the way up to her throat. 'But we can hardly count Selma as being part of this. Her mind's so shot away that she can hardly have been aware of what was going on in the basement, but it goes without saying that she'll be questioned about everything. She seems to have had an obsession with new toys. You ought to see the stuff in there, unbelievable! But I suppose her shopping sprees must have been a front for bringing in all the stuff needed for the factory. She must have been out of her mind,' Særós said, her hands spread wide.

'I saw it for myself,' Guðgeir said and then Særós's phone rang again.

He took the opportunity to watch what was going on around them. The area had been securely cordoned off and traffic blocked in both directions. The helicopter bringing the specialist team could hardly be far away. Only a year before he had gone on leave, these had been skills they would have had to bring in from Europol, but now they were coming from Reykjavík. Things had changed, and he hadn't had a chance to ask Særós for any details.

'That was the drug squad. They suspect that every possible smuggling route must have been used, in and out of the country,' she said. 'They're checking *Children in Crisis* to see how it fits in with all this. It's beyond belief how low people can go. *Children in Crisis*! Absolutely revolting to use something like that as a front. The thinking is that the payment buttons on the site send coded messages about shipments, prices and suchlike. But we'll figure that out and they're working on it now. Leifur said there's been very little traffic on the site, apparently just a narrow group of regular users.'

'And Sajee? How does she fit in with all this?' Guðgeir asked as he took in the deluge of information, and his thoughts returned to the woman from Sri Lanka.

'You know that the most popular pills these days have a child's head motif?' Særós asked instead of answering his question.

'What?'

'It's more or less a child's face. Víðir Jón reminded me just then, and now I can't wait to get inside and take a look at that tablet press.'

'It's disgusting,' Guðgeir said, scowling.

'Exactly.'

'Særós, you've done a fantastic job,' he said, reaching to pat her shoulder. 'Well done!'

'It's all thanks to you,' she replied, stamping warmth into her feet. 'It's hellishly cold. Shouldn't it be spring by now?'

'Looks like your first big case has a happy ending.' Guðgeir smiled. 'It's just as well you listened to all my bullshit.'

'Don't talk yourself down. You know I'm way too cool to take any notice,' she said with a laugh, clearly delighted with the day's success.

'You deserve every bit of it,' Guðgeir said with conviction. 'How far away is the helicopter?'

'It'll be a while yet,' she replied. 'Don't you want to head home? Not much is going to happen here for a while.'

She bit her lip, as if regretting what she had said, but Guðgeir pretended not to have heard.

'Sure. But once this is over the whole property will have to be searched,' he said, nodding towards the barn. 'Have you been in there?'

'A quick look. It looks like it was used to fix up cars. Ísak had other hobbies as well as producing drugs. We'll take a closer look afterwards. There were extra small washing up gloves under the sink and Ísak's explanation was that there was a Thai or Filipina woman who did some cleaning and that she only came once, so that could have been Sajee. They said she had also cleaned at Gröf, and the couple there should be able to confirm that.'

'Then why did they pretend to know nothing about her the time I came here?' Guðgeir, and the feeling of helplessness was making him anxious.

'That was what I was looking to ask, but hadn't go that far when it all kicked off in there. Personally, I find it very strange that Thormóður pretended not to remember the woman...' she said, and her voice faded away as her gaze went from the house to the sky and back. 'Isn't that the way it was?'

It was clear that her mind was elsewhere, and Guðgeir had become a distraction as she watched for the helicopter.

'That's it. And if he's put under any pressure, then he blames bad memory due to his former lifestyle. You'll have to bear that in mind in the interrogation and not let him play games with you,' Guðgeir said.

'Of course not.'

'Did you ask if the woman had a cleft palate?' he asked, and Særós sighed and shook her head.

'No. It wasn't easy to get through to her,' she said. 'Ísak looks like he's having a breakdown and Selma is clearly very sick, and in this instance we might have to accept that they're telling the truth.'

'I don't believe them,' Guðgeir muttered, running a hand over his head and rubbing his jaw. He had slept badly and hadn't bothered to shave.

'Look, none of us have seen Sajee, and she hasn't been reported missing,' Særós said, as her phone rang again. 'Hello?' she said quickly, and listened attentively.

Guðgeir could make out a few odd words, and couldn't fail to notice that her mood brightened as the conversation progressed.

'Fantastic! That's unbelievable,' she said again and again. 'Keep me informed. OK, thanks.'

She dropped the phone back into her pocket, and raised a hand in the air. It took him a moment to realise that this was a high-five invitation, something that was very unlike the serious and organised Særós, who was all about discipline and competitiveness, whether she was swimming, running or climbing mountains in all weathers. Now she was triumphant. Særós had reached her mountain peak.

'Wonderful,' he said. 'Congratulations!'

'It all worked out. They found drugs in a backpack at the hostel in Höfn and there were two bags of cash at the hostel in Reykjavík. They must have been struggling to get rid of all that money! The dogs are sniffing everywhere, so with any luck they should turn up even more.'

It all added up. He had seen Thormóður stacking stuff up in the local shop in Höfn and noticed that he had paid with five and ten thousand krónur notes, which was unusual now that almost everything was done electronically. Guðgeir recalled that at the time he had suspected a tax swindle, but the reality had been very different. The goods went to Bröttuskriður where production took place, hidden away behind an old-fashioned farmhouse. It looked like the backpacks went from there to the hostels to be distributed around the country, more than likely with couriers pretending to be tourists. The organisation had been hidden behind *Children in Crisis*.

Særós's phone rang again and this time she switched to speaker. This time Leifur was reporting that the charity's offices had been examined and the desk, the only piece of furniture in the place, had yielded a stack of CD cases. This seemed odd, as CDs had become practically obsolete, and the cases were empty – but this turned out to be yet another distribution method.

'This is all very complex…' he said, and Særós interrupted him.

'Leifur, to make your day, I can tell you that there's a load of *Children in Crisis* CD cases at Bröttuskriður,' she said and laughed. 'Straight to the back of the net, and so fast,' she said, as she ended the call.

'So were the hostels used to launder the cash?' Guðgeir asked.

'Maybe they were, or maybe not. Someone has to make a mistake somewhere along the line.'

'And Sajee? What about her?' Guðgeir asked again.

Særós frowned, showing that she was unsure whether to continue or step back.

'That's what I've been wondering about,' she said after an awkward pause. 'She could have left the country, or…' she drew a deep breath. 'Maybe we've constructed Sajee from more than one person. We don't have a picture of her. She's nowhere to be seen online. We can't pronounce her name properly, let alone know if we've even been able to write it down accurately.'

'What exactly do you mean?' Guðgeir asked, looking away to hide his disappointment. The insistent howl of the fox as it tugged at its chain by the barn wall and the cries of the fulmars could be heard in the distance. His discomfort was growing by the minute.

'I mean that there's a chance these people are telling the truth. They got some cleaner in and don't remember her name – and we're mixing up two different people.'

Guðgeir sat in silence.

'But if it didn't matter, we wouldn't have started looking for Sajee. And then we wouldn't have found the factory.'

44

It was the wailing that was driving her mad. It was a long drawn out screech that cut through her mind like a razor. She felt that her head was about to shatter into a thousand pieces with the needle-sharp pain that tortured every nerve. She tried to find some comfort on the bench, but the slightest movement set of the screech. Was she howling herself, or had the fox made its way down here to her?

45

Guðgeir was restless. He tried to lose himself in the TV, but gave up and went out to the car. As he drove around Höfn's quiet streets, Sigurður Guðmundsson's sweet music failed to calm his nerves. It wasn't long before he had been along every street in the town, but instead of going home, he decided to take a trip out to the airport, where everything turned out to be quiet. On the way back he called at the filling station for a coke and a hot dog, and ate it standing at the window. As he swallowed the final morsel, a man with a strong smell of the stable about him came in.

'Something weird going on up at the Lagoon,' he heard the man say as he paid for his fuel.

'What's that?' the assistant asked.

'Police cars and plenty of traffic,' the man said. 'Someone said there was a helicopter up there by the screes.'

Guðgeir picked up a paper and leafed innocently through the pages.

'Really? Who told you that?'

'Tómas, my pal at the stables. He reckoned there's something criminal going on up there. Said something about a drugs factory.'

'Up at the Lagoon?' the assistant laughed. 'That's a good one. More likely some wrinkly had a heart attack.'

'Yeah, probably,' the man replied. 'Give me a pack of red Opals as well, will you?'

Guðgeir screwed up the hot dog wrapper, dropped the coke can in a bin and checked his phone yet again. Not a word from Særós and there was nothing in the news. Back home he sat in front of the television, and around eleven he gave up and went back out, cruising the empty streets for half an hour before stopping at the police station. Every light inside the building was on, which told him that people were being questioned. He leaned the seat back, switched on the radio and listened to the midnight news bulletin. He was hugely relieved that there wasn't a word about drugs factory in the countryside being busted. Hopefully the media would allow the police elbow room before the morning news to get to grips with the case.

The radio repeated a programme from earlier in the day and he listened with little interest to a discussion about the bizarre decisions made by politicians. A light inside the building was switched off and a moment later Særós and two colleagues appeared. The pair waved to him as they drove away, but Særós marched straight over to his car. There was no indication that she might be tired after the long day.

'Anything about Sajee?' he asked as she took a seat next to him.

'No, unfortunately. Their accounts tie up.'

Thormóður brought in an Asian woman who cleaned the house at Bröttuskriður and for the couple at Gröf. She had been in trouble and wanted to earn enough money for a ticket to Reykjavík. Thormóður said he'd felt sorry for her, let her stay for a couple of nights free, and found her some cleaning work.'

'What about the name and the dates?'

'None of them said they could remember her name, and the dates don't tie up exactly. To be honest, we've had plenty to deal with and tomorrow I'll check up on the old couple at Gröf. Thormóður and Ísak will be taken to Reykjavík tomorrow and we're asking for a week's custody.'

'Sounds good. I was listening to the news just now and there wasn't anything about all this, but there are already rumours around the town. You don't have long.'

'I know,' Særós yawned. He could see now that she was exhausted, as if the energy inside her had suddenly been switched off. 'I hope this hotel we're staying at is reasonable? I need to get some sleep before we start again tomorrow.'

'I hear it's fine. Or I could drop you off at the Hostel by the Sea?' he said with a grin.

'No, thank you!' she said, yawning again. 'I need to be on my way. Thanks for everything today. I'll speak to you tomorrow.'

She took hold of the handle to open the door, and hesitated as she saw the look of concern on Guðgeir's face.

'And Sajee?' he said.

'We'll search properly tomorrow, when the factory has been dismantled,' Særós said, about to get out of the car. 'I had a message from Ragnhildur who used to employ her. She didn't manage to find a photo.'

'No luck with the Chinese women who rented the basement rooms?' he asked quickly.

'The landlord, Ísleifur, brought them down to the station. They didn't seem to understand a word of Icelandic, or pretended not to. Leifur said they were on edge, probably terrified they were going to be kicked out,' she said, opening the door and stepping out into the street. 'I'll walk up to the hotel. A breath of air will clear my mind.'

'What do you make of Ísleifur?'

'He's a shitbag landlord who screws everything he can out of people who are down on their luck. But we haven't found anything to pin on him otherwise.'

'Understood.'

'Guðgeir, we'll go over every inch of the place tomorrow and all the places they have in Reykjavík. The woman could be there, in some flat … if she exists at all. I mean, we could be mixing up two or more women,' Særós said. She was tired out and leaned against the car door. 'Plus we have to expect that imagination has taken us a long way and maybe taken us down blind alleys, but regardless of that, we have a result. According to Leifur, this is one of the largest narcotics cases for years, so the next few days are going to be interesting.'

'It all worked out,' he said slowly. 'Or almost.'

He stared out into the spring twilight so she wouldn't see his feelings in his expression. Her suggestion that Sajee was some kind of figment of his imagination irritated him.

'There's someone on duty up there, isn't there?' he asked, aware that he shouldn't have said anything.'

'Of course.'

'And did anyone notice the fox chained up by the barn?'

'Sure. Someone must have. I didn't go down there myself. It's been a busy day.'

She sat back down in the car, folded down the sunshade and looked at herself in the mirror. She rubbed her eyes, licked a fingertip and ran it over her eyelids. Særós always made sure she looked impeccable.

'I can't get that fox out of my mind,' Guðgeir said. 'The poor thing howled the whole time you were in the house today. It'll probably have to be put to sleep or released. Can you call the guy on duty and ask him to keep an eye on it?'

'No problem. I'll do that,' Særós said. Her blue eyes gazed at him fondly. 'You're so good-hearted, and I just don't understand…' she said and looked along the deserted street. 'Can you run me up to the hotel? I need to sleep. Right now. I'm almost asleep on my feet.'

'Call the duty officer up there,' he said, and drove slowly along Hafnarstræti. She had finished her call by the time he pulled up in front of the hotel.

'He'll check on the fox,' she said. 'Thanks, and speak to you tomorrow.'

'Sure. Good night. You'll let me know…'

'I promise.'

46

He couldn't sleep. The day's events and the nagging concerns about Sajee's fate combined with old memories magnified his discomfort. At three in the morning he got out of bed and went to the bathroom, and after weighing things up in his mind, he decided to take a sleeping pill. If he were going to function tomorrow, he'd need to get a few hours' sleep.

It was towards morning when he was startled from sleep and looked around. The air was heavy and the white walls seemed to be closing in on him. In the distance he could hear a strange sound, conscious of the pressure increasing and the oxygen level dropping. He called out for help, but little more than a croak escaped from his dry mouth. Andrés's eyes appeared in the darkness, and the image of the fear frozen into them would never leave him. Guðgeir thrashed as the nightmare took hold. He saw a bloody mouth, felt cold, rough hands take hold of him, tightening their grip as he fought to free himself. He could hardly breathe and in desperation fumbled in the gloom. He would have to wake himself up to escape from these depths. Finally he was awake, his heart hammering as he managed at last to open his eyes.

Disoriented, he shivered in discomfort and it took him a while to realise he was in the rented flat in Sveinn's basement. He stared at his surroundings and it was only after a few minutes that he sat up and held his head in his hands. He sat still for a while until he had relaxed enough to strip off and in the shower he let the cold water flow over his shoulders. He forced himself to remain under the icy deluge until he was thoroughly chilled. He was shivering when he finally reached for a towel, dried himself quickly and pulled on jeans and a lightweight sweater.

He filled the basin with hot water and searched through the bathroom cabinet for shaving soap and a razor, deciding that he ought to look respectable despite the bad night behind him. He lathered his face and slid the disposable razor over one cheek and then the other; throat, chin and upper lip were next. He pushed his tongue behind his lip to let the razor do its work, and noticed a drop of blood hit the surface of the water.

'Hell,' he muttered, covering the cut with a scrap of toilet paper just as another drop joined the first in the soapy water. He felt suddenly faint and held on to the basin to support himself. He closed his eyes, but that was worse, and he opened them wide to peer into the water. Another red drop appeared in the white froth. He pulled off the scrap of paper, looking up to see the image staring back at him, a cut above his lip. He could taste the blood and he closed his eyes, allowing last night's nightmare to come rushing back. A small, slim woman wearing jeans and a brightly-coloured scarf had come towards him. Her dark hair covered her face in soft waves and her brown eyes looked into his entreatingly. She came close and he could see there was blood behind her smile, as her face faded into darkness, replaced by the image of the fox, not howling as it had done all the time the police team had been at Bröttuskriður the previous day, but staring into his eyes.

He opened his eyes and recalled that the previous evening Særós had only mentioned the men. He snatched up his phone and listened to it ring as he slipped on shoes and a jacket.

'I said I'd be in touch when I have something to tell you,' she said as she answered the phone.

'Am I right in thinking that last night you only spoke to Ísak and Thormóður? What about Selma? Did you get anything out of her?' he asked quickly.

'No, she was in a real state and she was sedated.'

'When are you going to interview her?'

'The men will be going to Reykjavík on the midday flight and we'll start the site investigation around then. We'll get to Selma later today.'

'What…?'

'She had a breakdown and went wild in the car. We could hardly restrain her. Quite apart from the breakdown, it seems she hadn't left the farm for years, or so the doctor said. The poor woman's genuinely in a bad way.'

'I was sure you'd be taking her to the station when I saw you drive away yesterday,' Guðgeir said, unable to hide the disappointment in his voice. There was a deep unease growing inside him. 'Is she in hospital?'

'No, there are no facilities in Höfn and it's four hundred kilometres to the nearest hospital. But naturally we want her to have professional help as soon as possible,' Særós said. 'The doctor sedated her, as I said. He reckoned it would be best for her to be with people she feels she can trust, so she's at Gröf. Selma is in such a bad way that we didn't want to risk making things worse. The couple at Gröf sat with her until she fell asleep and they've been in regular contact. In any case, the officer on watch isn't far away.'

'Yes, but she's part of all this,' he insisted.

'Absolutely. But Selma isn't a priority as she isn't suspected of direct involvement in a large-scale narcotics operation. We feel that they abused her position. Guðgeir, you know as well as I do that I could never justify locking up an elderly, sick woman in a cell. Imagine the fallout if something had happened to her. Things like that have happened before, as you know. We'll decide what the next step is once we've assessed the situation, and as far as I'm aware, everything's quiet up there.'

'Særós, would you do me a favour and check? Make sure everything's all right?'

'Sure. I'll call you back in a moment.'

It was more than a few moments later as he was unlocking Hornafjörður Security's garage when his phone pinged as it received a text message. According to Særós, Selma was still sleeping and she had dispatched one of the team to Gröf to talk to her as soon as she was awake. Guðgeir forced himself to gulp down a cup of coffee in the tiny canteen and then set off on his usual route. Before he knew it, he had abandoned routine and was on his way up to the Lagoon. He was in the tunnel when Særós called.

'They said she was angry and agitated last night but she's sleeping now. The poor woman sees visions and hears all sorts of voices in her head. The doctor has promised to go up there once the clinic is closed for the day and our guy will stick around at Gröf.'

'Our guy? Who's that?'

'His name's Eiríkur. He was on duty overnight, so he's the closest one.'

'So there's nobody watching Bröttuskriður?' Guðgeir said, putting his foot down harder.

'Not right now. But we'll be on the way soon.'

A bank of dark cloud loomed overhead and the fulmars swooped over the river. On his previous visits Guðgeir hadn't noticed just how bleak the landscape was at the far end of the Lagoon. It was in keeping with his mood, as his head pounded and he drove with the window wide open to get a flow of clean air. He drove fast, not slowing down until he was close to Gröf. He turned off the main road and took the track to the farm slowly. A snipe shot from a ditch by the road, calling as it flew, and a couple of sheep watched calmly from a field as he passed by. There was a police car parked by the farm, and he sighed with relief. Eiríkur had to be inside and he hoped he would be keeping a close eye on Selma. Guðgeir turned around in the farmyard and drove back. At the junction he hesitated, and after a moment's thought he set off on the Eystrahorn road. The dark-haired woman from his dreams wasn't going to leave him in peace and he needed to see the place for himself.

The place had been cordoned off with yellow tape, so he walked up the track to Bröttuskriður, leaving the car by the road. The grey farmhouse looked desolate and he had a sudden vision of the walls undulating as if in a mirage. This couldn't be real. This couldn't happen on such a cool day up here below the mountain slopes. He looked from the farm down towards the sands and saw nothing out of the ordinary there. The pill he had taken and no more than a few hours's sleep had to be affecting his senses.

As he looked back up the slope towards the barn, he made out a movement. Something was there. He jogged towards the barn. A length of wood lay by the grey corrugated iron, a few sharp nails protruding from it. He didn't need to look closely to know that the dark stains were blood and a trail led into the barn. The first thing that came to mind was the fox. He pushed open the door and squeezed past an old Ford that had been parked half over a pit. He took out his phone and used it to illuminate the steps as he made his way down. There was nothing to be seen, but couldn't help noticing the foul stench, and a gap where one of the steel sheets of metal that clad the side of the pit was not flush with the next. As he put a hand to it and pushed hard, the metal gave way and opened into a passage. Stooping low, he was able to make his way, the phone in his hand. At the end was a little door, not much more than a hatch, that opened as he put a hand on it.

He stared in shock. A bench, a filthy duvet, a pillow and a blanket, and on a small shelf in one corner stood a little group of figurines. He saw a pile of clothes on the floor, jeans, a brightly patterned scarf and a pair of boots. He crawled as fast as he could back, out into the fresh air that he dragged deep into his lungs while he felt the blood pumping in his temples.

Still chained, the fox lay dead by the wall. Guðgeir glanced around quickly, saw nothing, but heard a faint sound of movement and set off to find its source. Now it was clearer, the crunch of a shovel punched into gravel, and the rattle of small stones. The iron gate of the family plot stood open and he jogged up the slope. He could make out Selma between the stunted trees. She must have trudged through mud and marshes all the way from Gröf, as she was filthy and covered in red-brown stains.

'No!' he yelled with all the force he had. His voice echoed from the rocks.

Selma ignored him, and carried on digging, shovelling to fill a grave.

'Stop,' he shouted, the rocks bouncing his voice back to him.

She looked around, raising the shovel high in the air as she rushed at him, a solid, grey-haired old woman with a blue apron tied around her waist. With a furious yell, threw himself at her, dodging the swinging shovel as managed to catch her in a lock and dragged her to the ground. She struggled to begin with, and gradually gave way. For a moment he heard only his own laboured breathing and the cries of the fulmars high above; and then he heard a long moan.

June

In the kitchen there were bluebells in a vase and on the table a welcome gift for the new tenant, duvet covers in bright, lively colours. The place was sparkling clean, but he still glanced around before he snapped shut his suitcase, hung his jacket over his arm and stepped out into the sunshine. He stood still and felt a wave of satisfaction pass through him. He locked the door for the last time and dropped the key in his trouser pocket. Matthildur was relaxing in the sunshine and she waved.

'Have a good trip,' she called out to him.

The plane was on the ground when he got to the airport and the car park was packed. On the way, he patted his pocket to make sure the key was in its place. At the check-in desk, he and Sveinn nodded to each other. The first passengers were making their way in and they watched in anticipation as each passenger passed by.

Sajee was the last to disembark, taking careful steps. She was cautious, as might be expected after her long stay in hospital followed by recuperation. The warm wind flicked her hair over her face and she deliberately pushed it back behind her ears before continuing.

Guðgeir's thoughts filled with a range of memories, some crystal-clear, some vague. He recalled his own howl of horror as he dug with his bare hands. She lay in a shallow grave, her face covered with earth. In desperation, he had cleared her airway, forced air into her and pumped her chest until he could detect a pulse. He remembered flashing lights, loud, urgent voices and the clatter of a helicopter.

Over the next few days, dreadfully undernourished and maltreated, Sajee had fought for her life.

'She's as tough as hell,' Sveinn said with the usual short bark of laughter.

Guðgeir smiled. Yes, she was certainly tough. He went over to her and folded his arms about her, then he took her hands in his.

'You'll have to promise me you'll look after these,' he said, looking down at them, and felt her tremble.

She looked into his eyes, took a deep breath and nodded.

'You know I have a job here, starting in the autumn.'

'Yes. At the old people's home. Congratulations.'

A broad smile spread across her face.

'And one day I'll open my own salon.'

'I don't doubt it. Not for a moment,' he said, taking the key from his pocket and pressing it into her hands. 'The flat is all yours.'

'I'm so lucky,' she said and gazed into his eyes. 'Hirumi is coming to see me next week.'

Guðgeir swallowed and looked away, overcome with relief at seeing how Sajee had recovered.

'Won't you sit down while Sveinn finishes up? You'll have to wait for him for a little while,' he said.

'Yes, that's best,' she answered and dragged her suitcase over to the imitation leather sofa.

'Good luck, Sajee,' he said as he left her.

'Thank you, and have a safe trip.'

He hummed a tune as he drove over the long bridge spanning the Hornafjörður estuary. The blue-grey mountains were at their most magnificent in the summer sunshine, and he was heading home.